BLAZE
RETURNS

BILL RUNNER

RUNNER HOUSE BOOKS, LONDON
www.bill-runner.com

First paperback edition December 2021

Illustrations by Abdul Qadir AQ Studio

ISBN 978-1-7398325-0-6

www.bill-runner.com

AXEL BLAZE

SKILLS

Unarmed combat
(Expert in joints/pressure points)
Armed combat
(Knives, guns)
Mountain climbing
60-yard dash in 6 seconds

EXPERIENCE

US army
(Ten years – four in Special Forces)
US Marshals
(Five years)

PHYSICAL STATS

Height: 6'2"
Weight: 200 pounds

USUALLY SEEN IN

Jeans and black T-shirt
Cowboy boots
(with boot knives)

CHAPTER 1

I wasn't expecting trouble when I pulled off the highway. It was meant to be a quick stopover for dinner.

The neon sign shining in the distance simply said "Bar". To the point. No fuss. A sign above the entrance claimed: "Best burger in town". I had been on the road for ten hours—so long as they had buns with meat inside, I didn't really care. But what town? It was the middle of nowhere.

The joint was a flat wooden structure, standing by itself, just east of the border between Utah and Nevada. Another 150 miles to my destination— Little Butte, Nevada. It would take a little over two hours. There weren't many vehicles on the highway.

I got out of my pickup and stretched. It was a cool, early April evening. Just about getting dark. The crunch of my cowboy boots on gravel filled the quiet evening as I walked towards the entrance.

The inside of the joint was as lacking in personality as the name on the sign outside. A rectangular set up with tables laid out along three walls. Tables with chairs, not booths. The fourth wall had a bar, with a door on each side—one leading to the kitchen, the other to the restrooms. There was a jukebox beside the restroom door. It didn't look like it worked.

The place was practically empty. That suited me fine. I'm not what folks call a "people person".

There were two men at the bar. The bartender had a bored look on his face. He clearly didn't give a hoot about the troubles the drunk was trying to share with him.

As I entered, the waitress standing beside the kitchen door looked up from her phone. Late thirties, pleasant face, bored look. Doing this a long time? Maybe too long.

I asked for the table in the far corner. Slightly hidden by the jukebox, but with a clear view of the entrance and the entire place. Restricting the directions of approach. It had become second nature—identifying positions of dominance in any terrain. I wasn't expecting trouble. But it doesn't hurt to be watchful.

"Take your pick. Not exactly rush hour," the waitress replied with a wry smile.

She was efficient. My drink was in front of me within three minutes. A double shot of bourbon. Spreading a map on the table, I studied the remainder of the route. I folded the map when the waitress appeared again with my burger.

She had just returned to her spot by the kitchen door when the main door was flung open. A hulk of a man occupied the frame. At least six foot five. Close to 300 pounds. The kind of man who doesn't go down with a single bullet.

I could see trouble written all over him. In large letters. I have spent years dealing with lowlifes— from terrorists during my days as a Special Forces Ranger to drug runners and gangsters as a US Marshal.

I knew the tell-tale signs. There hadn't been any warning of the man's arrival—no sound of any vehicle pulling in. He didn't look the walking type—he surely hadn't trekked to that joint out in the boonies. He must have parked his wheels at a distance and walked over. You wouldn't do that if your intentions were noble.

The hulk had a phone in his right hand. He glanced at it briefly as he stepped in, before pushing it back into his pocket. He held his left hand slightly crookedly over his loose shirt. I felt sure he was carrying a shotgun inside the shirt.

He was followed by another man. About my height—a couple of inches over six feet. But wiry, at least 25 pounds lighter than my 200. He seemed jumpy. Dilated pupils. Possibly high on meth.

I groaned. I was on a tight time frame. Places I was meant to be. Urgent matters to be dealt with. I didn't have time for messing with lowlifes.

"Where's Mitch?" the hulk asked the bartender.

"No idea, buddy. I haven't seen him for a few days," the bartender tried to sound friendly, but couldn't hide the tremor in his voice.

The hulk suddenly placed his hand on the side of the bartender's head and banged it down on the bar. It was fast. Unexpected. The drunk almost fell off his stool and moved away.

"You lie again, I crush your skull. I know he was here today," the hulk shouted. He took out his shotgun. A 12-gauge double barrel. Sawed off. Could be really messy in that enclosed space.

The drunk began edging towards the door. The wiry guy took out a Glock tucked inside the back of his jeans.

"No one's going anywhere today," he almost sounded excited.

The underlying threat of the words did not register on the drunk. He kept edging away.

Without another word, the wiry guy shot him in the chest. The waitress screamed as the man collapsed.

"What the f... Stop shooting, you damned junkie. We don't kill anyone until we get Mitch," the hulk yelled at the wiry man.

"I was aiming for the shoulder... But he was part of Mitch's crew. I've seen him dealing," the junkie replied in a whiny tone, trying to justify himself.

The shot man twitched and went still. The waitress screamed again. The hulk butted her face with the shotgun. That really made my blood boil.

"Shut up," he yelled at her.

The waitress whimpered. Her nose and upper lip had turned bloody. But she shut up, sobbing quietly.

"Who's in the kitchen?" the hulk yelled at her again.

"Just the cook," she replied, her voice quivering.

"You," he motioned to his partner, "get the cook here. And check that the back entrance is locked."

A few seconds later, the man returned with the cook. The hulk made the bartender, waitress and cook line up against the wall.

Their attention was focused on the bar area until then. They hadn't yet noticed me sitting in the corner. Clearly not professionals. Just thugs with guns.

I sipped my drink, weighing my options, my mind in combat mode. I realized they wouldn't stop once they found their guy Mitch. They were there to kill. They wouldn't be leaving any witnesses.

I wasn't carrying a gun. But I did have boot knives in the inbuilt sheaths in my cowboy boots.

They were handcrafted, with a 5.4-inch double-edged carbon steel blade. The symmetrical weight distribution also made them deadly accurate for throwing at a target. Those discreetly sheathed blades had seen me get out of many tough spots.

I raised each leg of my jeans one after the other, tugging each one behind the sheath. That gave me quick access to the knives. Two knives against two armed men, one with a shotgun. Not great odds. Especially with that distance between us.

Knives are deadly at close range. Can be deadlier than guns—if you know how to use them. But I would have to use them creatively. Maim, not kill. Killing would be easy once the targets were within reach. But there would be too much hassle to deal with later. I was a man on a mission, didn't have time for paperwork.

I just needed to incapacitate them. For that, I needed them closer. Take them out one at a time. Violently and painfully. Not just because they deserved it. It was simply a matter of surprise—that would be my main advantage. It makes guys freeze. That's what I needed. Strike first. And hard. Not give them a chance to react. Put them down. Fast. And be on my way.

I kept my drink on the table for a few seconds. Flexed my wrists and neck, got the circulation going. I hadn't touched the burger yet. Pushing the plate to one side, I picked the drink again.

It was then that the wiry guy spotted me. He jumped with nervous energy.

"Whoa! Can you believe this guy?"

He swaggered towards me. Stood in front of the jukebox, gun pointing towards the floor. But still beyond my reach. The hulk standing near the bar had the shotgun pointed in my direction. But he didn't have a clear shot—the wiry man was between me and the shotgun. Definitely not professionals.

"Excuse me, I hope I'm not disturbing you," the wiry man addressed me in a mocking tone.

Funny guy. I needed him closer.

"Now that you mention it, I did plan to have my dinner in peace," I replied.

"Oh, so sorry to be disturbing your dinner. And who might you be?" the man asked.

"Nobody. Just a man having his dinner."

"Well, Mr. Nobody, what are you doing here?"

"Minding my own business," I replied, keeping the glass down.

"Hey, we have a smartass here," the man called out to his partner.

Then he moved forward, stood in front of me, and lined the gun on me.

"Would you like some lead with your dinner," he asked, an evil grin on his face, revealing rotting teeth.

I wasn't happy with the meth head pointing his gun on me. But I finally had him exactly where I wanted.

"Don't push it, pal. You've got no beef with me. You don't want to be doing this."

I couldn't help menace entering my voice. A slightly confused look appeared on the man's face.

"Get him over here," the hulk shouted.

The man looked back towards the hulk. Bad move.

I rose explosively from my chair, grabbing his wrist with one hand, and the gun along with his trapped trigger finger with the other. I twisted the gun forcefully outward and upward. There were almost simultaneous cracks of bones snapping as his trigger finger broke, followed by his wrist. The man yelped in pain.

I needed to keep the gun out of the equation. If I tried shooting at the hulk, I and the wiry guy would be splattered with shotgun blast. But if I didn't have a gun, the hulk wouldn't use the shotgun with his partner in the way. I needed to stay unarmed and keep the junkie between us—standing, not flat on the ground.

Flinging the gun under the table, I slammed the man's broken wrist onto the table—hand flat, palm facing up. I grabbed the knife and slammed it hard through his palm. 5.4 inches of razor-sharp steel sliced through bone and flesh and got firmly embedded in the wood of the table, impaling his hand. At the same time, I pushed him slightly away and smashed my knee upwards in a roundhouse motion, just below the back of his elbow. There was a sickening crunch as ligaments and bones snapped. The broken end of his radius bone pierced outwards through his skin. The elbow got bent at a crooked angle. The man howled in agony.

In four seconds, the man went from an armed threat to a broken, contorted mess. He was still standing but completely immobile—palm glued to the table, elbow stuck at a crooked angle. Even a shiver sent ripples of pain through his body.

One down, one to go.

The hulk had remained frozen for those four seconds. Then he came to life. He aimed the shotgun in my direction but found his partner in the way. He decided to charge. Exactly what I wanted.

I pulled out the other knife and threw it at him. The razor-sharp blade sunk in just below his right shoulder bone, getting buried to the hilt in flesh and muscle, slicing through nerves and blood vessels. The shotgun fell from his hand.

I leaped forward, placed my hand on a table for leverage, and swung a mighty kick, the entire momentum of my body behind it. The steel capped toe of my cowboy boot hit him just below the chin, snapping his head back forcefully.

That kick would have knocked most men out. The hulk staggered back a couple of steps and was reeling, but still standing. Before he could recover, I kicked the shotgun away and, in a fluid motion, grabbed his wrist, stepped under his shoulder, twisted his arm, raised it, and pulled it down with force upon my own shoulder. The back of his arm above the elbow stopped at my shoulder, the rest of his arm below the elbow came crashing down. There was a loud crack as the elbow snapped and got bent at a crooked 90 degrees angle. The broken ends of the bones broke through the skin and stuck out. The man bellowed in pain. But he was still standing.

I took a step back and kicked him hard on the knee, the wooden heel of my boot pushing the top of his kneecap back into bone and soft tissue, rupturing ligaments and tendons, turning his knee to jelly. He flopped down. As he started falling, I swung my forearm and hit him on the side of his neck, on the brachial plexus, the network of nerves carrying signals from the spinal cord to the arms. His arms went limp. A hard kick on his temple completely knocked him out.

Twelve seconds. Both targets down.

I pulled my knife out of the man's shoulder, wiped the blood off on his shirt, and sheathed it. I went through his pockets and took out his phone. It was one of those fingerprint unlocking phones. I was curious about what he was looking at when he entered. I pressed his right thumb on the home button to unlock it. There was a man's photo on the screen. Taken inside the bar from a side angle. The man in the photo didn't seem to be aware he was being clicked. He looked like a regular clean-cut guy. I set the phone to permanent unlock and kept it in my pocket.

I turned towards the wiry man, who was still standing at a crooked angle. He whimpered as I moved towards him. He screamed when I pulled out the knife, wiped it on his shirt, and put it back in the sheath on the other boot. While I was deciding how to knock him out, he saved me the trouble by passing out. I found nothing in his pockets but a few dollars and an eight-ball of ice. As I suspected, he was a meth head. I shoved his stuff back in his pocket.

The three spectators were simply staring at me. Motionless.

I went to the waitress and examined her nose. It wasn't broken. I grabbed a handful of napkins, poured some water on them, and dabbed her nose and split lips.

"Hold it for a while. You'll be fine."

"Thanks," she said, her voice trembling. "Are they dead?"

"No. Maybe I should have killed them."

"Yes. Maybe you should have," she replied, her voice quivering with a mix of fear and anger.

"Yeah, I guess," I agreed, nodding. "But homicide becomes complicated. Even though scum like these two make it almost worth it. But don't worry. You're going to be fine."

She nodded.

"Who were these guys," I asked her.

"I've never seen them before," she replied.

"And who's this Mitch they were after?"

"Mitch Martin. He kind of owns this place. But he's not around much. He comes and goes," she replied.

I took out the hulk's phone from my pocket and showed her the man's photo.

"Is this Mitch?"

"Yes."

"This was in that big guy's pocket. Why were they after him?"

"I don't know."

She looked at the bartender. I turned to him.

"Why were these guys after Mitch?" I asked him.

"Uh... I don't know," he replied.

"You do realize why that hulk was carrying the photo? He wasn't looking for a chat with your boss. They were here to get him. And they weren't going to leave any witnesses. All of you would have been collateral damage. Dead."

The look of alarm on their faces told me they believed what I said.

"I know. Thanks for saving our asses. I really mean it, man," he replied.

"Chuck your thanks. Just tell me why these guys were here. They'd have killed me as well had I not put them down."

"I've never seen them before. Honest. Maybe it's about meth. Mitch has been dealing for a while. He said it would bring customers."

"Did it?"

"What?"

"Get customers in?"

"Not many. Mostly some lowlifes we didn't really want here," he looked at the dead man as he spoke. "And bikers."

"You serve them biker's coffee? Spike it with meth?"

"No... honest. They come in only when Mitch is around."

"Where was Mitch getting the stuff from?"

"I'm not sure. From across the border. Some big set up in Nevada. They're flooding it all over Utah, New Mexico, Arizona... most of the west, really."

"Where in Nevada?"

"Uh, I don't know. Are you DEA?"

"What do you think," I asked, irritation creeping into my voice.

"I don't know. Uh, I don't think so."

"Then why ask dumb questions? So, where in Nevada?"

"I don't know, man. It's not as if I'm dealing myself."

"There's some big set up north of Vegas," the waitress spoke up. "I heard Mitch on the phone. But no idea where."

"How about you?" I asked the bartender. "Where exactly north of Vegas? I'm sure you know."

"Honest, I don't know much. But Mitch has connections in a bar in a place called Little Butte.

He goes there a lot. They deal in that shit there. I really don't know more than that."

"Little Butte?" I was more than a little surprised. That was where I was headed.

"Some little dot on the map, man."

"Is that place called Bar as well?"

"No, man, that anonymity is just for us," he said with a sarcastic laugh. "That place is called Dawson Bar."

"Give me Mitch's number. He'll be hearing from me if I run into his pals again."

The guy didn't look so happy as he gave me the number. I had all the information I needed.

"Alright, here's the deal. I'll be locking the three of you in the washroom," I addressed all three.

"But..."

"Don't talk. Listen carefully if you want to stay alive. These two will have pals who might come looking for them. But you'll have the cops arriving here before that. You need to have a story for the cops, so those other guys don't come after you."

They nodded.

"Now, here's the story," I said. "These two guys came, shot that man, and locked you in the restroom. After that, you have no idea what happened. You just heard some voices and a struggle. Let the cops make what they will out of it. Got it?"

All three stared at me.

"You need to tell me you understand."

"Yes," all three replied at the same time.

"You better not mention me. You don't want these guys' pals breaking your bones to get more info about me. Best to stick to the story that you saw nothing."

They nodded.

"Where's the key to the restroom door?"

The waitress took it out of her pocket and handed it to me.

"All of you, inside the restroom," I said, herding them in.

They complied without a whimper.

"Remember, you're lucky to be alive. Stay that way. Call 911 once I lock the door. And stay away from this place for a couple of days after the cops have hauled these two away."

They nodded.

"What if they wake up?" the waitress asked.

"They won't. Not for a while. And when they do, they'll have to be carried out. Neither of them is going to be hurting anyone for a long time. Trust me."

She nodded. Looked convinced.

"Who are you?" the waitress asked.

"Nobody. Just a ghost."

I locked the door, wiped the key, put the hulk's prints on it, and put it in his pocket. Then I set about removing any traces of my presence.

The broken man lying next to my table was beginning to come around, groaning in a half-conscious state. I kicked him on the side of his head and put him back to sleep. I picked the Glock from under the table, wiped my prints off, got the man's prints on the gun, and flung it below a table in the far corner. I threw the shotgun in the same corner. Neither of the two would be visible if either one of the men woke up before the cops arrived. Even if they did, they wouldn't be able to do much apart from waiting to be carried out.

The last thing I did was to pick up the burger plate using a napkin and place it on the bar. I was still hungry. I decided to grab the burger.

Then I walked out, taking a huge bite. Got in my pickup and began driving.

CHAPTER 2

I called Flynn.

Assistant Director Mark Flynn. Head of the Tactical Operations Division of the US Marshal service. Based at Camp Beauregard, Louisiana.

The Special Operations Group (SOG) reported to Flynn. SOG was a tactical unit. On call 24/7, for apprehending the most-dangerous fugitives and high-risk witness relocation and security (Witsec). A Marshal's job is always tough but, when shit really goes down, you call in SOG. I used to head SOG. I was Supervisory Deputy United States Marshal Axel Blaze until six months ago, when I left the service. Now, a civilian, kind of retired at 36, I'm simply Axel Blaze.

"Are you there already?" Flynn answered with a question.

"Not yet," I replied. "Another couple of hours. There was a bit of trouble."

"Trouble? You alright?"

"I'm fine. But a couple of guys I ran into aren't."

"I thought civilian life would have mellowed you," Flynn chuckled.

"Didn't have a choice. Those guys were out to kill everyone at a diner. Something to do with meth. And guess what, Little Butte came up in the conversation."

"No kidding. That can't be just a coincidence."

"I know. I have a new lead I'll follow up as soon as I land there."

"Good. What about local cops. Any problems?"

"No. I walked away before they arrived."

"Can they track you?" Flynn asked.

"Nope. Wiped off all prints. There weren't any security cameras."

"Any witnesses?"

"Three. But they won't talk. Too scared for their own lives. They wouldn't want to get involved."

"Are you sure?"

"Positive."

"Well, let me know if there's a problem. I'll sort it out."

"I will. I'm sending you a number. Need the location. Guy called Mitch. Probably a low-level meth dealer. He should be in Little Butte. I've got the name of a bar he's likely to be at. Dawson Bar. It will be good to have confirmation he's there."

"I'll get on to it now. Little Butte is a small town. Triangulation may not be exact, but should be good enough."

"Roger that."

****

It all began with Flynn's call five days ago.

I was out camping in the Black Canyon. Trout fishing and rock climbing. That place was my back yard—I grew up on a spread that had the Black Canyon on the north and Colorado's San Juan Mountains on the south. Dad died while I was still in high school. Mom being a bit of a cowgirl, took on the handling of the ranch.

Cell phone signal in the canyon was almost non-existent. When I caught a flicker for a few minutes, Flynn called.

"How you doin', Blaze?"

It wasn't like Flynn to make a courtesy call.

"Can't complain. Everything alright?"

"Um... what have you been up to all these months?"

"Learning to live a civilian life. What's up, Flynn? You're not one for small talk."

"I know," he said, sighing. "How about getting your cowboy boots dirty? A little investigation?"

"I'm mostly a ranch hand now. Not a shamus."

"I'm not looking for a shamus. I need someone who understands Witsec."

"Uh-huh."

"We have a problem. Witnesses have been disappearing."

"I wouldn't be too worried, boss. Most of those guys aren't the most upright of citizens."

"You know the argument, Blaze. They help get the bigger fish."

"I know. I get it. But I'm out. You know why."

"I know. Well, I'm sending Carter to snoop around."

"Joe Carter?"

"Yes," Flynn replied.

"He'll get the job done."

"I'm sure. I was thinking an extra pair of independent eyes."

"Let Carter give it a shot. If he goes there and feels he needs a hand, I'll go. How about that?"

"Fair enough," he replied as he hung up.

Flynn had been a fair boss. And a good mentor. Working in the Marshals service wasn't something I had imagined doing. I mostly followed my big brother Ryan in whatever he did. Taller and heavier than me, Ryan was on track to become the star quarterback for Colorado State. I didn't have the bulk to go far in football. But, on good days, I could throw back-to-back pitches touching 95 mph. And pull a 60-yard dash in under 6.3 seconds. Never made it to the Rockies, though. Messed up my elbow before the trials.

Then 9/11 happened. Ryan enlisted. I followed a few months later—took me a while to convince mom to let me go as well.

In 2007, Ryan disappeared. Declared missing in action. All attempts to locate him were soon given up.

I became a dog with a bone. I was on my fifth tour of duty in Afghanistan, having joined the Special Forces by then, part of the 75th Ranger Regiment. I kept searching for clues on extended tours, grilling every contact while executing missions deep inside enemy territory.

It took two years to dig out the dirty truth—a colonel and two subordinates, transporting heroin made in the Taliban's labs into the US. When Ryan and another member of his unit overheard them, they were lured into a trap. And shot. They wanted to pass it off as "friendly fire", but that couldn't fly—all three were shot in the back.

I tracked down the killers. You don't kill my brother and live to talk about it.

After eleven years of active duty, I took early retirement. Mom was dying of cancer. I needed to be with her.

When I retired, the Commanding Officer of my Delta Force Sabre Squadron D was Lt Colonel Seamus Flynn. He recommended the Marshals service, asking me to contact his brother, Mark Flynn.

I was a Marshal for five years. They called me Cowboy. Not just because I grew up on a ranch. It was more because I would get frustrated with the legal process. Marshals would bust their asses apprehending fugitives, only to often see them get an easy deal. I sometimes took remedial measures.

While many witnesses going into Witsec were genuinely trying to do the right thing, some lowlifes were getting an easy deal in exchange for testimony. Small sacrifices for the greater good, I was told. I disagreed. In my book, justice was not served unless there was proper retribution. You have to pay your dues. Period.

I began doling out my own brand of justice at times. It started when I had to relocate a drug-dealing pimp to Arizona in exchange for testifying against a drug crew in San Francisco. He specialized in hooking minors on to heroin, raping them, and putting them on the street. We were going to let him loose with a new identity on an unsuspecting town. I knew he would be back doing the same shit as soon as he hit the ground.

I set him up in his new identity. But returned a few days later and caught him in the shadows. Made sure he would never walk straight again.

Then it happened with a second witness. And a third.

That began weighing on my conscience. I had taken an oath to faithfully execute my duties. Moonlighting as a vigilante didn't sit right with that. I didn't want my actions to cast a slur on the Marshals' fine reputation. I put in my papers.

Flynn couldn't understand why I was leaving. He tried his best to persuade me to stay. I kind of explained my reasons to him later. He kind of understood.

****

Four days later, Flynn called again. It was evening. I was packing my pickup to head back to the ranch.

"Carter has disappeared," Flynn blurted out the second I got on the call.

"Disappeared? What do you mean?"

"Just disappeared. Without a trace. Gave me updates for a couple of days. And then, nothing. Just fell off the radar. Cell phone off. It's been over 24 hours. He's in trouble. Or worse."

"What about the first couple of days? Did he find anything?"

"Something big seems to be going on out there. Drug related. He was still digging. The last call was yesterday, early afternoon. He was leaving for Vegas to follow up on a lead. Was going to call me in the evening. And then... nothing."

"No cell phone trace?"

"His phone's switched off. We can't get a location. The last call he made was to a burner. The call location was near a motel he was staying at. The motel says he checked out."

I went silent. Carter was a good investigator. Meticulous. My main worry was he didn't have the instinctive ruthlessness to get out of really bad shit. I felt a pang of guilt. I should have gone when Flynn asked me.

"You there," Flynn asked me.

"Huh? Yes. I agree—something's seriously wrong."

"That's why I called you. We need to know what's going on before we head in full force. I don't want whoever it is getting spooked and going underground."

"I'll go, Flynn. Any clues from local cops?"

"I haven't asked. Carter was kind of undercover. He didn't want to flash his badge until he knew what was up. He was certain some of the cops were dirty."

"Hmm... what do you want me to do?" I asked.

"Be our eyes and ears on the ground before I send in the boys. Sending them in blind won't help. But we don't have much time."

"Got it. Which place are we talking about? You didn't mention a name."

"Oh, it's a place called Little Butte. Heard of it?"

"Vaguely. One of Carter's witnesses was relocated there. Small town, Nevada, north of Vegas."

"That's the one."

"Is Carter's witness the one who disappeared?"

"No, he's fine. There were two others we relocated there. They went missing a week ago. Alarm bells were sounded when both missed their monthly check ins. When we tried contacting them... nothing, no trace," Flynn replied.

"Same day? Could they have gotten together to pull a job?"

"Not likely. They didn't know each other. Relocated there a couple of years apart. You know how it is, they wouldn't have even a remote connection to the same crowd. One was from Texas, the other from way up north, Washington."

"Did they have the same handler?"

"Yes. Scott. He retired last month."

"Who were they reassigned to?"

"No one specific, yet. The central team handles them until they get reassigned to a deputy."

"Could there be a leak?"

"Unlikely. They're all solid guys. But nothing can be ruled out. That's why I need you."

"Understood. I'll need a briefing. And hardware."

"Of course. We'll give you the recon vehicle. It has everything. I think it'll be best if I temporarily reassign you as a deputy. The badge always comes in handy if you're in a situation."

"Whatever you say, boss."

"I'm in Camp Beauregard. No point you heading east from Colorado when you need to go west. I'll fly in closer to where you are."

"Let's make it Salt Lake City. That's mid-way between me and Nevada. I'll hit the road early morning. I want to be at that motel tomorrow evening. That's the best place to start."

"I agree. Carter's witness could come in handy. Carter trusted him. I know he touched base with him."

"Right. I'll need his info."

"You'll have everything tomorrow," Flynn promised.

"Shall we meet at 1200 hours?"

"Roger that."

"At the field office?"

"Let's meet at the safe house."

"Roger that. And Flynn..."

"Yes?"

"It sounds like some gang-related thing is going on. It could become messy."

"I know, Blaze. Just don't go overboard piling up bodies."

"I always try not to. But you never know."

"I get it. You have my full backing. Just go find our boy."

"I will."

****

I headed back to the ranch to pack. My climbing gear was already in the pickup.

As I packed, I filled in Adriel about the mission. Adriel Claw, our foreman and manager, had been a part of my life ever since I was a kid. The only time he left the ranch was for four years during the early 1990s. He was a veteran of the Gulf and Bosnian wars. When dad died, he took early retirement to help mom run the ranch.

Adriel was unusually skilled with knives, even for a man deeply rooted in the Navajo warrior way. Powerfully built—about my height, but at least 20 pounds heavier. All muscle, despite being on the wrong side of 55.

He examined the knives in my kit while we talked, running his thumb along the sharp edges. Under his tutelage, knives had become as integral as guns for my preparations for any mission. I don't remember ever having cowboy boots without an inbuilt sheath.

Adriel had taken me under his wing early. With mom and Ryan gone, he felt even more obligated to watch out for me.

"I can come along, kid. You might need an extra pair of hands."

"I'll be fine, Adriel. It's a routine investigation."

He looked worried but said nothing.

****

Flynn was already at the safe house when I arrived in Salt Lake City. He briefed me about the two disappeared witnesses. There was no connection between them.

I was also given the new identity and location of Carter's witness. His cover was still intact. Went by the name Chico. We couldn't be sure if he could be trusted. I would have to make a judgment call.

A recon vehicle was waiting for me. A black Silverado pickup. A specially reinforced tonneau cover gave it a proper concealed trunk.

Installed with a GPS tracker that couldn't be tampered with, it had a weapons compartment that could only be accessed by pushing two buttons in sequence—one hidden behind the left taillight inside the trunk and the second inside the fuel tank flap. That opened the compartment hidden behind the driver's seat. A bit out of a Bond movie. You couldn't find the compartment unless you knew about it, or literally took the vehicle apart.

The pickup had a handy night-time surveillance feature—a button switched off all lights, interior as well as exterior. You could move like a ghost without any brake or cabin light giving you away.

The weapons were the standard guns used by Marshals. A Special Ops issue .40-caliber Glock-22-Gen4. Backed up by a 9mm Glock 48 for concealed carry. A screw-on silencer for use with either of them. For more firepower, there was a suppressed Colt 9mm submachine gun. With its closed bolt system, it's a dependable gun when you need to take out multiple targets. Shoots exactly where you point it.

I was given two shotguns. One was the standard Witsec Marshal issue, the Witness Protection 870, or WP870. The short barrel makes it easy to carry and maneuver. Good for hitting moving targets. It was backed up with a Mossberg 590M 12-gauge—the one with a 10-round magazine. In one pocket of the compartment were a few trackers, some burner phones, and a handful of flexicuffs.

Flynn finally handed me the US Marshal badge. A circle with the words "United States Marshal" written on it and enclosing a star. It brought up memories. Mostly good ones.

"All the best, deputy. Go find Carter," he said as we shook hands.

I left my Ford Raptor at the safe house. Took the Silverado and hit the road. Drove on the I-15 until it hit Highway 50. That snaked through a vast and mostly empty stretch of desert. Towns were few and far between. In the desolate expanse, all I had for company was the whisper of the wind. Once Highway 50 hit Nevada, it would become "The Loneliest Road in America". The best kind of road to travel on. But before that happened, I saw a neon sign shining in the distance, just as darkness had begun settling in.

The sign simply said "Bar". That's where all that shit happened with the two hitmen. After locking the bar workers in the restrooms, I was back on the road again.

CHAPTER 3

Night had fallen as I began approaching Little Butte two hours later.

"Welcome to Little Butte." The four words were written on two huge sandstone signs. Shaped like buttes. Standing on each side of the road. Lit up eerily by small lamps looking up from the ground.

"Welcome to Dawson Country." Four more words on a large billboard a couple of hundred yards further on.

Whoever these Dawsons were, they seemed to be in love with their name. I passed a new sign bearing the name every two hundred yards. Dawson Bar & Lounge. Dawson Hotel. Dawson Bank. And then a bigger sign: Dawson Pharma. Pharmacy or pharmaceutical company? I wasn't sure. Either way, it looked like these guys owned the town.

The Butte Motel came up on the right, half a mile before the town began. It didn't look like the most prosperous of establishments. The neon sign announcing its name to the world seemed unable to make up its mind—few seconds on, few seconds off, unending repetition. The Vacancy sign below it was working fine. There were a couple of beat-up pickups in the parking lot.

Carter had been staying at the motel before he mysteriously disappeared. The motel claimed he had checked out. I didn't buy that. I pulled in, but didn't exit the truck for a few seconds, considering my next move.

Apart from the motel, there were two leads I had to follow—Mitch, and Carter's contact, Chico.

Flynn's call at that moment decided the issue. Mitch's phone had been switched off in the area around Dawson Bar half an hour ago. I decided to head there first. The motel could come later. As I was pulling out, a red Mustang turned into the driveway. Single occupant. It was too dark to see a face.

I headed towards town. There was something strange about it. It was split in two starkly contrasting halves. The decaying part came first. Boarded up storefronts. Run down houses, many in various stages of collapse. Chico's diner lay at the end of it. There were a couple of vacant lots next to it.

Once I drove past the lots, it felt as if I was leaving a nightmare behind and waking up to the American Dream. That part of town was shiny new. Tree-lined avenues, shiny stores. A newly paved road gleamed between spanking new storefronts. Even the post office looked glamorous. The three-story Dawson Hotel located at the main crossing dominated the other flat structures. A neon sign outside the hotel advertised a Bar & Lounge. But the place looked dead.

I decided to get a feel of the town's layout before heading into the bar. Dawson Bank lay on the other side of the crossing, followed by Dawson Pharmacy. That meant the Dawson Pharma sign I saw earlier was a pharmaceutical company. These guys did own the town. A single-story building carrying the sign, Little Butte Police Headquarters, was located further down the road. Beyond it stood a water tower.

I took a U-turn and drove back to the main crossing. The road veering to the right seemed to be leading to an expensive neighborhood. The tree-lined avenue was in stark contrast to the road with the bombed out look I passed earlier.

I stopped outside the hotel and went in. A kid, looking barely out of high school, was manning the reception. Must have been a part-time gig for him as night manager. I was informed the new bar would open in a week's time, when it would move from its current location. The kid asked me to take the road going west from the crossing, the direction opposite to the tree-lined expensive neighborhood.

"We don't have a great crowd out there right now," the kid said as I began walking out. "It'll be different once this place opens up," he added.

It sounded like the bar was a dump. I drove down the road he pointed me towards. After about half a mile of unbuilt area, a neon sign proclaimed Dawson Bar & Lounge. As I pulled in, the first thing I noticed were six Harley-Davidsons in the parking. All were shiny, well cared for. Almost rendered the two cars in the driveway invisible.

When I opened the entrance door, it became evident this was a biker's bar. If the Harleys outside didn't quite make it clear, "Highway to Hell" booming inside removed any doubts.

The bar wasn't really a dump, but it wasn't the kind of place you would go looking for a hook up.

It was divided into two halves. The entrance led to the main area. It had the bar and about a dozen tables. Three of them were occupied. The other part was separated from the bar area by a wall with an arched entrance. It had a pool table, a few scattered chairs, and four tables. There was no one seated there except for a couple of bikers playing pool.

A door beside the bar led to the kitchen and restrooms. I checked them out before pulling a chair. Scope out the surroundings before making any move—one of the simple rules that keep people in my line alive. The door opened into a narrow corridor. There was a locked kitchen door on the left. A bit further on were two restrooms facing each other. There was another latched door to a supplies room further to the right. There was a woman in there, gathering some stuff. Small but shapely. Probably the waitress. Beyond the supplies room was the rear exit door.

Three bikers were sitting on one of the three occupied tables in the main bar area. All of them dressed in black. Same as the two bikers playing pool. Black leather trousers and vests over black T-shirts. Called themselves Nevada Devils.

Two guys on the table looked almost identical—long hair, ZZ Top kind of long beards, heavy build, layers of fat building over what were once muscular frames. The third guy was an even bigger bear of a man. Most probably the leader. Tattoos across both muscular arms. Sporting a mohawk. A barbed wire tattooed across his forehead.

Five bikers, six Harleys. I wondered where the sixth one was.

The bartender was medium height but stocky. Tattoos snaked out from under his shirt sleeves on to his thick forearms. He looked like he could handle himself. Not a friendly character. Not that I was looking to be best pals with anyone in there. All I wanted was to get my hands on Mitch and get a clue about what was up. My running into those other guys looking for him had been a coincidence, but I had a feeling that this was all related to what Carter had been investigating.

I ordered a single shot of bourbon but didn't outright ask the bartender about Mitch. I decided to hang around for a few minutes, hoping to see Mitch make an appearance. If he had switched off his phone here less than an hour ago, he could be lurking around.

The corner table was already occupied. I sat at a table to one side of the bar, back to the wall. Unobstructed view.

The waitress came out of the door, carrying a box full of packets of chips. She smiled at me before going behind the bar and putting them down. She seemed out of place in that bar populated by big, burly men. For one thing, she was tiny—not more than three inches over five feet, even in her high-heeled sandals. Not much over 100 pounds. But filled out in the right places.

She was in her mid-twenties. Pretty. Light brown hair done in a ponytail. Sparkling green eyes. The name tag said Ellie.

Ellie turned out to be very friendly. I didn't expect a ray of sunshine in that brooding place.

"Hi! Welcome to Dawson Bar and Lounge. I'm Ellie," she said pointing to her name tag. "You haven't been here before, have you?"

It was the kind of cheerful pitch I would have expected from a waitress at a family joint in Disneyworld. Not in that dingy bar.

"You got me, Ellie. I'm new in town. You don't get a lot of visitors out here, do you?"

"Well, not mostly. Although a big crowd descended here about a week ago. Some business convention organized by the Dawsons."

"Business convention? Little Butte is a business hub?"

"Well, not really. But the Dawsons have big plans. It was something to do with their company."

"Pharmaceutical company?"

"Yeah. They're rebuilding the entire town. There's a new bar opening in town next week. I'll be moving there. And they'll be building a casino as well. They'll need people in hospitality. That's why I'm hanging around here."

"And I thought you were here for this lovely crowd."

She smiled. "It's a job. They don't hassle me. And I have just been in town for a month. I've got plans."

"I hope they work out. Tell me, Ellie, does Mitch often hang around here?"

"Mitch? Yeah, he does. He was here a while ago. Got a call and rushed out."

"Any idea where I could find him?"

"Not really. He just comes and goes. No idea where when he's not here. Maybe Tats will know."

"Tats?"

"Yeah, the bartender."

"Curious name. Thanks. You've been a big help."

"Can I get you another drink? The cook's off today, so I can't offer much to eat apart from chips."

"Thanks. I'll be on the road soon. Not really in the mood for chips."

"I can rustle up a hotdog. That's the best I can do."

"Can't say no to a good old hotdog."

"On it. Enjoy your drink."

I knew Tats wouldn't be as forthcoming as Ellie. I waited a couple of minutes, then walked over to the bar.

"Mitch happen to come in today?"

"Yup, he was...," he began answering instinctively. But he caught himself and added, "I've never seen you around before. You're a stranger."

"That's very perceptive of you."

"We don't like nosy strangers asking questions," he said in a slightly raised voice, looking towards the bikers.

"That's not very friendly now, is it? Here I am, trying to get to know the pleasant folk of Little Butte."

"Why don't you have your drink and be on your way."

"Let me try and explain the concept of customer service. I'm a customer, you're a bartender. I pay, you pour. I ask, you answer. Simple, isn't it?"

"You've got your drink, wiseass. That's all the customer service you get out here."

"I don't think you got what I was trying to explain. The thing is, I know Mitch hangs around this place."

"Nope, never heard of him."

"Think again, you might remember."

"Told you man. I don't know any Mitch," he said a little loudly, looking at the bikers.

Ellie had in the meantime come back with my hotdog. A scared look appeared on her face when she heard the bartender deny any knowledge of

Mitch. I looked up at the mirrors behind the bar to observe the bikers. They were watching me.

I headed back to my table. The bartender went off to the far end of the bar.

I knew I had set something in motion. I waited for some reaction as I sat on my chair.

Ellie placed the plate on my table, trying to force a smile. But she looked nervous.

"Ellie, listen to me carefully," I said, locking eyes with her. "No one could hear us over the music. We never had that conversation about Mitch."

She looked about unsurely.

"They also can't hear what I'm saying to you now. Got it? But you need to act normal."

She nodded, looking a bit less unsure.

"Now, relax. Carry on with your stuff and ignore me. You don't want to arouse suspicion."

"Yes," she said, nodding. "Thanks."

"Don't worry. Put on a smile and carry on."

Ellie smiled.

"Thanks. These guys are dangerous. Careful."

"Don't worry about it."

Ellie almost had her cheerful expression on by the time she turned and walked back. She got the check for the customers at one of the tables who were getting ready to leave.

The leader of the bikers nodded at the other two, got up, and moved to the pool table. The other two bikers got up and walked towards the restroom. They exchanged glances with the bartender. He gave a slight nod. A minute later, he came over to my table.

"You wanted Mitch? He's at the back. Follow me," he said.

I knew it was a trap. Ellie looked at me with alarm in her eyes. She shook her head slightly, signaling me not to follow the bartender.

I had no option but to play the man's bluff. I must have hit some nerve. The bikers had decided to mess me up. They weren't even waiting for the customers at the one remaining table to leave.

It was clear I wasn't getting out of that place without a fight. The only thing up to me was finishing it quickly. Without using a knife. It would be a close quarter fight in the corridor. I couldn't avoid killing one of them if I had a knife in my hand.

A knife can act as a deterrent only in a fight with a single opponent. If you draw a blade against multiple adversaries, you need to be ready to stab and slash until most of them are down. If you have a problem with killing, it's best not to draw a knife in such a situation—you'll almost certainly be killed with that same knife otherwise.

If one of them died, it would mean the cops getting involved. End of my investigation. I was on a mission to find Carter—I could feel the clock ticking every second.

I needed three quick takedowns. In a narrow corridor. Almost zero maneuverability. No space for elbows or kicks. It would have to be fists. Each punch would need to be decisive.

One thing in my favor was the entrance was not in the line of sight of the guys at the pool table. And the music was loud. They wouldn't be able to see or hear what was going on in the passage. They would also be overconfident that three of their guys would easily take me down.

The bartender opened the door and waited for me to enter the passageway. I stopped and waved at him to lead the way. Feeling cocky about the trap, he walked in. I followed him. The door closed behind me.

The moment the bartender crossed the kitchen door within the corridor, I punched him full force on the back of his head, on the fleshy part just below the external occipital protuberance, the knobby part at the back of the head where the skull meets the top vertebra called Atlas. That punch would have killed a slenderer man. The bartender had a neck built like a tree trunk. He didn't die. But the punch blew his lights out. He never knew what hit him as he crashed forward. He would be wearing a neck brace for months.

The two bikers were lurking in the entrances to the two restrooms facing each other. Both were expecting me to go down. Both rushed out to kick the falling man. I hit the one on the left first, smashing the heel of my palm onto his temple. He hadn't yet completely exited the door. His head slammed against the door jamb. That knocked him out cold.

The first biker was falling to the floor by the time the second one realized what was happening. He began turning towards me. Bad move. Left him very vulnerable. I smashed my boot on the side of his knee just as he was turning on it. Ligaments snapped as the knee bent at an angle it wasn't supposed to. He began sinking. A forceful swing of my elbow onto his nose completely flattened it, smashing the bone. I grabbed his hair and slammed his head hard against the wall. Lights out for him as well.

All three targets down in under ten seconds.

But I had no time to relax. I couldn't hang around for the other three to come bursting through the door, checking on their pals. Without the element of surprise on my side, it would be tough taking on three large opponents in that confined space.

I opened the door to the supplies room and dragged the three men inside. None of them would be waking up for a while. I noticed a baseball bat on a shelf and grabbed it.

I shut and latched the door. But it didn't have a lock. I opened the rear exit door inward and placed a wedge beneath it, almost hiding the door of the supplies room.

I walked out the rear door, rounded the corner, placed the baseball bat on the ground beside the front entrance door, and walked into the bar again. John Kay was belting out "Born to be Wild". I was back at my table within two minutes of leaving it.

Ellie's eyes brightened when she saw me walking back. The three bikers around the pool table had stopped playing by that time and were standing together. They looked at me, then at each other, confusion written large on their faces. The leader of the trio nodded to one of the guys to go take a look. The biker got up and went towards the corridor.

In the meantime, the customers on the last remaining table paid their bill and left. Ellie went behind the bar and remained there. A minute later, the biker came in through the front entrance again. He walked back to his group, shrugging his shoulders.

The leader shouted at him, glared at me, and walked towards the passage to check for himself. It was time for my final move. I knew when he came back in, he and his gang would set upon me.

I got up and walked out the front door. The other two bikers got up in a hurry to follow me. I was ready with the baseball bat the moment the first guy came out, a knife in his hand. I swung the bat full force onto his shin. I heard a distinct crack as his tibia bone broke. The man howled in pain and doubled over, grabbing his leg.

The guy following him couldn't stop himself in time and tripped over him, putting his hands out to break his fall. I swung the bat just as he broke his fall, his body weight on his arms. It hit him just below the left elbow. He collapsed as the bone gave way. A quick, hard tap with the bat at the back of his head put him to sleep.

I kicked the knife way out of the reach of the other man and walked around towards the back entrance to catch the large guy as he came out. I reached the back door but found it shut from the inside. The leader was smarter than his gang. He must have checked the supplies room. I guessed he would be following me through the front door. I retraced my steps.

I heard him curse when he saw his broken boys. As I turned the corner, he rushed at me in fury, knife in one hand. As he began raising his hand to slash me with the knife, I rushed forward, holding the bat straight out, slamming it into his solar plexus. His own momentum made the impact even more severe. The bat plunged into his midsection. He doubled over, gasping for air. I didn't want to leave the bear of a man able enough to come back at me later. I stepped back and struck him hard just below the knee. That would keep him on crutches for a while. A tap on the side of his head knocked him out.

I went around to the front, raising the baseball bat over my head, stretching my shoulders. The biker with the broken shin bone was lying where I had left him, groaning.

"Where will I find Mitch," I asked calmly, still stretching.

"Fuck you," he shouted, voice breaking with pain and anger.

I didn't have the time and patience. I tapped the bat on his broken shin bone. The man bellowed in pain.

"Where will I find Mitch?"

This time, he was more communicative.

"He's at the motel," he said, gasping.

"Are you sure? Cause I'll be back if I don't find him there."

"I swear, man. That's where he went."

"What car does he drive?"

"A red Mustang."

The image of the Mustang pulling into the motel driveway flashed through my mind. That must have been Mitch. I kicked myself inwardly.

"Why were you guys trying to get me," I asked the biker.

"Get you? You're the one with a baseball bat... I'm the one on the ground with a broken leg."

"You know you would've stuck that knife in me if I gave you half a chance. I won't ask again. Why were you out to get me?"

"You were after Mitch. We're supposed to be protecting him."

"Protecting him from what?"

"I don't know, man. People are after him. You were the one looking for him. You tell me why."

"I wasn't after him, knucklehead. I just had a few questions for him."

"How was I to know that? Max asked us to get you, so we did."

"Who's Max?" I asked.

"Our president. The big guy who rushed at you back there."

"President? You gotta be kidding me. President of what?"

"Our bikers' club."

"What... five losers in leather tights need a president telling them what to do?"

"Six, including the bartender. That's the way it is with clubs, man."

"Yeah, sure. This is all about meth, isn't it? Are the Dawsons running your little meth racket?"

He didn't reply. I raised the bat.

"No, wait," he said. "I don't know much, man. I swear. The Dawsons run the meth supply. But we don't deal with them. We're way down the chain. We deal with Mitch. All we do is carry some of it over the border, to Utah, Idaho..."

"Where do the Dawsons get the meth?"

"I swear I don't know. No one knows where they get it. There have been a lot of Mexicans around town. Maybe it's coming from them."

I figured he didn't really know more. It was time to head to the motel.

"Now here's the deal," I said. "None of you guys is going to be riding for a while. And things are going to get ugly around here. There are real bad guys after Mitch. So, best clear out tonight. I'm giving you the chance you wouldn't have given me."

"I can't even get up, man. None of us can walk."

"Not my problem. You shouldn't have started it. If you want to avoid further pain, figure out a way to get away tonight. A couple of your pals in the supply room will have terrible headaches, but they can walk. Figure it out. I'm going in for a minute and will be on my way. Don't move until I'm gone. Got it?"

"Yes."

I went in. Ellie was calmly sitting on a stool behind the bar.

"All done?" she asked me.

"All done," I replied.

"Are they dead?"

"No, just out of action for a while."

"Oh," she said, and spoke again: "Who are you? They were six big guys, all tattooed and dangerous. I was worried they'd kill you. But they're lying broken, and not a scratch on you."

"I got lucky."

"Really? You knew you were walking into a trap. And you were ready for it."

"Yes, thanks for warning me."

"I don't think my warning mattered. Seriously, who are you? Why were these guys out to get you? Is this some gang war thing?"

"My name's Axel. All I can tell you for now is I'm one of the good guys. It's best you don't know more. I need a day to sort some things out. I'll tell you everything once I'm done. Can you trust me on that?"

"I guess. I do trust you."

"Good. You're safe. You've got nothing to worry about."

"Alright. If you believe that."

"I do. It's time to get away from this place."

"OK," Ellie replied.

"Where do you live? Do you have any family here?"

"No family, but I've got a small place in the old part of town."

"I don't think you're in any danger, but you better stay somewhere else for tonight. You've got someplace you can go?"

"Hmm... I can stay at a friend's. But... you said I was safe."

"You are. It's just a precaution."

"Is anyone going to come looking for me?"

"Only to try to find out about me. But I don't think anyone will. All these bikers will skip town tonight."

"How do you know?" Ellie asked.

"I asked them nicely. I think they'll take the hint."

"I see. What's going to happen here?"

"This place is going to be closed for a while."

"Mm-hmm."

"How do you travel? Do you have a car?"

"I do. But it broke down a couple of days ago. I've been hitching a ride."

"I'll drop you at your friend's. And be on my way from there."

"Are you leaving town?"

"Nope. I'm gonna be around. For a day or two at least. But we need to get moving now."

"OK," she said, coming out from behind the bar.

"There are a couple of guys lying outside. Just step around them. Don't stop."

"Alright."

I stepped out and stood in front of the only biker who was still conscious. I unlocked the pickup with my remote key. Ellie moved carefully around us and got inside.

I held out the baseball bat to the biker. He flinched.

"Use this as a crutch. Your pals are in the supply room. They might already be awake. Better skip town tonight. Those men will come looking for you if you don't. They're trying to get Mitch. They'll get you guys as well if you're in the way."

He nodded and grabbed the bat.

I got inside the pickup. Ellie gave me directions.

When we hit the old town, the contrast between the new and old parts of town struck me again. The streets were in a bad way.

"It's almost as if we're driving the streets of some shantytown. Why's half the town in such a bad shape?" I asked Ellie.

"Everyone wonders about that when they come here. The Dawsons just want to build everything from scratch. I'm not sure why?"

"Can I ask you a personal question?"

"Sure."

"What are you doing in this place?"

"Um... I was supposed to be in Vegas. But had to leave. Long story."

"And that thing about the casino?"

"That's why I'm sticking around. Daphne promised me a job if I stuck around long enough."

"Daphne?"

"Daphne Dawson. She's part of the family."

"Who are these Dawsons?"

"They own this town, as you already must have seen. There's old man Baxter and his three kids—Jasper, Grady and Daphne."

"That's it? The old man and his three kids?"

"Yes. They came to town from someplace else four, five years ago. And now own most of it."

"Interesting."

"Over there, to the left. I'll get down here," she said, pointing towards a house.

The house was one in a row of crumbling two-story buildings. Not all of them looked inhabited. The streets weren't too well lit.

"The bar will be closed tomorrow," I said, as we came to a stop.

"Are you sure?"

"Positive. You better stay put until you hear from me. Give me your number," I said, handing her my phone.

She looked at me curiously.

"That wasn't a line," I said.

"Didn't sound like one," she replied, handing back my phone after keying in her number. "So, are you a cop?"

"Not really. Let's just say I'm an investigator."

"I see. Thanks for looking out for me."

"You take care, Ellie. I'll be in touch soon."

Ellie touched my hand and gave it a slight squeeze before getting out. She walked over and pressed a doorbell. A light came out from inside and a woman appeared. I turned the pickup around and headed towards the motel.

CHAPTER 4

As I drove towards the motel, I figured the bikers might have sent a warning to Mitch. There might be a trap waiting for me. I stopped, opened the weapons compartment, took out a Glock, and placed it in the concealed holster in the back of my jeans. I also grabbed a couple of flexicuffs and shoved them in a back pocket.

I drove past the motel, keeping an eye out for Mitch's Mustang. I couldn't see it in the parking lot. One of the two pickups I had seen earlier was also missing.

I left the road a couple of hundred yards away from the motel and stopped the pickup at a distance from the road. It was all flat, unbuilt area. I moved off on foot, taking a detour around the motel to approach it from the back. The rear of the motel lay in complete darkness. The moon wasn't out that night.

The motel was laid out in a straight line facing the road. There was a single-story reception area on the left, followed by a rectangular block of twenty rooms laid out on two floors. I walked from the far end towards the reception area. There was a faint light coming out of one of the rooms. When I peeked through the rear window, I saw the room lights were off. The light was coming from the bathroom. There was someone in there. But I couldn't see who it was.

As I moved in the darkness towards the reception room, I bumped into a parked car.

Draped by a makeshift tarp cover. It was a Mustang. I couldn't make out the color in the darkness. But it had to be Mitch's car—no reason for anyone else trying to hide it.

I made my way to the reception and peeked in through the window. There was a man behind the counter. Latino. Shorter than me, but heavier. Less muscle, more fat. Talking on a cell phone. If he had been warned, he would most certainly have a shotgun under the counter. There was a partially closed door behind him, leading to a back office. Lights were on in there.

I moved towards the entrance door. It was open, but the reception counter was some distance from it. If there was a shotgun under the counter, the man couldn't be rushed. I gathered some pebbles and stood beside the door, hidden in the shadows. I threw one at the door of the pickup parked in front of the rooms. It made a distinct sound in the quiet night. The man looked up. Not hearing any other sound, he went back to his phone.

I waited a few seconds and threw another pebble. The man raised his head but didn't move. I threw a third pebble, not at the door, but at the tire hub. The sound was different and a bit muted. The man finally got up. He was about to step towards the door when he stopped, leaned back, and picked up a shotgun from under the counter. He then walked towards the door, shotgun in hand. I drew my gun and a boot knife.

The man stood at the door for a few seconds, looking towards the pickup. He finally took a step out. The moment he did that, I walked out of the shadows. I pushed the gun against his spine and pressed the knife on his throat. He drew in a sharp breath as the knife nicked him. He stopped breathing for a few seconds. A sharp blade on the throat has that effect—even more than a gun on the spine.

"Easy now," I whispered. "Take a breath."

The man began breathing again.

"Don't make a sound. My hands might twitch."

The man remained soundless.

"Pass me the shotgun, barrel first," I ordered.

He obediently followed my command. I kept the Glock back in the holster and grabbed the shotgun, slightly relieving the pressure on the knife. I pulled him back into the shadows.

"Is Mitch in the room behind the counter?"

"No."

I again pressed the blade on his throat.

"Lie once more and it'll go in deeper."

"I'm not lying, man. I swear. Mitch was here, but drove off a few minutes ago."

"What car does he drive?"

"A Mustang. But he didn't take that. He hid the Mustang at the back. Took a pickup. I swear man, you can check for yourself."

I knew that already. The man was telling the truth.

"Is there anyone else in the motel?"

"Just the motel owner in one of the rooms. Mitch got him packing some stuff."

"What stuff? Meth?"

"I don't know, man. Meth, coke, who knows... It's Mitch's thing. I'm not into all that shit, man. I swear," he replied, his voice getting a bit high pitched.

"OK. Keep your voice down."

He went quiet. Just nodded.

"Who's in the room behind the counter?"

"No one," he replied.

"Why were you carrying a shotgun? Were you expecting trouble?"

"Tucker, the motel owner—he told me to hang on to it. These guys are mixed up in some bad shit, man. Nothing to do with me. I swear."

"We're going to go in now. I'll be behind you. If it turns out there's anyone in that room, I'll shoot through you to get to him. Got it?"

"I know, man. There's no one here," he whispered in a shaky voice.

I sheathed the knife and led him inside. He stopped before the door and looked at me questioningly. I signaled him to open it.

The room was empty. It was just a back office. A computer, a couple of desks, and a few chairs.

"When's Mitch going to be back?"

"I don't know, man. I swear. He was in a mad rush. He told me to stay here and just left."

"And you're what, his bodyguard? Guarding this place while he's away."

"Bodyguard? Me? Are you kidding? I'm just a businessman. Nothing to do with this dump. I don't do guns, man. I'm not even supposed to be here," he said in a desperate whisper.

"So, why were you manning the reception?"

"Mitch asked me to. He's got some scary friends, man. Bikers and all. Real scary guys. Best do what he says if he asks you to do something. If it was up to me, I would've been back at my own joint. I've got a business to run, man."

The guy talked too much.

"Alright. Are you expecting anyone else?"

"No. But it's a motel, man. I know it looks like shit, but people might come over, looking for a room. Don't hold that against me, man."

"OK. In which room is Mitch's guy?"

"103."

I checked the key rack behind the counter. There were many keys missing.

"I thought you said there was only one guy in the motel. Where are these other keys?"

"Those biker dudes I told you about. I think they're staying in the rooms. They aren't around right now. I don't know, man. I don't work here, I swear."

I guessed he was talking about the bikers I left back at the bar.

"Where are the duplicate keys?"

"Uh, I don't know. I'll look for them," he looked desperately all over the room.

I found the duplicate keys on a wall at the back of the room. I picked the one for 103.

"I'm going to cuff you while I go talk to this other guy."

"C'mon, man. I've told you everything you asked me."

"Not yet. I have a few more questions. Don't worry, I don't plan to hurt you. But I can't have you running away. Turn around and put your hands behind you. I can do it the hard way if you want."

"Hard way isn't good, bro. I'm an easy guy," he turned around obediently and held his hands at the back. I cuffed him.

"Go sit on that chair in the corner. If I find you away from the chair when I get back, you'll be in trouble."

"My ass will be glued to this chair, bro," he said, quickly sitting down in the corner.

"Good. What's your name?"

"Chico."

"Chico?" My voice betrayed my surprise. That was the name of Carter's witness. I didn't expect to bump into him at the motel.

"Yeah. I'm kind of famous out here. Chico's Diner. The best joint in town. That's me, man. I told you I'm a businessman."

That was quite a coincidence. The man was Carter's witness who I was planning to check out later. He was supposed to be in witness protection but seemed involved in a meth racket. So much for protecting upright citizens in Witsec.

"Wait here. I'll be back."

I shut and latched the door behind me. Took out the cartridges from the shotgun and put it under the counter. I was exiting the main entrance to turn towards the motel rooms when I heard the sound of a vehicle. I stepped back towards the outer edge of the reception room and crept into the shadows.

A black van was speeding down the road from town. It turned towards the motel, its headlights sweeping across the entrance. I crouched behind some bushes.

The van stopped next to the pickup. Four armed Hispanic men exited the vehicle. Mini Uzis in the hands of two of them. The third man carried an AR-15 rifle. The fourth one had a shotgun. All guns had suppressors fitted on them.

This was no random group of men. It was an execution squad. The suppressors on their weapons and the way they moved made it clear.

Three of them walked towards room 103 and took up positions outside the door. One man with an Uzi and the one with the rifle stood on each side of the door. The man with the shotgun stood in front of it.

The fourth guy walked in my direction, Uzi in one hand. I stepped further back in the shadows. He entered the reception area cautiously, ready for any trouble. He stopped in front of the room behind the counter, undid the latch, opened the door, and looked in. I took a step forward and aimed my gun at his head. I would have to shoot him if he made a move to kill Chico.

But he didn't. He stepped back, shut the door again. I stepped back into the shadows again. The man walked out towards the van. He opened the front door, took out a couple of big, folded plastic sheets, handed one to the other men, and began walking back with the other sheet towards the reception room.

I could easily guess what the plastic sheet was for. This guy was going to the room to kill Chico. The sheet was to avoid leaving any trace of the killing. No blood + No bodies = No killing.

I couldn't let him do it. Chico was my only source of information. I wished I had grabbed the suppressor for my Glock. If I shot the guy, the loud sound would have the other three coming there in no time. My gun would be no match for the three with their heavy arsenal. I would have to get close enough to use the knife. And use it decisively. That man would have to be taken out silently and swiftly, without any struggle. I put my gun back into the holster and pulled out my boot knife.

As soon as the man entered the room, I got out of the shadows, tiptoed towards the door, and took up position beside it. I heard the muffled sound of the shotgun go off outside. Those three guys must have busted the door of room 103 and gone in.

The man inside the reception office placed his gun on a chair and began spreading the plastic sheet on a wide area of the floor. His body language was as relaxed as if he was covering the floor to paint the ceiling. His neck and face were covered with tattoos. The man had more ink on his face than most tattooed men have on their entire bodies. These men were cartel sicarios. Hard core assassins.

Chico seemed to be following my instructions like an obedient schoolkid. He was sitting transfixed in the chair, watching with terrified eyes as the man prepared to kill him.

While he was spreading the sheet, the killer momentarily turned his back to me and took a step backward. That was the moment I was waiting for. I took a quick step, slipped my right arm around his neck, pulled his head to the side, and plunged the knife into the exposed area of his neck. The blade sliced through the carotid artery and jugular vein. The hilt of the knife kept the blood from spurting, but it flowed out and down his body as if a hose pipe had been turned on. The man made a gurgling sound and went limp within seconds. I let him down on the floor.

"Hide behind the table and don't make a sound. There are three more killers out there. I'm going to turn off the lights," I whispered urgently to Chico.

He seemed to be in shock. He kept sitting on the chair, looking at the dead man. Not a word came out of him.

I picked the dead man's Uzi. Set it to semi-automatic mode. Then closed the door of the darkened room behind me.

As I headed out, I heard the muffled staccato sound of an Uzi. A short burst, lasting no more than a second. One of the assassins must have taken out the man in room 103. I knew they would be heading to the reception area soon. I crept back into the shadows. I saw one man come out of the room carrying a bag in one hand and an Uzi in the other. He put the bag in the passenger compartment before walking towards the back of the van.

Meanwhile, the other two men came out, carrying a body wrapped in plastic sheet. They headed to the back of the van. The third man opened the door, and they flung the body inside. The man closed the door and headed back towards room 103. The other two headed straight towards me. I pressed further into the shadows.

The moment the two men entered the reception to move towards the counter, I stepped out and shot the one closer to me. Point blank. Double tap just above the back of the neck, where the spinal cord meets the brain stem. The suppressed gun let out two muffled cracks. The man fell to the ground in a heap. He was dead before he began falling.

The other man began to turn. There was a distinctive snake tattoo on his face. I couldn't help noticing it just before I shot him—a coiled rattlesnake on the side of his face, its mouth baring its fangs just above the man's temple. A double tap just below the fangs made sure the man's killing days were over.

I threw the Uzi and picked up the dead man's AR-15 rifle. I placed the stock firmly in my shoulder, held the rifle straight out in front of me, cheek pressed against the stock, eye looking through the front sight, and moved towards room 103, ready to take down the fourth killer. As I was approaching the room, the man walked out. He saw me, but before he could even begin raising his Uzi, I put him down with three quick shots—two to the chest and a third to the head. There was a short, muffled burst from his Uzi as his finger twitched just as he died.

I went to the van and looked inside the passenger cabin. There was a bag on the seat. Full of packets of crystal meth. Under the bag were a couple of the plastic sheets those guys were carrying for their victims. Lying beside the bag were two shotguns, three AR-15 rifles, and a couple of suppressors. Something big was up—those guys were equipped to wage war.

I went to the back of the van and opened the door. I stepped back in shock when I looked inside. There were six bodies lying there. Wrapped in clear plastic sheets. I used the flashlight of my phone to look at the faces. I recognized five of them—four bikers and the bartender. All of them executed— bullet to the head.

I realized I had landed in the middle of a drug war.

CHAPTER 5

I walked back to the reception room, trying to get my head around the events unfolding like a chain reaction. I had been in town less than two hours. And here I was, standing outside a godforsaken motel surrounded by ten dead bodies. And I hadn't even begun my search for Carter. The way things were happening, my hopes of seeing him alive were fading. But my resolve to get to the bottom of this was getting set in stone.

I decided it was time to tighten the screws on Chico. I had already begun to believe he may have inadvertently gotten mixed up in all this—wrong place, wrong time. But I needed to push him more to be sure.

I went over his details in my mind. Original identity: Miguel Sanchez. New identity: Jesús Alvarez. Nickname: Chico.

I walked into the reception room and turned on the light. Chico was sitting hunched on a chair in a corner. His eyes got fixated on the body of his would-be assassin. I walked towards him and snapped my fingers in front of his face.

"Snap out of it. We've got work to do," I said as I cut off his cuffs with a knife. I stood against the wall and turned his chair towards me to shift his focus from the dead assassin lying a few feet away.

"Who are you?" he asked me, his voice sounding detached from reality. "Some super assassin black ops commando dude? I was like, damn, those were some bomb moves, man."

"Don't worry about me. Why were these killers out for your blood? If I hadn't landed in your mess, you would have been lying wrapped in that plastic sheet—a bullet between your eyes."

That brought him back to reality as he turned his head to look at the dead man, before quickly turning it back again.

"I know, brother. And I thank you from the bottom of my heart. I owe you, bro."

"Yeah, right. Quit stalling. Answer my question. Why were they out to kill you?"

"I swear, man, I've got no idea why they'd want to kill me. I'm a nice guy. Ask anyone."

"Really?"

"I told you, I'm just a small businessman. A man with a diner. A simple man trying to earn an honest living."

"Honest living? Really?"

"I swear, bro. I have never once had a problem with the law in Little Butte."

"And what about before Little Butte? What about Chicago, Miguel?"

His face lost color for a second. But he recovered quickly.

"Chicago? Miguel? You have me confused with someone else. I'm Chico, man. My name is..."

"Jesús Alvarez," I said, cutting him midway.

That shut him up.

"Time to cut out the bullshit. I'm here for Carter. And if I don't find him, you and all your gangster buddies are going to be wrapped in plastic sheets before I leave town. *Comprende*, amigo?"

"Carter? Are you a Marshal?" he asked, almost in a whisper.

"What do you think?"

"Yes. Of course. Oh man, you have no idea... I've been worried sick about Carter. That's the only reason I've been sticking with Mitch. There's this gang war thing going on, man. Mitch works for the Dawsons. They're real bad dudes. They've got this meth racket going on. But Mitch was also running his own little show on the side. I think maybe the Dawsons found out and don't like it. And then these Mexican *hombres* landed in town. And they're like, even badder dudes. And they think because I'm like, Latino, so I'm their amigo."

"Yeah, right. They were a friendly bunch, especially this one. Looked like he wanted to show you his love."

"Not these dudes, man. I have never seen this guy before. This town has been going crazy ever since they had this big gangster meet a week ago. I'll tell you all about it, man. My life's on the line. I've been living in mortal fear every day."

"Fear of what? Have there been other guys after you?"

"Not before this one. But Carter suddenly vanishing really rattled me. I've got no idea what's going on. He was my handler, for Christ's sake. And if my handler goes missing, who do I ask for help."

"We'll talk about that. Do you have Mitch's location?"

"Yes. I do. And I swear, no more bullshit. Cross my heart. Nothing but the truth will come out of my mouth."

"Where's he?"

"There's an abandoned gas station three miles out of town. He's hiding there. That Mustang he used to prance around in has now become a pain in the ass for him, so he left it at the back and took Tucker's pickup. He left twenty minutes before you came."

"Who's Tucker?" I asked him.

"The motel owner. The guy in room 103. Mitch had a load of crystal stacked in the room, hidden in the false ceiling. He wanted me to pack it for him, but I said no. I don't touch that shit, man. Not after Chicago. You know how hard it is leaving your life in the city and living in a shithole like Little Butte. My mama, bless her soul, she never let me hear the end of it. She even picked my new name, Jesús, hoping it would make me a good man. And it did, I mean, look at me, man. I'm like, super respectable now..."

"Focus, Chico. I'll listen to your life story later."

"Yeah, sure, so... what were you saying?"

"We have to get out of this place. I need quick answers. What's Mitch's deal? Does he distribute meth for the Dawsons?"

"He's kind of a manager. Does a lot of shit for them. But not the main man. The Dawsons have a big network and a large-scale meth production set up. I've got no idea where. But they've been supplying it across Nevada. I think even other states. But I'm not sure."

"What's the deal with the bikers?"

"They work with Mitch. Carry his meth all over. But someone came looking for Mitch and messed them up real bad today. That's why Mitch ran away."

"Where do the Mexicans come in?"

"The cartel is pissed off with the Dawsons for some reason. I'm not sure why. They are scary dudes, man. You don't want them pissed off with you."

"Which cartel is it?"

"I don't know, man. I'm no expert. But I've heard people calling them SDC. That's short for '*serpientes de cascabel*'. That's rattlesnakes in Spanish."

That made sense. I recalled the rattlesnake tattoo on the face of the man I had just shot.

"Where do you come into all this? I want the straight facts. There are nine dead bodies lying outside the door. This shit is more serious than you think."

"Nine bodies! Are you serious? Whose? What's going on, man?"

"That's what I'm trying to figure out. It's actually ten bodies, including this guy," I nodded towards the dead man behind Chico.

"Whoa!"

"Keep talking. Where do you fit into all this?"

"Mitch keeps asking me to do stuff for him. He was trying to use my diner to store some of his shit. I kept saying no. I never ever want to go back to all that Chicago shit I left behind. But today, Mitch threatened to have the bikers trash my place if I didn't keep watch on the motel. I'm also keeping an eye on him ever since Carter disappeared."

"What's happened to Carter? I'm here for him. If anyone's done anything to him, they're going to die. Painfully."

"I feel your anger, bro. You know how we Witsec dudes are completely dependent on you Marshals. I've got nowhere to go without my cover. If the Chicago crew ever find me... it's game over. *Finito*.

Carter has been my handler all these years. I'm lost without him."

"So, what happened?"

"He came over three days ago. Just landed at my diner. I check in with him on the phone every month, but that's like talking to an answering machine. Mechanical questions, yes/no answers. The last time I'd seen him before that was when he relocated me to this place five years ago. Anyway, I was, like, in the kitchen, and when I came out, I saw him coolly having a coffee and pie. I almost fell, bro."

That was Carter alright.

"What happened then?"

"I told him everything I'm telling you. The Dawsons, the Mexicans. He told me about the two guys who'd gone missing. I had no idea all these years there were other Witsec dudes in this place. But when he told me, my first thought was it may have something to do with that gangster meet the Dawsons organized."

"Yeah, I heard about that. I was told it was a pharmaceutical company meeting."

"Pharmaceutical my ass. It was all about dope, man. They were hard core narcos. A real mean-looking bunch came to town. Maybe someone recognized those witnesses. I don't know, man. The only other possibility is that someone at your end has gone rogue. Carter was following up on both theories. All I know is that he was going to Vegas to meet some guy for information about the Dawsons. It smelled like a trap. And well, no sign of him for two days. I was hoping to get something out of Mitch. That's why I've been hanging around this place."

"And what about the motel? Carter stayed here, right?"

"Yes. That's why I hung around the reception tonight. I checked the register. It has Carter's signature for checking in, but nothing for check out."

"And which room was he staying in?"

"105. I was waiting for Tucker to leave before I could check it out."

"I'll check it now. And I hope for your sake you stick to telling the truth."

"I will, man. I need you guys to stay alive. I've been completely on the level ever since I landed in Little Butte. I never once lied to Carter. He even made me kind of a deputy, dude… OK, maybe not a deputy, but junior deputy… OK, not junior, but like trainee deputy… I'll show you when you come to my diner, bro. I've got a cool surveillance set up going on there."

"Fine. Now, first things first. We've got a pile of bodies lying outside. We'll have to get the hell out of this place. There's no way to explain all this to the cops. I'll have to save that for later. I don't want anyone getting in my way until I find Carter."

"Whatever you say, man. But who are all those bodies?"

"This guy," I motioned to the man behind Chico, "had three more partners. His three partners killed the guy in room 103. That makes it five. And they came in a big van. There were already five bodies inside the van."

"Jesus Christ! Who are the guys in the van?"

"Bikers."

"Hell, man. Bikers? It can't be Mitch's guys. They called him half an hour ago. Some guy had messed them up, but they were alive."

"It's the same bikers. I was the guy who messed them up. They were looking to get me when I asked about Mitch. I left them broken and bruised, but alive."

"You left six guys broken and bruised? That's some serious badass shit, man. Who are you? Robocop?"

"Just a man on a mission. But there were six of them and... only five bodies in the van. One of them must have somehow gotten lucky. These Mexicans must have landed there after I left the place."

"They landed there and killed everyone? Jesus!"

"They're killers on a job. Someone must have ordered them to take these guys out. I'll deal with them if they get in my way, but my top priority is Carter."

"Got it. And believe me, I want Carter back as well. But, man, I'll have to skip town when they see me helping you. You won't leave me to the dogs, bro?"

"You help me get to the bottom of this and I'll lookout for you. You snitch on me and I'll deliver you to them myself. Got it? I'm not leaving this place until the dust settles."

"Got it, dude. I have no doubt about you being badass and all. I thought I was dead when that sicario walked into the room. I know I shouldn't badmouth the dead but, man, what a mean bastard. My heart stopped when he looked me with those dead eyes. You saved me, man. And I don't even know your name."

"Blaze."

"Blaze? I knew it would be a badass name like that. Got it, Marshal."

"I'm technically retired. But it doesn't matter. I'm a Deputy until I find Carter. Let's move. I need to go get some answers from Mitch."

"He's a crafty devil. But I have a feeling you'll get him talking."

"We'll see. First, I need to remove our traces from the crime scene. Was that your own shotgun you were carrying?"

"No. Tucker's."

"Right. I'll leave that under the counter after wiping our prints. And what about that pickup in front of the rooms? Is that yours?"

"Yes."

"What was the plan? Was Mitch coming back here or were you guys going to him?"

"Tucker was to take the bag to Mitch in the Mustang. I was supposed to manage the motel until he came back. I think Mitch is skipping town."

"Looks like it," I agreed. "Too many people looking for him. So, here's the plan. I have my pickup parked nearby. I'll need to move it to somewhere it won't be noticed for a couple of hours. This place is going to become a major crime scene the minute someone comes to the motel. The cops will seal off everything."

"There are vacant lots next to my diner. You can leave it there. No one will bat an eyelid."

"Good. I'll follow you in my pickup. Once I've parked it, drop me back here and I'll take the Mustang and grab Mitch. You stay at the diner. The less you're involved, the better for you."

"Whatever you say, boss. Are you sure you don't need me after that?"

"I will. Once I get what I need from Mitch, I'll need a ride back to my pickup. I don't want to be flashing that Mustang in town."

"You're right, bro. That thing has a bull's eye painted on its ass."

"I'll give you a ring. Pick me up and leave me near the pickup."

"Cool. Let me give you my number."

"I have it. I was planning to check you out after I was done with Mitch. I didn't expect to bump into you here."

"Oh... right. Dude, you almost made me shit my pants when you mentioned Chicago."

"That was the whole point."

"Anything else you need me to do?"

"The keys to the Mustang?"

"Should be under the counter. I'll get them on the way out."

"Right, let's get moving. I'll check out room 105, see if there are any clues. Don't freak out when you walk out of the room. It's a bloodbath out there. Walk carefully. Don't step on any bodies."

I turned and began walking out before he had a chance to reply. I grabbed the keys to room 105. But there weren't any clues waiting for me in there. It had been made up, with no trace left of Carter's stay. They must have taken extra care of that. On the way back to the reception, I took out my phone to get a photo of the killer lying dead in front of room 103.

I came back to the reception and clicked photos of the three men lying dead in there. I wiped my prints off the keys and put them back. Then wiped my prints off the Uzi and the AR-15 and replaced them with those of the dead men. I would eventually have to tell everything to Flynn and the cops, but now wasn't the time for it. I had to find Carter first. I needed to remain a ghost that night.

Chico grabbed the car keys on the way out but didn't linger in the reception area. He was standing at the back of the van, looking at the bodies in there. His face looked drained.

The neon lights going off and on periodically added to the eeriness of the place. I clicked photos of each dead man lying in there. The flashes made the scene even more sinister.

"Jesus Christ. What in god's name is going on here?" Chico asked.

"That's what we need to find out. Let's get going," I replied, wiping the prints off the door handles. "Don't leave any other prints."

We got into Chico's pickup. As he was reversing it, I asked him for the exact location of the gas station.

"It's simple. This road runs towards the town on the right. The gas station is to the left, away from town. Almost exactly three miles straight on. You can't miss it even in the dark. There's nothing else out there. No other buildings. Just wilderness."

"Does Mitch have anyone else with him?"

"I don't think so. With the bikers and Tucker gone, I don't think he has any friends left. I'm not sure why, but he seems to have fallen out with the Dawsons, otherwise he wouldn't be hiding in that dump."

"If he's scared and without a friend, that's a good thing. It will be easier to get him talking."

"Dude, you can be real scary without even trying. I'm sure you'll have him singing."

"Let's see. Now, take a left, drop me off after a couple of hundred yards. I'll get my pickup and follow you into town."

I got down and walked out in the darkness towards my pickup. Before I got in, I decided to equip myself with more weapons. I had come across too many men with an intention to kill in the last few hours. I had been lucky so far, but didn't want to push it. I was expecting Mitch to be alone, but an assassination team might turn up out of nowhere.

I opened the weapons compartment of the pickup and took out the heavier arsenal. I put the Colt 9mm SMG and a shotgun inside a large duffel bag. I picked the silencer for the Glock as well. Then I drove out towards the road and followed Chico to his diner. I parked the pickup in the vacant lot, grabbed the duffel bag, and jumped into his pickup. He dropped me back at the motel.

"Thanks. You better head back now. I'll go find Mitch."

"Sure you don't need anything else?" Chico asked.

"I'll let you know once I've got my hands on Mitch."

"Got it. Good luck," he shouted, driving off.

I walked towards the back of the motel. The car was a 2000 Mustang GT. This Mitch guy did have taste. As I turned the key, the 4.6L V8 engine roared to life, raring to go.

I eased it onto the road. Once I got on the tarmac, I let it go. I was finally on my way to corner the elusive Mitch.

CHAPTER 6

Chico's estimate was accurate. The gas station appeared exactly three miles away. It must have been a thriving business once—there were two substantial structures behind the skeletons of the gas pumps in the foreground. What must once have been a convenience store was in a bad state— just bits of broken glass in the façade and a partially caved in roof. The other building was still more or less whole. A rusted billboard on top declared it an auto repair shop.

The place evoked the same feeling of wistfulness you get when you pass by any ghost town on Route 66. Something once flourishing and vibrant gone to decay. It felt like staring at a corpse. The person I was looking for was hidden somewhere within its rotting bowels.

I knew Mitch would be armed. And desperate. That makes even regular men dangerous. From what I had heard, Mitch was a crafty weasel. I would need to draw him out. I figured the best way would be to maintain the appearance of normality. Mitch was expecting Tucker to arrive in the Mustang and drive over straight to the courtyard, without a hesitant approach. That's how I decided to make my entrance.

I turned into the gas station and stopped the car in the courtyard, between the gas pumps and the convenience store. I kept the beams on high and kept the engine running. The convenience store was bare and empty. I figured Mitch would be in the repair shop.

I waited for less than half a minute before I noticed in the rear-view mirror, someone approaching the car from behind. Mitch must have circled behind the convenience store. He was carrying a shotgun and approaching the car from directly behind, so he wouldn't be visible in the side mirrors. The moment he got to within five feet of the car, I put it in reverse and lightly pressed the throttle. The car lurched backwards before I jammed the brakes. The bump from the car sent Mitch flying. He landed flat on the ground. The shotgun flew out of his hands.

I got out immediately, shotgun in hand, pumping it more for effect. The clackety-clack sound is enough to make people freeze. But it didn't matter—Mitch was too dazed to react.

I looked at his face in the eerie red haze created by the rear lights and exhaust fumes. It was the man in the photo. I finally had Mitch.

He was shorter and lighter than me. I took out flexicuffs from my back pocket, cuffed his hands behind him, and threw him into the trunk. I pulled out a few seconds later. I wasn't sure if Mitch had a partner waiting in the shadows. I didn't want to find out the hard way.

I headed a further couple of miles away from town. While studying the map at the Bar earlier, I had noticed a narrow trail five miles from town, running towards a small mountain range. Reading and memorizing maps are essential survival skills for Army Rangers. And I was good at it. You can't rely on GPS while out chasing terrorists in the Hindu Kush mountains in Afghanistan. Maps become clear as photos once you know how to read them.

The trail was meant for SUVs with high ground clearance. Not really fit territory for a Mustang. But all I needed was to be a few hundred yards away from the road, to avoid the worry of a vehicle suddenly coming up.

I kept my eyes peeled for the trail, which finally appeared on the left. I turned into it. After about three hundred yards, the trail curved around a group of rocks. Beyond them was complete wilderness. The rocks hid any view of the highway. The night was pitch dark. All you could see were the dark shapes of looming rocks. They looked scary. Perfect place to get someone talking, especially when that person has been shut in the dark confines of a trunk.

If I had to find Carter, Mitch was my best shot. The guy seemed good at saving his skin when things were going down. I would have to put the fear of death in him to get all the answers I needed.

Before exiting the car, I took the magazine out of the Glock. I already had the scary visual atmosphere of that dark, desolate place. Loading the gun while standing over him like an executioner would enhance the effect.

I opened the trunk, pulled him out, and frisked him. Found a wad of cash, a wallet and phone. No hidden guns. I kicked his legs from under him and dumped him on the ground.

"Hey, listen to me, man. You don't need to do this," he pleaded in a scared whisper.

I kept quiet. Placed a foot on his shoulder and began loading the magazine. The click of the magazine followed by the sound of racking the slide made the scene even more ominous.

"Listen to me, man. Please. I've got money. I have four pounds of meth in a bag. That's easily 200 grand. I can get it for you, man. Please."

He was scared. Sounded desperate.

"Where did you get the meth?" I asked him, speaking in a measured tone.

"What? Never mind where I got it, man. It's all yours. I can get it for you," he replied with a flicker of hope in his voice.

I took my foot off him, grabbed his collar, and hauled him up against a rock.

"Shut up and listen carefully. You can't buy your way out of this. You're a marked man. Any friends you had back in Little Butte are either dead or out for your blood. All your biker buddies are dead. Killed by sicarios, who are now roaming the streets to kill you. Get it?"

He nodded, licking his lips, which had gone dry.

"You're completely out of options," I continued. "I'm the only one standing between life and death for you. But I haven't yet made up my mind if you're worth saving. I'll give you one chance to convince me. If I'm not convinced, I'll put a bullet in your knee, dump your ass back in the trunk, and leave your Mustang in the middle of town. The sicarios will do the rest. Got it?"

"Yes," he said, voice heavy with dread.

My words were having the intended effect. I had done this hundreds of times. Make it clear to a potential informant he's out of options. Once he gets that, offer him a way out. The entire Witsec program ran on that system.

"Now, here's the deal," I said. "And it's a pretty good one as there's an option you might get away from this place alive. I'll ask some questions. I know the answers to most of them. If I catch you lying to even one, this conversation is over. It'll be a bullet in the knee for you. And then over to the Mexicans. Get it?"

"Yes. I won't lie. I know I'm fucked," he replied in a shaky voice.

"Good. Why were you hiding out at the gas station?"

"I got a call someone was looking for me. I got scared. There are people out to get me."

"Why?"

"I don't know, man. It just began in the last few hours. There was an attack on a bar in another place. And then someone came looking for me here. I really don't know why."

"Really? You have no idea why?" I asked, my tone dripping with sarcasm.

"I don't know, man. It's been very sudden. Things were fine until today."

"How long have you been dealing meth?"

"Are you a cop?"

"Wrong answer. You don't ask questions. You just answer them. I'll give this one a pass, as it wasn't a lie. One more question or lie out of you and your ass is back in the trunk. I don't have the time or patience for it. Got it?"

"Yes."

"How long have you been dealing meth?"

"Two years."

"Who supplies the meth? Dawsons?"

"I can't, man. They'll kill me."

I didn't reply. Just walked to the car, took out the silencer, and began screwing it on.

"You should have listened to me. The Dawsons are out to kill you. I was giving you a way out. Too late now," I said, placing the muzzle of the Glock on his kneecap.

"No, no, wait, please, listen to me. I swear, I'll tell you all," he almost shouted, and kept speaking non-stop. "It's the Dawsons. They make the meth. Huge quantities of it. Ever since Baxter got the idea in his head that making meth is a better use of pseudoephedrine than making cough medicine. They divert pseudoephedrine from their pharma set up to cook meth. I didn't even want to get involved. They were a regular pharma company before that. I was just a salesman. They made me do it, man. I swear."

"Who gave them the meth idea?"

"Jasper. He's the real scammer. He gave the old man the idea when a couple of years ago, they got a big shipment of pseudoephedrine from China. Around four tons. They declared it missing. Then used it for cooking meth. That shipment alone lasted for a year."

"Where do they cook it? Inside their pharma plant?"

"No, man. They wouldn't risk that. There are too many checks by the FDA. They can't screw around with their legit operation. They source pseudoephedrine from their pharma plant, but keep the cooking away from it. And they keep moving it. It used to be in the old part of town. They moved it to the casino site a couple of months ago. But I don't think they're cooking right now. They've got a big stash and are covered for a while.

They're also keeping things quiet... some Senator is supposed to come for a visit before they get the casino license."

"Who cooks it? One of the Dawsons?"

"Dawsons don't have the brains for it. It was Rixon initially, the chemist from their pharma business. He trained a few guys. I think they do most of it."

"Why are all these guys looking to kill you? I think I already know the answer, so don't try to bullshit me."

He sighed before he began speaking.

"The Dawsons have thrown me to the dogs. You saw the sicarios."

"That doesn't tell me why they're out to kill you."

"The Dawsons became greedy. Not a good idea when you're dealing with the Mexican cartel. No one realized until last week how ruthless they are."

"Which cartel? The rattlesnakes? SDC?"

"You know that?"

"I told you I know most of the things I'm asking you. I need you to fill in a few missing pieces."

"I've been honest with you, man. You won't feed me to those rattlers, will you?"

"You haven't told me much yet. Keep talking. If you're honest, I'll offer you a way out. I promise. Without me, you're a dead man. Even if I give you the keys to your car, you've got nowhere to go. You'll be dead before morning."

"I know. What's happened to the others? Are they all dead?"

"I'll tell you soon. Keep talking. What's the beef between the Dawsons and the cartel?"

"When the Dawsons began cooking, they didn't have a clue about distribution. That's where the Mexicans came in. They could move any quantity. Began with Nevada. Then spread it across other states. Each state was under a local crew. The Mexicans were taking a big cut, but it was going fine until the Dawsons began getting greedy. They started shifting some of it on their own. That's where the bikers came in. We used to deal a bit of crystal at the bar. The bikers used to come there. That's how I met them. They were breakaways from a club in Vegas. Trying to form their own club. Or chapter. Whatever they call it. They were broke, needed some easy dough."

"Were they using the bar as their club?"

"Kind of. They weren't a rowdy bunch, so it wasn't a problem. The Dawsons have built a new bar in town. That old place wasn't going to be part of the new scenery."

"So what ticked off the Mexicans?"

"The bikers began moving stuff in small quantities in Nevada, Utah, Oregon. Then other gangs began complaining. The Mexicans forced the Dawsons to organize a meeting to settle things."

"That was the one a week ago?"

"Yes. Gangs handling distribution all over the west landed in town, along with the Mexicans. I haven't seen so many mean-looking guys in one place. The Dawsons got scared and made us the fall guys."

"Us?"

"Me, the bikers, Rollie."

He went quiet for a few seconds.

"Who's Rollie?"

"Just a kid. Harmless. Used to help out at the bar, packing meth in the bikes, stuff like that. They shot him to save their asses."

"Who shot him?"

"Hector Alvarez. Top lieutenant of the cartel. In front of all those gangs gathered in Dawson hotel in the middle of town. Jasper shifted all blame on us to save his ass. Told me to keep my mouth shut or he'd get Grady to kill me."

"Who's Grady?"

"Jasper's psycho brother. He's dim, but built like a bull. Smashes anyone Jasper sets him upon. Jasper is half his size, but Grady blindly follows his every command."

"So, what happened at the hotel?"

"They called me and Rollie into the conference room. Made me promise never to move any meth on my own again. Rollie was standing next to me. Jasper was doing a tough guy routine, twirling a gun, threatening to shoot both of us if we ever strayed again. That Mexican psycho got up, took the gun from Jasper's hand, and shot Rollie in the head. Didn't say a word. Just handed the gun back to Jasper, went back to his seat, and began rubbing his ear. The top half of his left ear is missing. Lucky escape from a bullet."

"Why shoot Rollie? And not you?"

"It was just chance. Rollie was closer to him, I guess," he said, a shiver running through him at the memory.

"What happened after that?"

"Once the gangs left town, Jasper ordered me to carry on distributing meth in Utah. When I protested, he told me to take it up with Grady. That's when I knew I would have to split to stay alive. Then two days ago, some guy turned up in town, asking questions. A couple of local guys had gone missing when the gangsters were in town. But this dude asking all those questions made the Dawsons very nervous."

"Who were the guys who went missing?"

"I don't know, man. I didn't know them. I just heard one of them was called Charlie. The other was an Indian guy, Lou."

"Why did they go missing?"

"I only know what I heard. Those guys had some gang connections before they came to Little Butte. I think when all these gangs came to town last week, someone recognized them. Charlie worked at the pharma factory. I think his girl works at the salon. The other guy was a loner. Worked at the auto repair shop."

"What about the guy who came looking for them? What happened to him?"

"I don't know, man. I saw him once at the bar. He was asking about those two. But I've been too busy with my own shit these last few days."

"Who could tell me more about him?"

"I don't know. Maybe Jasper. He got really spooked when he heard about this guy."

"Alright," I said, taking out a boot knife. "Turn around and hold still."

Mitch began rubbing his wrists as soon as I cut the cuffs off.

"I'll do what I can to help you stay alive," I said. "What was your plan?"

"I was skipping town tonight. There's this stash of meth. That would have been enough for a fresh start somewhere far away."

"As in the bar in the middle of nowhere on the Utah border?"

"You know about that? Who are you? A cop?"

"Kind of. I'll come to that later. What's your deal at that bar?"

"I bought a share in it six months ago when I came into some money. It was in the middle of nowhere, came pretty cheap."

"Were you there earlier today?"

"I was. Headed out for Little Butte after lunch."

"That bar is going to be off limits for you. I was there earlier in the evening."

"Jesus! Were you the one who put down those two guys?"

"Yeah, that was me. Lucky for your crew I happened to be there. Those guys would have killed all three of them."

"I know. That's what they told me."

"I had no idea who you were and decided to check you out at the Dawson bar."

"Oh, man, were you the one who messed up the bikers?"

"Yeah."

"You messed up all six of them?"

"Yes."

"Who are you, man?"

"You'll know soon enough."

"But you just beat them up. You didn't kill them, right? They called me after that. So, they aren't dead, right?"

"Unfortunately, they are. I left them broken, but very much alive. I went to the motel from there, when these four sicarios turned up in a black van. They had the bodies of the bikers in the back."

"Jesus."

"I saw five bodies, including the bartender. More like stumbled upon them. They looked like gangland executions. Double taps to the head."

"Fuck. That's bad. Oh, man. But you saw five bodies. So, the sixth one is still alive?"

"Maybe. I think the sicarios must have landed at the bar, got information about you, and then killed whoever was there. If the remaining biker managed to hide, he might have survived. But if he shows his face in town again, I doubt he'll live long."

"What about the sicarios? How did you manage to get away?"

"They weren't the kind you have conversations with. I killed them."

"You killed them all?"

"No other option. They were out there to kill you and the bikers. You've been lucky—one step ahead of everyone sent to kill you."

"Oh, man. I'm so completely screwed. I'm dead."

"Not yet. We'll try to figure something out. The first thing you need to know is your stash of meth is gone. All you have is this cash you had in your pocket," I held out the wad of notes in front of him. "It can help out for a while, but not long. Taking my help means your drug dealing days are over. Got it?"

"Yes. Completely. Believe me, man, I'm sick of this business. It wasn't as if I was a big shit narco or something. All it got me was this Mustang, the rest of it was just peanuts—the Dawsons piled the money and treated me like shit."

"Talking of your Mustang, you'll have to dump it if you want to stay alive. It's a highly visible target."

"I know," he groaned. "That's why I hid it back at the motel," he said, sighing. Then, after a pause, "Was there anyone else at the motel?"

"You mean Tucker? He's dead."

"Oh, man."

"There was a guy at the reception. Chico. He's alive."

"Oh. Right," he said, sounding not too bothered either way.

"Is he part of your crew as well?"

"Not really. He's too pussy for all this stuff."

That statement raised Chico's credibility a bit more. But Mitch hadn't figured Chico. He had acquired a mile-long rap sheet on the streets of Chicago before he got into Witsec.

"He would have died like the rest of them. It was just chance that I happened to land there. You're mixed up in some real bad shit, Mitch. What do I do with you?"

"I've got nowhere to go, man. Help me. Please."

"I'll make a deal with you. Help me find the guy who was looking for those other two. He's a US Marshal. His name is Carter. That's the only thing that matters to me. If I find him, I'll help you get into Witsec. But that will be in return for your testimony against the Dawsons and the cartel."

"I'll be dead if I testify against them."

"You're already good as dead. You still think you've got a chance without me? The Dawsons have kill orders out for you. But if I get you into Witsec, no one can touch you. That's what Marshals do. And they do it really well. But it's your choice. If you think you can manage on your own, you're free to go."

I held out the car keys.

"No, no. I'll do it. The asshole's have screwed me over. I'll help you get them."

"My priority is Carter."

"I get it, man. I'll do my best. I hope he's alive. So, are you a Marshal?"

"Yes. The name's Blaze. I'm here to find Carter. But we need to find a place for you to lie low until this blows over. Somewhere they won't come looking for you."

"I'm clueless, man. Everywhere I thought I was safe, I've got people coming to find me."

"I'll figure something out."

I went to the car, took out the duffel bag with my guns inside it, then handed the keys to Mitch.

"If you need to grab anything from the car, get it now while I make the call. We'll be leaving it at the gas station."

"Oh, man, that's gonna hurt. I love this babe," he said, real passion in his voice.

I kind of understood the passion. It was a mean machine. But certainly not worth losing your life over.

I walked off some distance and called Flynn. I needed to get Mitch away from that place if there was any chance of him surviving. I told Flynn he was my best bet to get to Carter. Flynn arranged for me to meet with a deputy at a motel just off Route 93. About an hour's drive away. The plan was to take Mitch there, get all information I needed for my investigations, and hand him to the deputy to take to a safe house.

Then came the difficult bit of the conversation.

"I'll forward some photos, Flynn. If you can get them ID'd, it'll help put the pieces in place. This

79

town is buzzing with Mexican cartel. There's some kind of gang war going on out here."

"Mexican cartel? Up in Little Butte? You sure?"

"Positive. You can see for yourself in the photos. Cartel called SDC. Short for rattlesnakes in Spanish. Faces tattooed with gang symbols and shit. Name of the top lieutenant is Hector Alvarez."

"Well, I'll be damned. That's good work, Blaze. You've just been there a couple of hours. How did you manage to get those photos?"

"That wasn't difficult. They were.. uh... dead."

"Dead? How?"

"Shot."

"By whom?"

"They were sicarios. A group of four. About to take out Chico, Carter's witness. I had to shoot them."

"You killed all four?"

"Yeah. Didn't have a choice, Flynn. It was them or Chico."

"Whoa, hang on there, cowboy. Didn't we have a conversation... something on the lines of, don't go overboard piling up bodies."

"Yes, boss, but I told you it could get messy if this turned out to be a gang thing. And guess what?"

"Yeah, I know. So, how come they were after this Chico character? Is he involved as well?"

"No, he seems clean. Just happened to be in the wrong place, wrong time. Those guys were on a killing spree. Turned up at the motel where Carter stayed. With a pile of bodies in the back of their van."

"Pile of bodies? You sure you haven't crossed the border into Mexico? You're in Little Butte, Nevada, right?"

"That's the thing that's got me worried, Flynn. These guys were cold-blooded killers. If they had a hand in Carter's disappearance, there isn't much hope of finding him."

"Just say the word, Blaze, and I'll send in the Tac team. I'll ask them to fly in and be on standby at the Vegas field office. These are your own boys from SOG. They know you're on the case. I've had a hard time keeping them on a leash—they're raring to go."

"I can imagine," I said, unable to restrain a smile at the thought of the wild bunch in the Marshal's Special Operations Group. "Good to have them on standby. There's something strange going on here. Kill orders out for Mitch. A pile of bodies lying in the motel."

"You be careful, Blaze. The team will be in place in Vegas by daybreak. After that, they can be with you at two hours' notice."

"Roger that. I'll get moving now. I'll rendezvous soon with the deputy at the motel on Route 93."

I could hear an incoming call while I was talking to Flynn. When I checked my phone, the screen showed a missed call from Adriel. That was unexpected. When I drove out from the ranch in the morning, I didn't expect to talk to Adriel until I was back home again. Something wasn't right. I called back immediately.

"Kid," he said. He was the only person in the world who called me that.

"Adriel. Everything alright back at the ranch?"

"One of the missing men you're looking for was a Navajo kid. Lou."

"You sure?"

"I didn't know until his sister called me today. The kid got mixed up with the wrong crowd in Texas. Then decided to go straight, testified against them. Your guys moved him to Little Butte under Witsec."

"And the sister knew that?"

"Yes, the two were close. He told her. She never told anyone until she called me today after he went missing."

"I see."

"She asked me for help. You mind if I come over? Won't get in your way."

"No problem. You won't be in the way. What's your plan?"

"I'll head out before daybreak. Should be there in the afternoon."

"Sounds good. I'll turn on the location finder in my phone. In case I can't take a call, you'll know where I am when you come in tomorrow."

"Good idea. See you tomorrow."

"Roger that. And Adriel... come armed. Things are more serious than I thought. Mexican cartel's involved. Looks like there's a war brewing."

I gave him a quick brief of what had happened in the couple of hours I had been in town.

"I'll be prepared. You take care, kid."

I next called Chico and asked him to pick me up at the gas station.

"Turn on your phone. I might need to call you," I told Mitch as we drove towards the gas station.

"I will," he replied. Then, after a pause, "How did you know it was off."

"I'm with the Marshal's service, remember. We were tracking your phone until you switched it off a couple of hours ago."

"Oh. I got scared when I got the call about the attack at that other bar. I thought maybe someone could track me."

"They wouldn't have turned up at the bar if they were tracking you. And it's not that easy to track phones. The Dawsons seem to be some kind of a big deal out here, but even they won't be able to do it unless they have the police chief and some judge in their pocket."

"They do have Graves in their pocket."

"Graves? Who's that?"

"Earl Graves. Chief of police."

"Oh. I guess it had to be if they're running their operation on such a big scale. How big is the police department? Are all of them dirty?"

"There are five of them, including Graves and a detective. I don't think all of them are dirty. But the Dawsons manage to get their way. Graves looks like a kindly old granddad, but he's crooked. I'm not sure about the rest of them, but Nash is a real boy scout. That's Hunter Nash, the deputy. He can't stand the Dawsons."

Mitch pulled into the gas station and stopped outside the repair shop.

"Hide it well. Maybe inside the repair shop. I don't suppose people come out here much."

"No. That's why I felt safe enough to lie low here. Until you came and busted me," he replied.

"Yeah, well, I'll call you when I arrive. We don't want you rushing out to meet the wrong guys."

"Not a chance of that, man. I've got too many people out to kill me."

"Good. Stay hidden until I'm back."

"Sure thing."

Chico arrived at that moment. I got into his pickup and we got going.

The motel was deathly quiet as we drove past it. No one seemed to have landed there yet. Maybe no one would until morning. The black van stood menacingly in the parking lot. The thought of the bodies inside it was chilling.

"Sweet mother of Jesus," Chico said in a quivering voice. "It's the silence of death. The town's going to go loco when the bodies are discovered."

"I'm sure it will rock the Dawsons boat. But I need to get away before that happens. If I get detained, I'll have to reveal my identity. I can't lose the element of surprise. There are many leads I need to follow up tomorrow."

A couple of minutes later, Chico stopped beside my pickup.

"Don't go trusting Mitch too much," he cautioned, as I opened the door to get out.

"It's not about trust. He knows I'm his only chance of getting out alive. The Dawsons have thrown him to the dogs. They're saving their own skin. He'll squeal on them just to stay alive and get back at them."

"That's something I can believe. You take care, Marshal. Anything you want from me, just say the word."

"I'll need you tomorrow. If we bump into each other and there's someone around, act like you don't know me."

"Got it, boss. I'll ignore you like you're a girl I just dumped. Not that I dump girls all the time.

But, you know, there was a time chicks used to dig this package, dude... up in Chicago. But now, I'm like, super respectable Chico."

"Yeah, right. Off you go, Casanova," I said, watching him drive off.

I placed my duffel bag on the front passenger seat. As I was walking towards the driver's door to get in, I saw a dark van coming from town. It looked very much like the van the sicarios had brought to the hotel. The one with the bodies dumped at the back.

I tried to look inside. There were four men in the van. It was too dark to make out the three passengers, but I could clearly see the driver. Hispanic. Mean looking. Thick moustaches drooping down to the chin. Tattoos on the face. Our eyes locked for a second before the van passed. The vibes we exchanged weren't the least bit friendly.

The guys in the van were probably a second party of killers, looking for the ones I killed an hour ago. All hell could break loose once they discovered their partners were lying dead at the motel.

CHAPTER 7

I drove towards the motel in darkness, headlights switched off. The special feature in the vehicle to turn off all lights was a lifesaver. Giving those guys any indication I was following them was dangerous. I couldn't even risk the brake light coming on—it was a dark night, the red haze of the lights could become visible in a side mirror of the van.

It was a straight drive to the motel. I drove in a direct line towards the neon sign and veered the truck away from the road before rolling to a stop a hundred yards before the motel. It was all flat, unbuilt area. The pickup came to a rest in the darkness some 30 yards away from the road.

I got out and walked towards the motel, watching the parking lot through my binoculars. It was a dark night. Those men were in a lighted area—they couldn't possibly peer into the darkness to see me.

There was a lot of animated activity in the parking lot. The two vans were parked beside each other. The men were well armed—each one had a suppressed mini Uzi slung across his torso on nylon straps. I was sure they had more guns inside the van. I wouldn't have a chance in a straight-out firefight with the four of them.

They had just opened the rear door of the van and discovered the bodies. One man was making a phone call while the others were peering at the bodies, trying to figure out who they were. They finally shut the door and began looking around.

One of the men began heading towards room 103. The body of the assassin I had shot was lying just outside the room door. The man called the other three over. They consulted for a few seconds before moving the body inside the room.

They came out of the room, shut the door, and began walking towards the reception area. The bodies of the three other assassins I had killed were lying in there. I was sure they would be in there for a while.

I knew they wouldn't be leaving the bodies to be discovered by the cops. I debated whether to call 911 or try and track the vans. If I called the cops, there would definitely be a shootout. I doubted the local cops would be trained enough to take on those killers. The dead would certainly include some cops. And the state police would be all over the place in a few hours. That would drive the Dawsons and the cartel underground. My best chance of finding Carter was to remain undercover until I had some clue about the operation and hideouts of these guys.

I decided against calling the cops. My best bet was to track the vehicles. I rushed back to my pickup, opened the weapons compartment, and stuffed a couple of trackers in a pocket. Then grabbed a Glock and a suppressor, closed the compartment, and ran towards the motel, screwing the suppressor on the gun.

There was no time to make a concealed approach. The men wouldn't stay inside long. They also might have another team coming in. I knew if they came out at once, I would be a sitting duck for their Uzis. I had to bank on the probability that not more than one or two of them would come out initially. I had managed to scrape through situations in the past where the probability of staying alive had been much lower.

I sprinted in a straight line towards the vans and stopped in the concealed space between them. It took me half a minute to install a tracker inside the tire wells of both vans. I was about to sprint back to my pickup when I saw the headlights of a vehicle coming from town. I pressed back against the side of the van, waiting for it to pass. But the vehicle turned into the parking lot and stopped in front of the reception room. It was a jacked-up Ford pickup.

I watched from behind the vans as two men got out. The man in the driver's seat was huge. The truck bounced on its suspension as he got out of the driver's side. He must have been about six feet four, and over 250 pounds. Even under the loose, untucked shirt, I could make out the massive chest, thick shoulders, and powerful arms—this was a guy who could do serious damage with his bare hands. He had a very unkempt look, occasionally scratching his dark beard.

The second man, although not too short in height, was about half the other one's girth. He had long straw-colored hair done in a ponytail, and a droopy moustache going almost to the chin, which he kept smoothening every now and then with a thumb and index finger. He wore a black sleeveless vest over black trousers. The man didn't look too shabby but seemed to be in the wrong time zone— he looked more like a porn star from the eighties. He was on the phone as he exited the vehicle.

From the description Mitch gave me earlier, I guessed those two were the Dawson brothers—Jasper and Grady. It kind of made sense—if the cartel faced a tricky situation in Little Butte, they would call the Dawsons to sort things out.

One of the Mexicans came to the door and signaled them to come in. The moment all three walked in, I readied myself to sprint back across the road to my pickup. But I had barely taken two steps when another pair of headlights came into sight, coming from town. And this time, it wasn't just any pair of headlights. It was a cop car, red and blue strobing lights tearing through the darkness between the town and the motel. The sirens, however, were off. I had no option but to hide behind the vans again.

The police car pulled in and came to a stop next to the jacked-up pickup. A clean-shaven man of about sixty, with receding hair, stepped out of the car. The moment he got out, he grabbed a cowboy hat and put it on. There was no doubt the cop was crooked. He was there to help the Dawsons deal with the shit I had created for them. Otherwise, there would have been cars rushing towards the motel, sirens wailing.

The three men who had gone inside came out and joined him. The four men stood just a few yards from where I was hiding. I had no option but to get down on the ground and slither under the van farthest from them. It turned out to be a good idea as all four began walking towards the van with the bodies. The Mexican opened its back door to show the bodies to the others.

I was able to make out from the conversation that the cop who had just come in was Earl Graves, the police chief. Mitch had been right. Graves was crooked as a corkscrew.

A couple of minutes later, they closed the van door and headed towards the reception area. It was time for me to make a dash towards the cover of darkness.

I decided not to head straight for my pickup. There were too many men in the reception area. Someone could come out any second. I didn't want a bullet in my back while still running across the road. I decided to run towards the other end of the motel, the far end of the rooms, and hide in the darkness beyond the walls.

The moment they went in, I scrambled out from under the van and sprinted in that direction. I made it to darkness and safety in under ten seconds. But I was too far off to be able to watch them.

I took the same route behind the motel that I had taken earlier. Walked around the back in complete darkness to arrive at the other end, beside the reception room. I remained in the shadows and peeked inside. All three bodies had been stacked near the door. The Mexicans were cleaning up as much of the blood as they could. Jasper and Graves stood discussing options about disposing the bodies. Grady stood behind Jasper, scratching his beard.

I was able to catch parts of the conversation. Graves was doing most of the planning. He made it clear that the immediate priority was to get the bodies out of there before someone else turned up. They agreed to put all the bodies in one van and hide them temporarily in the abandoned gas station, until they could figure out a plan.

That created a problem. I would need to alert Mitch to get the hell away from the gas station. I slunk back into the shadows and called him. He picked it on the first ring. I told him about a change of plan. Asked him to get into the Mustang and drive it back to the place I had taken him earlier. He began to get a bit hysterical about the sudden change of plan.

"You're going to be safe. I have arranged safe custody for you and will take you there. But you need to get out of there immediately. The Mexicans will be landing there to hide some stuff," I told him.

"Fuck, man, they're gonna kill me."

"Shut up and listen to me. No one knows you're there. Just get in your car and drive the hell out of there."

"I'm not sure I know the exact location of that place."

"It's almost exactly two miles from the gas station. Keep your eyes peeled. You'll see it on your left. Send me a message once you're there, then wait for me. Get moving. Now."

I went back to watch the men again. One of them had reversed the van near the reception entrance. The others were putting the three bodies inside it. Grady had meanwhile walked into room 103 and was carrying the fourth body. The back of the van was packed as they shut the door. I zoomed the phone's camera to maximum and clicked photos to get all their faces.

Grady talked to one of the Mexicans, who led him to the second van. Grady looked inside the passenger cabin and picked two guns. Heckler & Koch MP5 submachine guns. With the 50-round box magazines. These guys were carrying some serious firepower. It would be best to avoid a full-on firefight with them.

Grady handed one of the guns to Jasper. That seemed a bit pointless—the way Jasper wielded it, it didn't look like he knew how to handle it.

The Dawson brothers got into their pickup and began driving slowly towards the gas station. Two of the Mexicans got into the van and drove behind them. The two remaining Mexicans went back into the reception area to continue the clean up.

Graves stood beside his car for a while, talking on his phone. He finally got in his car, reversed it, and swerved it out of the parking lot, onto the road. The sweep of the headlights across the darkness made my pickup momentarily visible. I was hoping Graves might have missed it—it was visible for less than half a second. But it caught his eye.

Graves drove across the road, got out of his car, and looked all around. He walked toward the pickup with a flashlight. He circled it, looking inside carefully. It was a good thing I had managed to shut the weapons compartment before rushing towards the motel. Graves wouldn't find anything suspicious in there. It was a different matter that a pickup standing by itself on the deserted highway, across the road from the motel where the police chief found a pile of bodies, was the very definition of a suspicious object.

I could imagine the thoughts that must have been going through his head. He couldn't officially confiscate it, because that would mean alerting his office, which would result in other cops getting to know there was something going on at the motel.

Unless the entire police department was dirty, that was something he would avoid. I really doubted an entire department could be crooked. It was a good thing the Dawsons and the two Mexicans had already driven away. Or else, they would have figured a way to tow my truck as well.

Graves seemed to be in a hurry to get back. He noted the license plate number, rushed back to his car, and drove off towards town. The moment his taillights receded in the distance, I received a text from Mitch. He was waiting for me at the "scary place".

I kept the phone in my pocket and stepped forward to peek into the reception again, almost bumping into a man. It was one of the Mexicans. The letters SDC tattooed on his right temple, a snake tattooed on the left forearm.

Both of us were equally surprised. Our reaction time was identical. We pushed each other back with our left hands. The one thing working in my favor was my silenced Glock was already in my right hand. By the time he got his hand on the mini Uzi slung on his side and began raising it, my gun was already pointed at his midsection.

I shot him point blank in the middle of his chest, the bullet ripping through his heart. His body simply folded as he went down. Had I been half a second late, he would have emptied the Uzi's magazine into my gut.

I didn't have time to recover. I heard the other Mexican rush towards the entrance and stepped back hastily, tripping over a thick branch lying on the ground. The gun flew out of my hand as I landed hard on my back. That turned out to be a good thing. At the same instant as I fell, the man leaped out of the entrance and let go with a burst of his Uzi.

Luckily for me, he had moved from a lighted room into darkness and was shooting completely blind. He let go a wide burst aimed at waist height. Had I been standing, it would have drilled my gut. I heard the muffled staccato blast of the suppressed gun as 32 bullets from the Uzi's magazine zipped through the air above me, spent cases raining down all around me. I counted to two—that was when the magazine would go empty. The mini Uzi fires 950 rounds per minute in automatic mode. The 32-round magazine gets emptied in two seconds.

The guy was a pro. The empty magazine was falling to the ground as he grabbed a new one from his pocket. It would have taken him not more than three seconds from the time the magazine emptied before he began firing again. But that time was enough for me to launch myself from the ground, push him back while trapping his hand holding the magazine in the pit of my hand, and force his forearm forward with a jerk, breaking his elbow.

The man yelled in pain. But he had enough presence of mind to reach for a gun hidden in the back of his trousers with his other hand. He pulled the gun out and began moving his hand forward to get it into position to fire at me. The gun hand was too far away from me to block. I raised one leg, pulled the knife from my boot, and pushed it into the man's throat, burying it to the hilt. The gun fell from his hand. He staggered back a couple of steps, making a gurgling sound as blood spurted out. Then he collapsed.

I retrieved the knife, found the Glock that had fallen from my hands, and left the scene. I ran over to my pickup, got in, and was out of there like a shot. As I passed the gas station, I saw the faint shape of the Dawsons' jacked-up truck in the dark. There was a faint light in the repair shop, where they were hiding the van. I sped up, in case they got curious about the vehicle moving on that deserted highway late in the night. I looked at my watch. It was just getting to midnight.

I checked the rear-view mirror before turning onto the path. There was no other vehicle on the road. I soon came up behind the parked Mustang. I turned off the headlights but remained inside the pickup, gun ready for any unforeseen event. There was no sign of Mitch. I called him on the phone. He was hiding behind some rocks. He came out when he heard my voice on the phone.

The moment he got in, I drove out onto the highway, moving away from Little Butte, on my way to rendezvous with the deputy at the motel on Route 93.

Mitch filled me in on the Dawsons' operation on the way to the motel. To find Carter, I would need to press hard on the Dawsons. To do that, I needed to bring them out in the open as criminals. I would have to find their meth lab and the huge meth stock they had. The only man, apart from the Dawsons, who could lead me there was Peter Rixon—the head chemist at Dawson Pharma. He sounded like a half-hearted criminal, liked the perks that came with his job, but didn't want to be seen as a criminal. I had come across many such fence sitters in the past. They were the easiest to turn.

Rixon had helped Jasper set up the meth cooking lab, getting the right equipment and the proper cooking process to get high-grade purity, something the hundreds of barely-literate morons posing as cooks couldn't achieve in their half-assed cooking labs mostly spread across California. That's how the Dawson's product grabbed most of the market in Nevada's neighboring states and the entire west coast.

Rixon was one of the many chemists employed by the company. But he was made the head of the pharmaceutical division once he showed the Dawsons his cooking prowess. He loved the perks—a large house and fancy car—but saw himself as a scientist rather than a criminal. He trained a couple of other guys who didn't have qualms about being labelled meth cooks. The Dawsons allowed Rixon to take a step back so long as he still oversaw quality control.

But the previous week had shaken his cozy little set up, as it had done the entire Dawson operation. The Mexicans didn't trust the Dawsons anymore. They were planning to shift the cooking operation to a place called Las Hermosas, south of Tucson in Arizona, close to the Mexican border—an area the SDC cartel controlled.

But shifting the cooking base meant the cartel wanted to take Rixon along. That would make him simply a meth cook, not the head chemist for a semi-respectable set up. Rixon hated the prospect, but didn't have a choice. When the SDC cartel tells you they want something, you shut up and do it. Unless you have the balls to say no. Rixon was a man known for his meth cooking, not for the size of his balls.

The Dawsons would become minor players, mainly restricted to the supply of pseudoephedrine for the cartel's cooking operation.

Pseudoephedrine, the usual starting point for making meth, was the main stumbling block when it came to running a large-scale meth lab. You can't get it in large quantities simply by using runners to buy cold medicines from pharmacies.

The Dawsons would have to divert huge quantities regularly from the pharma business. That wasn't something they were happy about as it was a recipe for getting caught by the authorities sooner or later. They had begun their meth operation two years ago when they received a shipment of four tons of pseudoephedrine from China, which they were able to declare missing. That gave them enough raw material for an entire year.

We arrived at the motel in less than an hour. It was a little before one in the night. Deputy Teller was waiting for us. I knew he wouldn't have been too happy about having to stay up late to babysit Mitch. But it was all part of a Marshal's job.

Mitch would remain with Teller until I sorted out whatever the hell was going on in Little Butte. Teller had taken a room at the motel. But we decided it was best he drove out straightaway with Mitch, taking him to a safe house located southeast of Vegas, a little short of Boulder City.

I thought about exchanging my pickup for a different one as Graves had noted my license plate while inspecting it. I finally decided against it. If I came face-to-face with Graves, I wanted to call his bluff. My plan was to shake things up until I got clues to Carter.

It was past one in the night. It had been a long day. I planned to crash in Teller's room. Just before I could do that, the phone rang again. It was Flynn.

"The damnedest thing just happened, Blaze. I got a message from Carter's phone."

"What? So... he's alright?" I felt a sense of relief.

"I'm not sure. All I got was a message. When I tried calling back, the phone was switched off. It was only turned on for a minute to send the message. The location was Little Butte."

"Right here in town? Could you get a precise location?"

"I could get a half-mile radius. It was in the southern end of the town. The area from the Dawson hotel at one end and the police station on the other. It's difficult to be more precise than that. It's a small town with a limited number of cell towers."

"What did the message say?"

"Just a couple of lines. I'll read it out. Hold on, now where did I leave my glasses...ah, 'Investigation going well. Need to stay low for a few days. Will be in touch later. Carter.' That's it."

"It's not Carter. Why wouldn't he simply call?"

"I thought so as well."

"But that's good news. They've got him but he's alive. Had it been otherwise, they would have destroyed the phone as well."

"That's true."

"That message was from whoever has got him. I have really rocked the Dawsons' boat in the last few hours. A pile of bodies they will find difficult explaining to the cartel. I think they're desperate now, trying to avoid the feds and state police swarming all over town."

"I get the same feeling. I'm gathering all info on the SDC cartel. Two of the guys in the photos you sent have a record in Mexico. As you said, cartel hitmen. And the lieutenant, Hector Alvarez, is considered extremely dangerous. Ex-Mexican army. Deserter. Took a couple of his men with him to the cartel. They're his team of bodyguards. These guys are lethal, Blaze. You've gotta watch out."

"Roger that. And one more thing, the police chief in town is definitely dirty. I've got photos. He was helping the Dawsons hide the bodies I told you about. He's going down when this is over."

"You bet. Where was this? At the motel?"

"Yes. There was another group of sicarios in a van. I have installed trackers in both the vans. I'll send you the coordinates after this call."

"Good work. No one saw you?"

"No one that mattered?"

"That doesn't sound comforting."

"A couple of sicarios saw me when everyone left."

"And?"

"They're dead."

"Jesus. Are you trying to set some record?"

"It was kill or be killed, Flynn."

"I know," he sighed. "I also know they're getting scared because of you. That's why someone sent the message."

"I think so. I'll find Carter by the end of tomorrow. I'll dig up the entire fucking town if I have to."

"I know. Where are you now?"

"At the motel. Teller has taken Mitch to the safe house. I'll catch some sleep and be on my way again early morning. Nothing much I can do this time of the night."

"Makes sense. Good work, Blaze. Keep me posted."

"Roger that. Let me know if there's any more activity on Carter's phone."

"I will."

I ended the call. Crashed into bed. Slept like a log for four hours.

CHAPTER 8

I was on the road again at 0600 hours.

I began approaching Little Butte less than an hour later. Everything about the journey and the destination appeared different in the early morning light. The folks who named Little Butte were probably being funny. The butte overlooking the town wasn't little by any standards. The flat-topped, steep-sided red sandstone structure rising straight out of mostly flat surrounding land stood out starkly against the horizon. It caught the eye long before the first sign announcing the town came into sight.

I had sent the tracker coordinates to Flynn last night. He put a techie on the job of monitoring them. I was informed early morning that one van was still parked at the gas station. With two more bodies waiting for Jasper and his bunch when they arrived back at the motel, they must have gotten really flustered. The two bodies would either have been hidden inside the motel, or taken to some other location.

The other van was parked outside Dawson Hotel in the center of town. That didn't surprise me. I had created a real mess for the Dawsons last night. Their credibility with the cartel must have fallen even lower after six of the Mexican shooters ended up dead in their little town. The Mexicans wouldn't be planning on leaving town for a while.

As the abandoned gas station came into view, there was nothing there to suggest that a van full of bodies lay hidden within its crumbling remains. But I noticed a pickup parked in front of the repair shop. A man was sitting inside. The Dawsons must have posted him there to make sure no one would stumble upon the van.

I wasn't planning on exposing the bodies and the complicity of the police chief yet. Not until I had definite information about Carter. But something about the idea of a tough guy shooing away people riled me. I pulled in and came to a stop beside the dry gas pumps.

Before getting out, I tucked a gun in the back of my jeans, underneath my T-shirt. If the previous night was anything to go by, it promised to be a day full of action. I didn't want to be caught out without some basic firepower. That gun would be with me all day.

I got down and stretched. Reached inside the truck, picked a map, and sat on the hood, pretending to be studying the map, waiting for the man in the pickup to react. He did so a couple of seconds later, pressing his horn. I looked up once, saw him waving me away, ignored him, and got back to my map. He pressed the horn a few more times. I kept my eyes on the map.

"Hey, you, can't you hear me honking? You can't stop here. Get moving," the man got his head out of the driver's window and shouted at me.

I kept studying the map.

The man got out of the pickup. I looked up for a second. He was a large guy. Not more than 25, about six feet three, weighing about 230 pounds. He wore a tight-fitting T-shirt, which showed off the hours spent pumping iron. Dumb muscle. Looks good. Helpful if you want to push a truck stuck in mud, or shove people around in a half-assed scuffle outside a bar. Less useful in a real threat situation—where you kill or be killed. Guys like him sometimes get lucky and cruise through life without getting into that situation. But more often than not, there's a lot of hard learning they end up doing.

"What's wrong with you, asshole? Are you deaf? Get the hell away from here," he shouted as he strode towards me aggressively.

I folded the map, placed it on the hood beside me, and looked at him. My silence infuriated him further.

"Didn't you hear me? I told you to clear off," he said, coming to a stop a couple of feet from me.

"Don't," I said.

"Don't what?"

"Don't be rude to people. It's not nice."

"Nice? Get the fuck off..." he began saying as he raised his right arm to grab me by my left elbow to push me off the hood.

Bad move. Leaving his forearm open for punishment. Wrist and forearm holds are basic techniques for taking down uncooperative fugitives before cuffing them. A correct hold with the right amount of twist could bring even a 400-pound hulk to his knees. After years of experience, it had become second nature.

His sentence got cut-off midway as I caught the outer edge of his palm in one hand and his wrist in the other, and twisted them anti-clockwise to the point of breaking his bones. The only way for him to avoid that was to kneel on the ground. I slid off the hood without letting go and stood in front of the kneeling man. His face was contorted in pain—

I didn't let off the slightest bit of pressure on his twisted wrist.

"As I was saying, it's not nice to be rude to people. Is that getting into your thick head now?" I asked, giving his wrist a little extra twist, which made him yelp.

"Yes, yes... please," he begged.

"I twist another inch and your wrist and forearm bones will shatter. To be specific, the scaphoid and radius bones. Got that?"

"Yes," he replied, panting.

"Which bones did I just mention?"

"Huh... scaph something... radius... please."

"If you ever talk to me like that again, those two will be the least of your problems. Got it?"

"Yes."

I let go. He stood up and held his right hand as tenderly with his other hand as if holding a new-born baby. But he wasn't done yet. As the pain subsided, his broken expression began changing into an angry one. He reached into his trouser pocket with his left hand. It came out with brass knuckles around it.

"Asshole," he shouted and threw a solid punch with his left hand.

That punch could have seriously hurt me had it landed. But he made three basic mistakes. Alerted me with his expression and his curse rather than taking me by surprise. Second, he used his weaker left hand for the punch, which came in slower. Third, he didn't get it from the lesson I taught him half a minute ago that I was particularly skilled in tackling sudden attacks. Taking a swing is a usual reaction of a fugitive about to be apprehended. That is, if the fugitive doesn't have a gun. This bodybuilder certainly didn't have one on him, although I was sure there would be a shotgun in his truck.

I sidestepped and swayed to my right. His punch missed me by many inches. I slapped his forearm away with a strike behind his elbow, which made him turn slightly away from me. I grabbed his elbow with one hand, struck him at the back of his shoulder to push him away and forward, slipped my arm over his punching arm and around the front of his neck, moved one leg behind him, and pushed his neck backward and downward, making him trip over my leg. He hit the ground hard, the wind getting knocked out of him.

This time, I didn't plan to show any mercy. I grabbed his right arm, held it straight, and swung my knee onto the back of his elbow. There was a loud crack as the bones of his forearm snapped.

The man yelled in pain.

I left him lying there and went to his pickup to check it. As I thought, there was a shotgun on the front seat, along with a baseball bat. Overconfidence in his size had let him down. Had he grabbed one of the two, he would have had a better chance, although the end result would most probably still have been the same. He just wasn't experienced enough in combat to take me by surprise.

His key was still in the ignition. I took it out and pocketed it. I picked the shotgun, walked back to my pickup, and threw it on the passenger seat.

"Get up," I ordered him.

He was moaning, pain shooting across his broken arm. But by now, he knew better than to ignore me. He got up on his feet, dropping the brass knuckles on the ground.

I frisked him, found a phone on him, and slipped it into my pocket.

"Get inside your pickup."

He walked over, opened the door, and got in.

"What's your name?"

"Spencer."

"A piece of advice, Spencer, if you're ever given such a job again, be polite with strangers. You don't want to run into someone like me again."

He nodded meekly, face contorted in pain. I began walking away.

"At least give me the keys." After a pause, he added, "Please."

"Good that you're learning manners. Sit here for a while. Think about your life's choices. I'm sure someone will come over to pick you."

I walked back to my pickup, got in, and drove off. I purposely avoided looking into the repair shop. I wanted the Dawsons to think the bodies were still their secret.

I stopped about a mile from the gas station, almost halfway to the motel. Got out, emptied the shotgun, and threw it far away into the wilderness. The man's keys, phone and cartridges followed the shotgun.

I got into the pickup and headed towards town. I slowed down as I approached the motel a couple of minutes later. It seemed abandoned. I pulled in and stopped in front of the reception area. The doors were locked. A makeshift sign declared: "Closed for Repairs".

With the amount of blood that was spilt in there a few hours ago, it would take buckets of bleach to clear the evidence. I planned to put a stop to the Dawsons' little game before that happened. By the time I was done, they wouldn't be able to keep up the pretense of being a law-abiding pharma company in that sleepy little town.

I inspected the area beside the reception entrance, where I had taken down the two killers. All traces of the fight were clearly visible. There was a spot with dried blood, where the man stabbed through the throat had fallen. There were several empty casings lying scattered around, the ones from the Uzi's magazine he had emptied before getting stabbed.

I must have reduced their manpower to such an extent that they could not clean up the area during the night. I doubted if they would risk getting around to it before darkness fell again. I took a few photos and left things as they were.

I was about to walk towards the pickup when I heard something. Someone moving stealthily. The faint sound of slow, careful steps. The kind of steps you take when you're trying to sneak up on someone. I drew my Glock and pressed my body against the wall, close to the edge.

The first thing I saw inching out around the edge of the wall was another Glock at chest height. A pair of arms followed, holding the gun out straight. Just as the man began turning the corner, I pushed his gun skywards with one hand while pressing my own gun into the man's gut. It was the biker from the previous night. One of the two big guys with long hair and ZZ Top beard. The one I took out in the passageway beside the bar counter. The only one who somehow managed to escape the sicarios and stay alive.

"Take the shot," he said in an emotionless voice, "I'll keep coming after you until one of us is dead."

He was clearly past the point where he cared for his life. Revenge was his only driving force. I felt bad for him. I had been there. I knew how it burns up your insides.

"What have you got against me?" I asked him in a calm tone.

"You've got some nerve asking that," a touch of emotion entered his impassive tone. "First you mess us all up, then send your men to take us out..."

"Whoa, hold on. You're mistaken. I did mess you up, but that was because you and your pals were going all gangster on me. If I wanted to kill you, I didn't need to send anyone else. All six of you were lying knocked out unconscious in that bar. It wouldn't have taken any effort to put bullets in all of you. Think about it."

An unsure look appeared on his face. I used that moment of indecision to wrench the gun out of his hands and move back a step.

"It wasn't me who killed your friends," I said.

"Brothers. Not just friends. We were brothers. Wore the same patch," he muttered, almost to himself.

"Brothers. I get it. But it wasn't me who got them killed. Think about it."

He gazed vacantly into the distance for a few seconds.

"Those killers were all wetbacks... So, you didn't send them?" he asked me, his voice sounding very unsure.

"You know I didn't. Those were Mexican cartel sicarios. Sent there by the Dawsons. They are the ones who let you down. Made you scapegoats to save their own skins."

"But we had nothing to do with the Dawsons. We did nothing against them. We just used to deal with Mitch."

"They were after Mitch. All of them. The Mexicans were getting mad the Dawsons were using Mitch to get you guys to distribute meth out of Nevada. But the Dawsons are weasels. Shifted all blame on to Mitch. Told them he was doing it without their knowledge. To save their skins, they gave the Mexicans a target—Mitch and his crew. You guys had nothing to do with it, but got caught in the territorial dispute."

He didn't reply. Just kept looking at me, trying to make up his mind.

"Why don't you tell me what happened after I left? I'll fill you in on the rest," I said.

"Alright, man. Maybe you're right... Well, after you left, Gurtie came in hobbling, using a baseball bat as a crutch. He said you'd given it to him, after you broke his leg with it. That's some weird shit, man."

"You know why I had to do that."

"I guess. Gurtie told us we needed to clear out from that place. People were coming looking for us. You told him that?"

"I did. I wouldn't have done that if I wanted you guys dead."

"I guess. Well, I was the only one fit enough to ride. I was going to go into town, get a truck, haul us and the bikes away from that place. I was just about to get on my bike when I decided to take a leak in the bushes. That's when those wetbacks came there in that van. Heavily armed, Uzis, AR-

15s, shotguns, serious firepower, all with suppressors on. All I could do was hide and watch. I don't know what happened inside, but they soon carried all of them outside, wrapped in plastic sheets, dumped them in the van, and took off. All I could do was watch like a pussy," he said, his voice breaking on the last words.

"I'm going to kill them all," he added in a firmer voice.

"What happened after they left?"

"I just kept sitting there for a long time. Couldn't decide what to do. Finally, got on my bike, came to the motel. The reception was locked. I just went to my room. I've been lying low in there, trying to think how to get back at them, until you just came in. I could have left town, but I'm not leaving until I get who killed them."

"You have no idea what a charmed life you've been living last night. Missed death by a whisker, not once but twice. If you'd come to the motel a little earlier, it would've been a different story."

I told him all that happened at the motel last night. Told him about finding Mitch. Everything I had learned about the Dawsons, the cartel. I had no doubt that this man wasn't a threat. We had a common enemy. That made us natural allies.

"You killed them all? Those Mexicans, with all that serious hardware they had?" he asked me.

"Yes, I got lucky."

"You don't get lucky against that arsenal. And the way you went through six of us... not a scratch on you. You're not just some random guy. Who are you, man?"

"Those weren't the first killers I've taken down."

"No shit. So... they're all dead?"

"The four who killed your brothers? Yes. And two of their pals. Right here," I said, pointing to the spot of dried blood.

"Bastards," he said, spitting. "But it's not over. I'm going after the Dawsons."

"Don't go rushing in like a bull... the way you rushed at me."

"I know, man. My head's still throbbing," he said, tenderly massaging the side of his head, which I had banged against the doorjamb.

"If you go head on, chances are you'll end up getting killed. There are too many of them. At least five I know of. There might be more. And the Dawsons and their men."

"I don't care. I won't let them get away."

"You'll get your chance. Make sure you're good and ready when you take it. Until then, be patient."

"Alright, man. Whatever you say. What have you got against them?"

"A friend has gone missing. That's why I was looking for Mitch. To get information. I've spent all night investigating. I know the Dawsons have a hand in it."

"Let's get them. Tell me what to do. Whatever it takes. I'm not leaving this place until they're finished."

"I need all the help I can get," I said, holding out my hand. "I'm Blaze."

"Brick," he said, taking my hand.

"The first thing to do is to make you safe. You stick out too much in your biker gear. The Mexicans will kill you if they see you like this. Change your look before you do anything."

"This is what I've worn for years, man. I know it's all gone now," he said, pain over his loss making his voice quaver.

"We'll make the Dawsons pay. You've got my word. Do you have any regular people clothes? Maybe jeans and T-shirt?"

"Yeah."

"Good. How about a razor? Ever seen one?"

"Not for twenty years. But I've got scissors."

"They'll help. Lose that beard, cut your hair, and get into regular clothes. You'll be unrecognizable. I'll give you a razor. Where's your bike?"

"At the back over there," he said, pointing to the back of the motel.

"That won't do, pal. It's going to get you killed if they find it."

"They won't. It's way out back there, behind some rocks, under a tarp."

"Well, alright then. But you better head back to your room. Change your look. Don't get out until you hear from me. Give me your number," I said, handing him my phone.

He keyed it in and handed it back.

"Keep this," I said, handing him his Glock. "You need to work on your stealth skills, pal, I could hear you coming a mile away."

"I know, man. You got the drop on me. Twice."

"Now better head back inside. But be careful. I don't think they're going to be cleaning up this mess before dark. But you never know."

He nodded and headed to his room.

I got into the pickup and drove towards town. It was time to get acquainted with the folks of Little Butte.

CHAPTER 9

I was as surprised by the bombed-out look of the first half of town as I was the night before. It wasn't as if I hadn't seen streets with whitewashed windows, boarded up storefronts, vacant lots, ramshackle houses... Drive the length and breadth of America and you will come across dozens of towns taking their last breaths—pale reminders of smothered aspirations that somehow fell off the wagon that was the American dream.

It was the stark contrast of the new part of town that made the distinction even more striking. I pulled in where the two halves met. Chico's diner lay exactly at that point.

I parked the pickup in one of the lots that had a partially standing boundary wall in front of it. That didn't really hide it, but the license plate was no longer visible to any passerby. I wasn't ready yet to bait the police chief.

As I walked toward the diner, I looked at the large billboard on top of it—the words Chico's Diner screamed out in striking red on a yellow background. One of the specials displayed near the entrance mentioned a chef's special burger with a Mexican touch—served with guacamole and salsa.

But apart from the billboard and chef's special, the rest of the place had the menu and traditional floorplan of any diner in the American heartland. A service counter ran almost across the entire length, with floor-mounted bar stools in front of it. A row of booths was set up against the front wall and at the ends.

When I entered the diner, a pleasant-faced woman standing behind the counter welcomed me with a somewhat hesitant smile. I couldn't figure out if she was worried about something or just plain tired. I looked around at the occupants of the place.

The table near the entrance end was occupied. Two guys from the Mexican cartel were sitting there. One of them was the man I had locked eyes with last night when he drove past me in the van. Despite getting only a fleeting look at him, I had no doubt it was the same man. Small eyes, thick moustaches drooping to the chin, a rattlesnake tattoo on the right temple. Those two were the surviving members of the second van's occupants, the two who had driven the van full of bodies to the abandoned gas station. No wonder the woman behind the counter had a strained smile. She must have known they were cartel—the tattoos on their faces left no doubt about that.

I no more than glanced toward the Mexicans' table before beginning to walk towards the other end. Although I recognized the man instantly, I saw no trace of a recognition, or any other emotion, in his eyes. Those were cold, dead eyes. Eyes of a killer.

I walked toward the far end of the diner. The corner table was empty. I noticed three of the tables were occupied. There was a man of about seventy on one of them. He had a full head of hair, all white, having a coffee, immersed in a crossword puzzle in the newspaper on the table. A couple of clean-shaved young guys in cheap business suits and cheap imitation leather briefcases were sitting at the second table. The word salesman was almost tattooed across their foreheads. They were getting their first caffeine shots of the day. There was a couple at a third table, both in their 30s, having a quick breakfast, probably on their way to work.

The woman came out from behind the counter to take my order. There wasn't any sign of Chico. I ordered coffee. And eggs and bacon on toast.

I noticed the Mexican at the other end of the diner staring at me. I started getting the feeling he remembered me from our very brief encounter. And if he remembered me, it was logical he would be suspicious about me—he had seen me standing by the side of the road in the dead of night, minutes before two of his pals got killed.

I had left town straight from the motel and had met no one in town apart from Ellie, Chico and Mitch. There was the kid at the hotel reception, but he must have crashed out by then after his night shift. For all intents and purposes, I had just arrived in town that morning. That was the line I planned to stick with.

A bus came to a stop near the diner. It was a shiny new silver-grey coach. Dawson Pharma was written in large blue letters on the side. Must be transporting employees to their morning shift at the pharma factory. There were a handful of people sitting inside it. The two salesmen and the couple paid their bill and got on as well. But the bus did not move. Probably waiting for more passengers.

The only other customers left inside the diner were the old man and the Mexicans. The waitress came over with my order. She still had that strained smile on. She laid the plate and coffee on the table along with a set of napkins. She turned up the napkins slightly to show me a note beneath them. Then covered the note again, looked pointedly at me, and went back.

I picked up the napkins and read the note. It was from Chico. He was hiding out at the back to avoid the Mexicans. Asked me to call him after breakfast to arrange a place to meet.

It wasn't clear why he was hiding. I guessed he hadn't gotten over the scare from last night. I couldn't blame him. Watching a killer spreading out plastic sheet, preparing to kill him would have been nerve wracking. These guys were merciless killers—it would be best for most men not to cross paths with them. But until I found Carter, I couldn't apply that advice to myself. I would have to actively seek them out and ensure that when our paths crossed, it would be the end of the road for them.

I had just begun eating when the jacked-up Ford pickup I saw last night came to a stop behind the bus. Jasper and Grady Dawson got out. Jasper was attired differently from when I last saw him. He had a light cotton blazer on top of a black vest. Possibly his respectable work clothes. He still didn't look anywhere like a sharply dressed businessman, but didn't look as seedy as he did without the blazer.

Grady had clean clothes on as well, although not much different than what he was wearing the previous night—a half-sleeved tucked in shirt with sleeves rolled up further to reveal his huge biceps. He stood scratching his beard while Jasper entered the bus, had a word with someone, and came out. Both of them headed for the diner.

Jasper had a whispered conversation with the Mexicans. He then turned around and acted as if he was looking around the diner. But I knew he was checking me out—his glance rested on me half a second more than it normally should have. The Mexican must have told him about me.

"Where's that lazy Chico, Anna May?" Jasper asked the woman.

He was trying to sound playful, but there was a nervous edge to his voice.

"He opened up early morning and went back home. Said he wasn't feeling well," the woman replied.

"Is that so? Why don't you give him a call? I'll ask about his health."

"His phone's switched off. I tried. He must be sleeping."

"Hmm... not a busy morning?" he said, looking at the old man and then resting his eyes on me.

"There were more customers. Just got on the bus."

"Ah, right. I see Quint's busy with the crossword," Jasper said, looking at the old man.

The old man didn't react, and kept his eyes glued to the crossword.

"Oh, hello, we have a new face," Jasper pretended to have just noticed me.

I ignored him and continued eating. Jasper walked towards me, stopped a couple of steps before my table, and addressed me.

"Hello, stranger. You've got some business in town?"

I glanced at him, then got back to my plate for another bite.

"As I was asking, what're you doing in town?" he persisted.

"Minding my own business."

"Oh, a tough guy. I'm Jasper. Jasper Dawson. You might have heard the name."

"Nope."

I ignored him and kept eating.

"And what might your name be?" he asked.

"Stranger."

"That's funny," he sniggered.

I ignored him.

"New in town?" he persisted.

"Yup."

"Came in last night?"

"Nope."

"Oh?"

Jasper kept waiting for a response, losing his swagger with each passing second. I carried on eating.

"Well, then, you arrived this morning?" he persisted.

"Yup."

In the meantime, Grady moved and stood behind Jasper. That brought back some of his cockiness.

"Not a talkative man, I see," he observed.

"Nope," I replied.

I placed my cutlery on the plate and stood up suddenly. Jasper took a quick step back, as if scared I was going to hit him, and bumped into Grady. I stepped towards the empty table next to me, picked a ketchup bottle, and sat back on my seat.

Jasper was stuck in a difficult situation. He had been embarrassed by his nervous reaction to my standing up. He would further lose face if he backed down. He decided to persist.

"Out here, we consider it mighty impolite to turn down a conversation."

"That so? Where I come from, it's considered mighty impolite to disturb a person having his breakfast in peace."

"Fair enough, I can wait until you've finished eating," he replied, trying to appear in control, although he was clearly flustered. He held a hand out to Grady, who seemed ready to pounce upon me like an angry gorilla. They sat down at the table next to mine.

I continued eating. I was finally done after a few minutes. But for Jasper, the man forced to cool his heels while I ate, time must have dragged excruciatingly slowly. Grady was venting his frustration on a fork, twisting it into a contorted mess.

I finally pushed my plate aside, wiped my mouth with a napkin, had a sip of coffee, and looked at him.

"You were saying?" I addressed Jasper.

"Mighty obliged you can finally talk to me. I was asking when you came into town."

"I don't see how that's any of your business, but looking at how you've been waiting so patiently, I'll oblige you this once. I arrived this morning."

"Well, that's where I'm confused. My friend over there swears he saw you last night."

"Well, your friend's mistaken."

"You saying he's lying?"

"Your words, not mine."

"I think the man's an honest *hombre*."

"Yeah, right. I almost mistook him for a priest. I thought those tattoos on his face were holy symbols."

Jasper sniggered.

"You aiming to stick around town?" he asked.

"Depends."

"On what."

"How much I like this place."

"We don't like strangers acting all smart," Grady spoke for the first time. He had a gruff voice.

"Friendly little place, this town of yours. The two of you and those rays of sunshine at that table by the door. I think I'm beginning to like it here."

"I think you might change your mind soon," Jasper replied. "Have you heard of the Dawsons?"

"Nope. But I have a feeling you'll tell me they're some kind of big deal in this little hole."

"Pops is the mayor. We own this town," Grady spoke up.

At that moment, a black Cadillac came to a stop behind the pickup. A man of around 65, dressed in a black suit and matching cowboy hat, stepped out of the driver's side. Long white hair peeped out of his black cowboy hat. His white moustaches were like Jasper's, drooping down almost to the chin. But between the white hair and moustaches, his eyebrows were dark, hardly a speck of white in them. It made for a very striking appearance.

A young man of around 25, built like a linebacker, exited quickly and stood behind the older man. The man had a similar height and weight to the guy I had just left broken at the gas station. Weighing around 250 pounds and four inches over six feet. He had a light cotton jacket on, mostly to conceal a shoulder holster.

A woman was sitting on the back seat. Honey blonde flowing hair on an attractive face with sunglasses on. Made a pretty picture.

The older man walked into the diner, followed by the bodyguard. He stood near the entrance and beckoned to Jasper and Grady. I figured it was Baxter Dawson.

"Looks like daddy's here. Time to run off, boys," I said.

They gave me dark looks as they stood up. Clearly obedient to the old man.

"This ain't over, mister," Grady said as he got up, kept the fork he had twisted and squeezed into a contorted mess on my table, and walked towards the entrance.

"You bet it ain't. I was just beginning to enjoy our conversation," I replied.

"We're in a rush right now. But I'm hoping you don't leave town without a taste of our hospitality," Jasper said, his voice laced with menace, as he followed Grady.

"Oh, I'll be around. You can bet on it."

The two talked to Baxter in conspiratorial whispers. Baxter looked at me, walked over, and spoke in a deep voice with a distinctly southern accent.

"I see you're new in town. Pardon me, I happen to be in a rush and can't stay long to make your acquaintance. Folks call me Baxter Dawson," he said, tipping his hat slightly.

"They call me Blaze."

"My boys don't take kindly to strangers. I hope you stick around for a spell to get acquainted with us."

He was clearly the most dangerous of the lot. Not easy to figure out. His words and tone made it difficult to make out if he was being polite or delivering veiled threats.

"I'll be around," I replied.

"Good day to you," he said, turned around, and began walking out. He stopped for a second before the table where the old man was sitting, said "Quint", touched his hat and walked out. Quint nodded but didn't reply.

Jasper, Grady and the bodyguard stood near the entrance all this while, glaring at me. The moment Baxter walked out, they followed him. The Mexicans got up as well and followed them.

The Cadillac was the first to drive off, followed by the pickup and the bus.

Quint, busy in his crossword until that moment, folded his paper and spoke to me directly.

"Your name happen to be Charlie Bronson, son?" he said.

"No. Why?" I couldn't help smiling as I replied.

"I have never seen a man with such a death wish. Them Dawsons are a mean bunch. Them and those two gangsters at that table. Better watch your back, son," he said, sincere concern in his voice.

"Appreciate your concern. I thought you were too engrossed in that crossword," I replied.

"I was hanging on to every word. The tension was so thick, you could cut the air with a knife. I wanted to whoop the way you put them down. I'm Quint, by the way."

"I'm Blaze," I replied.

"There's a hardware store at the south end of town. I don't have a license to sell guns, but if you're ever in need of a hammer, or a chainsaw,

I'm your man. Gotta run now," he said, getting up and folding the newspaper.

Quint was tall and slender, and moved with a relaxed gait. He was a pleasant, likeable man. I decided I would pay him a visit later.

The moment Quint walked out, Chico made an entry from behind the counter.

"Whoa, Marshal, that was some serious Wyatt Earp shit," he said excitedly.

"Where have you been hiding?"

"These cartel *hombres*, they're bad news, Marshal. After last night, I don't know if they're coming to my place to order a taco, or to whack me," Chico replied.

"Why was Jasper looking for you?"

"I honestly don't know, man. Maybe someone saw me talking to Mitch yesterday, when he came in here. I don't know. And I don't care. After last night, I don't want to be within a mile of any of them. I couldn't sleep all night, bro. Every time I close my eyes, I see that killer's tattooed face."

"Good idea to stay away from them. But what if Jasper started looking for you? Were you in the kitchen?"

"Anna May doesn't let just anyone walk into the kitchen," he replied. Lowering his voice into a whisper, "She's like psycho about cleanliness, bro, washing hands, shit like that. And even if Jasper bullied his way through, I've got escape routes. Come on, I'll show you," he pulled at my arm.

I followed him to the back of the counter. Chico led me through one side of the kitchen to a small room at the other end.

"I was here, behind this locked door," he said, slipping a key into the door lock.

"How did you know what was going on out there?"

"Watch and be amazed, dude" he said, opening the door and waving me inside.

There were a couple of monitors on a desk getting a feed from two security cameras installed at both ends of the diner. A pair of headphones were lying beside them.

"It's real high-tech shit, bro. I already had the security cameras in my place. When Carter came in, he installed four microphones as well. Now, I've got eyes and ears. I can hear anything right from the entrance to the other end, where you whupped Jasper's ass."

"That's handy. Were you able to listen in on what they were whispering among themselves?"

"Nothing goes on out there that Chico doesn't know about. Seriously, you're impressed, aren't you? Didn't I tell you I was, like, trainee Marshal."

"Alright, Chico Earp. What were they talking about?"

"Yeah, right, let me think... OK, right, they're like, having a big meeting at their office. At the pharma plant. Some cartel big shit is going to be there."

"So that's where they were off to early in the morning? They must be in deep shit with the cartel."

"Right, bro, sounded like they have really blown it. And... there was something else. Let me think. Yeah, right, the Mexican guy was saying he's sure he saw you last night. What was that all about, Marshal? I thought you had popped all four at the motel. Was he with them?"

"No, it happened after you dropped me and drove off home. There was another group of four in a van. They passed by me. I barely locked eyes with that guy for a second. But he remembers me."

"Whoa, that's bad news. Be careful, Marshal. I know you do your Robocop shit, deadly and all, but, you know…"

"I know."

"And what's going on at the motel? I thought things would be going loco this morning, what with those piles of bodies in the van."

"They moved the van at night. Those two Mexicans from this morning. They hid it in that abandoned gas station."

"Whoa, that's crazy, dude. This place is becoming full on cartel land. But why hide the bodies? I thought the vans were to make them disappear without a trace."

"The plan was to hide them there until they could clean up their mess at the motel. But things didn't go as planned."

I filled in Chico on what happened at the motel.

"That's crazy shit, Marshal. You mean Graves was there helping hide the bodies? I know he's crooked, but this is way out, man—helping the cartel hide bodies… Maybe you should call in your Marshal buddies and clear this shit once and for all?"

"All this is going to end by the time I'm done. But I need to locate Carter first. If I call in the boys, we'll blow any chance we have of finding him."

"You're the boss, whatever you say."

"I also ran into one of the bikers this morning. Brick, you know him?"

"Not by name. Is he one of Mitch's guys?"

"Yup."

"Then I'll know him by face. Their leader was a dangerous dude with a mohawk. And there were a couple of hairy guys, beard, long hair and all. Like those ZZ Top dudes, you know."

"He's one of those ZZ Top dudes."

I told Chico about my encounter with Brick.

"Whoa, that's one lucky dude, bro. Escaped those psychos twice."

"He sure is. I'll go get him later today. It'll be good to have an extra hand."

"Count me in, Marshal. What should I do?"

"Best no one sees you with me. Stick to the diner. See if you can find out anything with your surveillance set up. I'll go about rattling their cage until someone leads me to Carter."

"Whatever you say, boss."

"What's the deal with Quint? He seems like a nice guy. Didn't seem to like the Dawsons."

"That's Quint Madison, Marshal. One of the original Little Butte families. This used to be a mining town. Full of silver. But the mines closed ten years ago. The town was dying out. Land was going cheap. That's when the Dawsons came and bought up most of the land for the new part of town. There was nothing there before they came. Baxter began steamrolling all other businesses. That's why you see this ghost town."

"Right, I've been wondering about that. So, that's the Dawsons' doing?"

"Yup. These are nasty guys, Marshal. Force businesses to shut down and buy space from them. Some gave in, others moved away. Quint is one of the few who're still holding on."

"And what about you?"

"They haven't begun pushing me yet, but I'm sure they will, bro. I've got the only eating place in town, so they have let me be for now. But I know it won't be for long. I'm on the wrong side of town."

"You can forget about the Dawsons pushing you out. Their operation will be over by tomorrow. I'll gather enough evidence by the end of the day to shut down anything they've touched. I think I'll go pay Quint a visit. Did Carter meet Quint?"

"I don't think so. He never came up in our conversation."

"OK. Get some paper. Draw me a map of the town. The main locations, mainly the Dawsons."

Chico gave me the layout. The pharma factory and offices were located on the southern end. The Dawson family lived in three identical houses located beyond the factory, well out of town. Baxter and Daphne lived on their own. Jasper and Grady shared a house. The three houses were well fortified, surrounded by a seven feet high wall, with a guarded front gate.

The casino was being built next to the butte. The construction site was fenced in a way that the butte formed an impenetrable back wall.

The other Dawson businesses were located in the center of the new part of town. The three-story Dawson Hotel with the new Bar & Lounge, a Bank bearing their name, and a pharmacy.

I had all I needed to get started. It was time to further shake the Dawsons' set up.

CHAPTER 10

I took the diner's back exit and made my way around to the pickup.

I had just gotten in the driving seat when I received a message on my phone. The van parked near the hotel had begun to move. I began tracking its movement on the app on my phone. The van was moving towards the diner. I sat low inside the pickup and kept my eyes peeled on the road. As the van passed by, I saw the two Mexicans from the diner driving it.

I kept tracking the van. It moved past the motel and came to a stop at the abandoned gas station. It looked like they were going to move the van with the bodies.

I waited for their next move. There were only two choices open to them. They could drive away from town, towards the north. But I doubted there would be places where you could dump a dozen bodies without a trace. They couldn't take the chance of the bodies being discovered.

The second option was to drive through town to someplace the Dawsons would help them get rid of the bodies. But that seemed too brazen in broad daylight. Two Mexicans with gang-related tattoos all over their faces driving a suspicious-looking van through town—chances were they would be stopped by a cop. Provided, of course, there were a few honest cops in town. I wasn't willing to believe all of them were dirty.

At that moment, a police car cruised past me in the direction of the van. The cop inside was a new face. There was no way to figure out if he was clean or dirty. The next few minutes would reveal that, I guessed. I kept glancing at the tracking app on my phone. After around ten minutes, both vans began moving. They were coming towards the diner, on their way towards town.

Three vehicles soon filed past me, moving single file. The cop car was in front. It turned out to be a dirty cop after all. I had no more than a second to click a photo of the cop car. The two Mexicans had split up, driving one van each. I began following them, using the directions from the phone app, keeping a couple of hundred yards behind them.

The vehicles turned right at the main crossing and headed towards the bar. Beyond the bar, about a mile further on, loomed the butte, beneath which was the casino construction site. The vehicles drove straight towards it.

As I drove past the bar, I saw a "Closed" sign displayed prominently outside the entrance. The path going to the back of the bar was blocked with a makeshift wooden structure. It was clear the Dawsons were getting nervous. They didn't trust the Mexicans to have done a clean job with the bikers at the bar. They must have decided it was safer to keep it closed; out of bounds for anyone who could chance upon any proof of the murders that took place there less than 12 hours ago.

I figured the cop car would escort the vans up to the site and head back. I didn't want the cop getting any hint he was being followed. I left the road beside the bar, drove around it, and stopped behind it, hidden from the road.

I got out and walked to a point from where I could see the road. Less than five minutes later, the cop car passed me, making its way back to town.

I went back to the pickup and began driving towards the casino site by the butte. For a small town the size of Little Butte, the site was massive, although set against the backdrop of the butte, didn't appear that way from a distance.

As I closed in, I saw that it was completely secured. An opaque grey pre-fabricated ten feet high wall topped with barbed wire ran along three sides of the site. The butte formed an impregnable back wall.

Even the entrance to the site didn't provide a peek inside—it was blocked by heavy sliding doors, same height as the fence. A small window on the side of the gate opened into a guard's cabin. It was clear that the opaque perimeter wall was meant to keep prying eyes from discovering what went on inside.

There were security cameras across the perimeter, most of them pointed towards the road. That seemed like too much security for a construction site. There was surely something more going on.

I noticed a camera on the fence moving, tracing my approach towards the site. A face soon appeared on the window of the guard's cabin, watching me. The road approached the site and continued on the left, hugging the fence. I drove along the road, without stopping. I knew that the road ran around the site, went on to go halfway around the butte, before winding its way to the main north-south highway passing through town.

I kept driving slowly, watching the perimeter for any breaks. But couldn't find any. I carried on until any view of the road from the site was completely blocked by the butte. I pulled up once I reached the back of the butte.

It looked even more imposing from up close. The red sandstone walls, around 300 feet in height, rose straight up from the ground. I used my binoculars to scan the walls, trying to work out a path to the top.

This wasn't going to be an easy climb. Apart from the steepness, there were overhangs near the middle and the top, where the walls bulged out. Clearly a technical difficulty grading over 5.11.

I finally worked out a possible route to the top. There looked to be sufficient hand and footholds on most of it, but not on the entire route. It was a tough, technical climb. I would need my climbing gear and shoes—on portions with barely any footholds, smearing against the wall with the shoes would be the only way to get some friction.

Coming down wouldn't be a problem. Climbing down a steep rockface is usually harder than going up. There's the extra difficulty of not being able to see holds from above. But I had my ropes with me. I could easily rappel down after a free climb to the top. I would need to carry two lengths of 60-meter ropes for the rappel. Good thing I had all my climbing gear in the pickup.

No one guarding the site would expect anyone to try and make an entry from the top of the butte. To an inexperienced climber, it would look like an impossible task. But I had spent most of my youth scaling clifftops in the Rockies.

I would need the cover of darkness if I was to try and descend into the casino site from the top of the butte. There was no cover during the day. Anyone within the site or even driving down the road from town could easily spot me. I didn't want to be stuck on a rope, with someone on the ground taking pot-shots with a rifle. But climbing the butte at night would be close to impossible.

The only way out was to make two trips. Once during the day, to go up, fix a rope at the top, do a recon of the site, and rappel down the rope. Then make a second trip under the cover of darkness, using the rope to climb the butte and descend from its other edge into the casino site.

I didn't want to hang around the place for too long. I had driven slowly across the front of the site, checking out the perimeter. Someone from the site could become suspicious and decide to investigate. I decided to come back later.

I got back in the pickup and drove on, meeting the main road just outside the southern end of town. As I turned towards town, I drove past the Dawson's houses and their factory, before coming across the only operating gas station. It was a Chevron. I half-expected it to have a Dawson sign. As I was filling the pickup, I glanced towards town. My eyes rested on a sign: Madison Hardware. It was time to get acquainted with Quint Madison.

I drove to the hardware store, parked, and went in. It was a little past nine in the morning. The place had just about opened for business.

It wasn't huge like a lot of hardware stores, but with an area of around 5,000 feet, big enough for a town the size of Little Butte, with a population of under 2,000.

A skylight window in the middle of the ceiling gave the store a lot of natural illumination. The place looked like it had been in business for a while. The wooden floor looked worn; the signs above some of the narrow aisles looked faded. A display area near the payment counter had an arrangement of power tools and fishing tackles.

There was a kid of no more than twenty behind the counter. Thin, nerdy-looking bespectacled boy—he would have been more at home playing video games than managing a hardware store. He was taking payment for a can of paint from a middle-aged woman.

"Is Quint around?" I asked the kid, as soon as the woman left.

"Uh, not really. Can I help you?"

"Not really? That's a curious answer. Could you give him a call? Tell him it's Charlie Bronson? I'm a friend."

The kid looked unsure. But picked a phone, pressed a button, and spoke into it.

"Blaze, come on in back here," Quint called out from the back of the store.

"Down there," the kid pointed towards an aisle. I walked through it into a small office.

"I was passing by... Hope I'm not intruding," I said, taking a seat on a chair opposite him.

"Not at all. It's not as if I'm very busy," he said, pointing to the crossword still open on his desk. "Dewey out there just saves me the bother of unwanted visitors."

"You get many of those."

"Sometimes. You saw how the Dawsons have a habit of poking their noses into everyone's affairs. They don't like people not agreeing with them."

"And you're one of those people?"

"Yeah. It may turn out to be a losing battle. But can't give up the fight, can we?"

"No, don't give it up. It might not turn out to be a losing battle."

"How much do you know about it?"

"Not much. That's what I'm here to find out. By the time I'm done with what I'm here for, the Dawsons won't be bothering anyone."

"If you don't mind my asking, who are you, Blaze? I don't think you're just a traveler passing through town."

"You're right. I didn't just come wandering. I'm looking for someone who went missing. A good man. The best really. I know the Dawsons had a hand in that. But not sure how."

"Can I do anything to help?"

"I'm still putting the pieces together. I've been told you're best placed to give me an idea of what the Dawsons are up to."

"They're a family of rogues. Except for that gal, Daphne. Them all arrived in town five years ago. Little Butte was a mining town. Silver mines. A rich streak ran from the butte. But that dried out. All mines closed ten years ago."

"I heard about that. So, what happened?"

"Well, land was cheap and Baxter had endless amounts of cash. He floated the line that he came into money selling family land up north. But I know for a fact he was in the weed business in Tennessee—him and his two pups. They built the weed business the same way they're doing it here—bullied families to sell their land cheap. When they began getting too much heat, they sold it off and came here. Bought a lot of land and an ailing pharmaceutical plant. Acted respectable for a spell. But you know what they say—no matter how many times a snake sheds its skin, it'll always be a snake. They were soon in the meth business."

"Is that common knowledge in town? Does everyone know the Dawsons make meth?"

"I think so, unless you've got your head buried in the sand. They were able to keep it under wraps for some time. But then, strange characters started appearing in town. Also, Baxter needed to launder his money. Daphne mostly set up the pharma business for him. Then she got him a license for a bank. She used to work in a bank before she came here. Hard to believe she belongs to that family of crooks."

"Banking? That's interesting."

"Yeah, isn't it? But the bank alone wasn't enough. Construction was another easy business for laundering cash. So, they're building this new town. They force old businesses to shut shop and move into new properties they built. Rent free for starters. Then they begin turning the screws. They've got a lot of muscle to make life difficult for those who don't give in."

"That's why you asked the kid out there to tell people you're not in?"

"Yeah. There are a couple of rednecks working at the gas station across the road. They come over visiting sometimes. I'm not afraid of them, but they spoil my day every time I see them."

"What about the cops? Don't they intervene?"

"They mostly don't do much damage to make it worth a police complaint. Just create a little ruckus, scare customers away."

"But would the cops help if you asked?"

"I don't lay much faith in them, mainly because Graves is the chief. He's sold his soul to the Dawsons. And it wasn't as if he was always a bad cop. He was alright until them devils came to town. Baxter threw money around, became town council president. He made Graves the chief. Callaway, the one before him, was forced to retire. Ever since Graves became chief, he has been on Baxter's payroll."

"What about the rest of the force?"

"Not much of a force. There are four others apart from Graves. I can vouch for two of them— Hunter Nash and Betsy Adams. Hunter is a local boy, brought up the right way, old southern values. I've known him since he was a pup. He's the only reason I still have hope. But the boy can't do much when Graves calls the shots. The only reason he has a job is he's a good cop. And some of us old-timers still have some say in the town council. Graves is retiring next month. We're hoping Hunter will be the next chief. But who knows what them devils will get up to?"

"And what about Betsy Adams?"

"Nice lass, God bless her. Her heart knows no evil. But she's just the dispatcher. Doesn't do much policing."

"And the others?"

"There's Elliot Birdie. Scum of the earth. Does all of Graves' dirty work. I'm not sure about Owens. The detective, Lester Johnson, looks like he has a good head on his shoulders."

"And what about Daphne? You said she isn't as bad as her family?"

"I ain't saying she's an angel, but she seems different. Educated. And I've seen her do good for some youngsters in town. Anyone with a helpful spirit can't be all bad. But she doesn't matter much, with them other three calling the shots. Baxter uses her to get deals done for the respectable part of his business. Things like the bank and pharma company."

"Interesting."

"She's a pretty gal. You haven't met her yet, have you?"

"No."

"She was in the Cadillac this morning. Dawsons have been using her to get their casino license through."

"I think I saw the construction site."

"Did you? They're guarding it like they have gold buried there. They have no business building a casino, they haven't even got a license yet. Although I think it could happen any day. Baxter has a deal with a Senator. What I've heard is he needs the casino—he's spread himself too thin with all the construction and big plans. The casino will bring in cash... launder more money."

"So, that's what it's all about? He can't afford a scandal right now."

"You got that right. If he doesn't get that license, things are going to be difficult for him. I hear the license will be pushed through by the Senator next week."

"Right. That's why they're desperate. Tell me one more thing, Quint... was there some big gang business going on in town a week ago?"

"There was. A whole bunch of crooks descended here for a couple of days. A godless pack. You could see just by looking at them."

"Have you heard of anyone going missing after they left?"

"No one I know of. Why? Has something happened?"

"I think so. That's what I have to find out. And you wouldn't happen to have come across a man called Carter these last couple of days."

"No. Is he the one you're looking for?"

"Yes. He's a good man. Two men went missing last week, after those gangsters came to town. Carter was looking into that. But he went missing as well."

"God almighty. Has it come to this—people disappearing? This Carter, was he a cop?"

"US Marshal. I might as well tell you about myself. I was a Marshal. Left the service a few months ago. Carter was a good friend. That's why I've come looking. I have a strong feeling the Dawsons are mixed up in this."

"I'll be surprised if they aren't," Quint replied. "Tell you what, let me make some calls. I'll see if anyone has heard about them missing people."

"That'll be very helpful. Just don't mention Carter by name. Word might spread I'm here looking for him. I don't want the Dawsons catching wind of that. Not until I'm good and ready for them."

"Got it. I'll take care."

I waited while Quint made the calls. Five minutes later, he put the phone down, a troubled look on his face.

"You were right. There were two men who went missing. And someone did come looking for them."

"So, what happened?"

"One of the men gone missing was a factory worker called Charlie Bird. I don't know him. Must be from out of town—I don't recall any Bird family around here. He worked at the Dawsons' pharma factory. His girl works at the salon in town. What was the name..." he looked at a notebook in front of him, "yes, Clarise. She's been to the cops, but nothing has come out of it."

"Hmm... and the other one?"

"It's the mechanic in the auto repair shop in the old part of town. I've seen him there. Indian kid called Lou. Hard to miss—you don't see many natives in town. He was a bit of a drifter. Appeared in town one day. Knew his job. Lived in a room by the repair shop. His stuff is still there, it seems."

"No one looking for him?"

"I don't think so. It might be best to talk to Aldon, owner of Baker's Auto Repair. He's a good man. Tell him I sent you."

"Thanks. I'll do that. Anything about Carter?"

"He did go asking around town. But no one seems to remember his name. I think he went to the cops as well. But I couldn't find out anything more than that."

"That's more than enough, Quint. It's time to make a few investigations of my own."

"Anything else I can do, just say the word. It's time someone took them black-hearted devils to account."

"They will be taken to account, you can bet on it. And if Carter has come to any harm..." I left the sentence unfinished.

"I know."

I was getting up to leave, when Quint looked at a security camera feed and groaned.

"Problem?" I asked.

"Here they come again," he replied.

"The guys from the gas station?"

"Yes. And they have a couple of partners this time," he turned the monitor towards me. There was a pickup outside, four men inside it.

"They must be planning to dial it up a notch. I can't let them do it," Quint said.

He opened a cupboard and took out a shotgun and cartridges.

"Let me handle this, if you don't mind."

"I appreciate the offer. But it's not your fight."

"Don't rise to their bait, Quint. That's what they want you to do. Gives them a reason to trash this place. Thugs like them don't mind spending a night in the slammer. Even if you call the cops, Baxter will have them out on bail. But if that shotgun gets fired, it will be trouble for you. Bringing a gun into the picture complicates things. Even if you take a self-defense plea. Believe me, I've been doing this for years."

"I can't let you risk your life for this."

"Risk my life? With those clowns? Trust me, I deal with chumps worse than them all the time."

He remained silent, trying to make up his mind either way.

"I've been meaning to get the Dawsons all riled up. This just gives me another chance. Take my word for it, you won't have to deal with this long," I said, standing up and holding out my hand. Quint took it.

"I'll deal with them on my way out. You stay in here. We don't want them getting the impression I'm doing this for you. I'm just a customer in the shop. Alright?"

"Alright."

"If the cops get involved, all you and the kid know is I was a customer they were harassing. It'll all get recorded in the security camera. Makes sense?"

"It does. Much appreciated," he said.

"No bother at all. I'll be seeing you later," I said and walked out of the office.

As I walked through the aisles towards the counter, I saw three men get out of the pickup. They walked in while the fourth guy remained seated in the truck, music blaring out loud.

The largest of the trio who walked in was heavyset, thick neck and shoulders, close-cropped hair. There was an excessive swing to the shoulders as he walked—showing the world how tough he was. He had a cocky expression on his face, which became more pronounced when he saw the nerdy kid, Dewey, behind the counter.

The other two guys were slightly smaller versions of the first one. But that made them feel obligated to be even more obnoxious. One of them bumped into a display stand beside the counter. Clearly on purpose.

"Oops," he said, in a tone suggesting he was being very funny.

"Watch it, Riley. You don't want Dewey getting mad at you," the larger guy said.

All three laughed. I stood near another display, looking at fishing tackles. I knew they would try and act fresh with me soon.

They walked towards the aisles, spilling a box of screws as they went. When they came back towards the counter again, one of the smaller guys was carrying a can of paint, holding it by the handle, his arm held straight out at shoulder height. It was the same guy who had bumped into the display earlier—the funny one. He let go of the can so it would fall less than a foot from my boots.

He was opening his mouth to say "Oops", but never got the chance. I caught the can's handle before it touched the ground.

"Easy, pal. You might end up hurting someone."

"Uh... so what?"

He wasn't expecting this turn of events. He struggled to come up with anything else.

"Not a nice thing to say. The proper thing to do is apologize for being so clumsy," I replied.

He tried to grab the can from me.

"Not a good idea," I said, moving my arm holding the can away, putting the can down beside me, away from him. "You go on pay for it. I'll hand it to you on the way out. We don't want you having another clumsy accident before that."

"Who are you calling clumsy?"

"I see only one person in the store bumping into things left and right. I know you're not bright, but try figuring it out for yourself."

"You trying to act smart, mister?" the larger guy, who was standing behind the clumsy one, spoke up.

"With your buddy around, I don't really need to try."

"Uh... I think you're trying to make fun of me," the clumsy one spoke up.

"Hey, you're getting smarter by the minute. Wouldn't it be swell if you learned some manners as well?"

"You looking for trouble?"

"Not especially. So long as you behave politely," I replied.

"You planning to walk out of here in one piece?"

"Now you're starting to scare me. Do you mean you're going to be waiting for me when I walk out?"

"That's exactly what I mean."

"Before we commit to it, let me warn you, clumsy man, it's not a good idea. Think once more about it."

"There's nothing to think. You're dead meat."

"I see. In that case, let's go outside. I'll try to explain my point once again."

They smiled at each other and began walking out. I handed the can of paint to Dewey. His eyes had gone bigger behind his spectacles.

The three guys had walked up to the fourth one by that time and were quickly whispering to him. The parking lot beside the store was mostly empty. But it faced the main street. I didn't want any cop passing by to break the fight and haul all of us in. I had too many tasks planned for the day.

I took a few quick steps backwards towards the area behind the store. Apart from some trash cans and a few empty boxes, it was mostly vacant. Plenty of space to have a brawl. Although a brawl wasn't what I was after.

In a fight with multiple opponents, it's not about how many punches or kicks you throw in. It's more about reducing numbers quickly and decisively—one at a time. That comes down to surprise. Quick entry, fast strike, rapid exit. Repeat. Until they are all down.

The three felt even more confident when they saw me backing away. The fourth one was taking his time getting out. He didn't really think he would need to get involved.

"Have another think about it. I don't really want to hurt you. You can still apologize and walk off in one piece," I cautioned the three as they approached me.

"Hurt us?" the big guy smirked.

He decided to make a sudden rush at me. Dumb move. It would have been better for them had they spread out and come at me from different directions. The guy made it too simple by coming between me and his partners.

He threw a punch with all his body weight behind it. He was a big guy, could maybe deadlift over four hundred pounds. But this wasn't a weightlifting competition.

The punch could have knocked me out had it landed. But I saw it coming a mile away. I sidestepped and struck him on the throat, with what in unarmed combat training we used to call tiger's mouth—the arc formed by the thumb and index finger. It's the lowest joint bone of the index finger, the metacarpal phalangeal joint, that you thrust into the throat of your opponent. Strike it forcefully just below the Adam's apple—you can kill a man.

I didn't plan on killing him. I held back a little, applied maybe 70% of my force in the thrust. That was enough to stop him in his tracks. His hands went to his throat, gurgling and croaking sounds coming out of his mouth. I stepped back and drove my heel into the side of his knee, forceful enough to break a couple of ligaments, mainly the medial collateral ligament. That would leave him on crutches for a while. He fell flat onto the ground, still clutching his throat, still making those strange sounds.

Quick entry, fast strike, rapid exit. It took no more than five seconds. I took a step back, ready for the other two.

The big guy lying between us complicated things for them. They did have the sense to coordinate their attack. Both of them rushed towards me at the same time. But they had to take a somewhat circular path, stepping around the fallen man. That meant I could take them out one at a time.

The man on the right went into a crouch and rushed at me, trying to grab me around the body. I took a step forward and made a quick, hard strike on the side of his neck with the edge of my hand, on the part between the ear and the chin. That's where the vagus nerve lies hidden, between the carotid artery and the jugular vein. The vagus connects the brain with the heart and lungs. A hard tap on the area causes a momentary break in blood flow to the brain. Instant knock out. You see that happening in MMA fights, although that's usually more by dumb luck than by design. I hit that man on the vagus on purpose. I knew what the result would be—he collapsed in a heap.

Quick entry, fast strike, rapid exit. Game over for him within two seconds.

I immediately turned to face the third guy. He had dropped his head and was rushing at me like a bull. I sidestepped, turned a little, and drove my elbow into his temple. He went out like a light.

All three down in ten seconds.

The fourth guy, who was halfway between his truck and me, had by that time realized that fighting me wouldn't be a cakewalk. He rushed back and grabbed a baseball bat.

I didn't give him time to think. I rushed towards him before he began swinging the bat behind him, preparing for a powerful strike. He never got around to completing it. I was two steps away from him as he swung back the bat. I took one quick lunging step on the ground, and the second step onto his knee. I smashed the wooden heel of my boot onto the top of his kneecap, pushing his knee way beyond its normal range of motion, snapping ligaments and tendons. His knee collapsed and he began flopping towards the ground. I grabbed his head and swung my other knee hard on his temple. Lights out for him.

All four targets neutralized.

They wouldn't be feeling well enough to bother Quint for a few days. I would be finished with the Dawsons much before that. Once I was done, Little Butte would go back to being a friendly little town.

As I walked back to my pickup, I saw Dewey rushing back towards the entrance. All this time, he had been hiding around the corner, watching.

Once he reached the shop entrance, he turned, gave me a big smile, and waved. I waved back, got in the pickup, and headed towards the auto repair shop.

CHAPTER 11

The repair shop was on the outer edge of the crumbling part of town. A dusty medium-sized billboard displayed the words "Baker's Auto Repair" in dull colors. It was easy to miss unless you were looking for it. No wonder I didn't spot it while driving in during the morning.

But it was a different matter at around ten in the morning. There were a couple of cars parked outside, both with hoods open. Aldon Baker was leaning under the hood of an old Chevy. I waited for a minute until he finally stood up and gave some directions to a mechanic.

Aldon must have been in his mid-sixties. Hair mostly gone grey. His hands told me he was a workman—strong hands, veins crisscrossing the still-muscular forearms visible under the folded-up sleeves of the shirt he wore under his work overalls.

He was a pleasant-faced guy. But stuck in a situation where his main man had gone missing, he came across as frustrated and irate. The furrows on his brows said so.

But the moment I mentioned Quint's name, the furrows disappeared. The frown was replaced with a smile as he held out a hand.

"Quint just gave me a call. Give me your hand, mister. It'll be my pleasure to shake hands with the man who taught a lesson to them devils. I'll be glad to be of any help," he said, taking my hand and heartily pumping it.

He took me aside so we could talk in private.

"Thanks. You in the same boat as Quint? Baxter making life tough for you as well?"

"God damn him. Them Dawsons are a scourge we can't see any end to."

"The end might come sooner than you think. But I'm here to ask about Lou. Could you tell me how he went missing?"

"Just disappeared. I remember the date—March 25th. He was here all morning. I went home for lunch. When I came back, there was no one around. The garage was open, a car he was working on stood with its hood open. His tools scattered on the floor. I waited until late in the evening, but there was no sign of him."

"Did you go to the cops?"

"I did, after a couple of days. But Graves just brushed it off. Said Lou was a drifter. Must have wandered on to someplace else."

"You buy that?"

"Not on my life. Lou was a bit of a mystery man, but he was no hobo. He landed in town four years ago. Came looking for a job. I tested him. He knew his way around cars. I hired him on the spot. Things were good back then. Them devils hadn't begun to bare their fangs at that time."

"The Dawsons?"

"Who else? I don't believe for a second that he'd just leave."

"Was there anything unusual you noticed in the last day or two before he disappeared?"

"Well, there were a lot of unsavory characters in town. Them Dawsons collected a bunch of crooks. But I don't know if that's got anything to do with Lou going missing."

"And those crooks you're talking about? Were they still in town after that?"

"I don't know... let me think... hmm... well, I'll be damned if you haven't got something there. Them crooks left town the same day. You think Lou went with them?"

"I'd say he was taken unwillingly."

"You mean kidnapped? But why?"

"That's what I mean to find out. I have a feeling Graves knows the answer why."

"I wouldn't be surprised. He's been in Baxter's pocket for a long while. So... that means Baxter has a hand in this?"

"Most likely."

"God almighty. Will be there be no end to that devil's wickedness?"

"That end isn't far. Upstanding folk like you and Quint will have their day, I promise you."

"Bless you for saying that."

"Would you know anything about another man who went missing the same day?"

"I didn't until Quint told me about it. I wish I did. You think they're connected?"

"I'm not sure. I'll find out soon. Was there anyone else apart from the cops who came asking about Lou?"

"No, and it wasn't as if the cops were coming around much. But hold on, there was someone. Maybe three days ago. I wasn't keeping well and had taken the day off. Mason, the kid who's helping me out now that Lou's not here, he did mention someone came around asking for Lou. But I didn't meet him."

"Could you ask Mason if he remembers anything about the man?"

"Sure. Mason!" Aldon shouted out to the mechanic working on a car. "Come on here, will you?"

A young guy of no more than 25, sandy hair falling across his forehead, came over.

"Who was that man who had come looking for Lou the other day?"

"What man," Mason asked, furrowing his brows, scratching the back of his head.

"You were the one that told me. That day, when I was home sick?"

"Ah, right. Carter, he said his name was. Said he knew Lou from way back."

"He did? You didn't tell me that."

"Didn't I? I told you a man came looking. You were busy with a truck, shooed me away."

"Did he say anything else?" I asked.

"He asked to look at Lou's room. Said he was some kind of detective. I took him around. And he went away. Why, did he take something from the room? I was there with him, I'm sure I kept an eye."

"There isn't anything worth taking in the poor man's room," Aldon said. "You go on, get on with that car."

"OK, boss," Mason turned and walked back.

"Could I have a look at Lou's room?" I asked Aldon.

"Sure," he went to a counter in the shop, picked a key, and led me around the side of the shop to a room at the back.

Everything in the room seemed to suggest the man who lived there hadn't made a planned departure. There was milk and food in the refrigerator. A pile of washing was lying in a corner—possibly to be taken to a laundromat in the evening.

I knew there wouldn't be any point looking for any other clues. Lou was transferred from Texas under Witsec. That meant not a trace of his past life would be found in that room.

As I got into my pickup, I received a message from Flynn's techie guy—one of the vans had moved from the construction site. The new location where it was parked was Dawson Hotel.

I had barely driven half a mile when I saw the flashing lights of a cop car in my rear-view mirror. I pulled over to the side. The car stopped behind me. The man who stepped out was Earl Graves. It was time to get acquainted with the police chief.

Graves put on his cowboy hat as he got out. He walked over to stand by my window and looked at me carefully. He didn't quite fit the profile of the hard-bitten crooked cop that he was. The face before me was that of a world-weary man. But the eyes were alert, no sign of weariness in them as he quickly scanned the inside of the pickup.

"License and registration please," he said in a crisp cop voice.

I handed both things to him.

"New in town?" he asked.

"Yup."

"When did you arrive?"

"This morning?"

"I want you to think carefully, sir. This vehicle was seen in town yesterday?"

"By whom?"

"We have witnesses."

"That's curious. Witnesses for what? Has there been any crime committed?"

He looked at me carefully, trying to gauge what I knew. He didn't get much from my face. He couldn't possibly say he saw the pickup while helping the Dawsons hide the bodies.

"No crime. We run a peaceful town here."

"Strange you feel that way. I've been hearing stories about gangsters coming to town, people going missing. I was almost thinking of getting away from this place."

I waited for my words to have some effect. His face remained impassive. Decades of practice of keeping his emotions in check.

"Someone has been feeding you stories. We don't have any gangsters or missing people," Graves replied.

"Well, then you have a lot of paranoid nut jobs with conspiracy theories in town."

"I don't know about that. You seem to know a lot for a man who's just arrived in town."

"People warm up to me, I guess. You ought to try listening to them, Officer. I was even told there were sounds of gunfire late at night. Mexican gangsters roaming about town."

This time my words had some effect. A momentary hint of doubt appeared on his face. But he checked it immediately. I would have missed it had I not been looking carefully.

He scrutinized my face again.

"Are you planning to stay in town?"

"Not decided yet. I saw the motel has been closed for repairs. Didn't look like there was any work going on there."

"I guess there must be, if there's a sign saying so. That's the owner's business."

"And who might the owner be?" I asked, waiting to see what he would say about the owner the Mexicans killed last night.

"Tucker," he said abruptly. "Maybe you best move on. That's the only motel in town."

"I'll think about it. This being such a peaceful town, maybe I'll stick around, enjoy the calm."

He didn't reply.

"You didn't tell me about the witnesses who saw my pickup," I prodded him again.

"Must've been an error. Have a nice day."

He handed back my license and registration.

"I will. You have a nice day in this peaceful town."

He glared at me but didn't reply and went back to his car. I had given him a lot to think about. The message would soon reach the Dawsons—something wasn't right about the stranger in town.

I drove on towards Dawson Hotel. Not seeing the van parked in front, I drove around to the back and found it in a parking lot. It was a secure lot for hotel guests, accessible using a magnetic key card.

I decided to take a room at the hotel. I knew it would be like walking into the devil's lair. The Dawsons owned it. The two Mexicans were staying there. Chico had also mentioned some cartel big shot was in town. He too would most probably set up camp there.

I had too much to do, too many leads to follow, and didn't plan on using the room. But having access to the hotel might come in handy.

CHAPTER 12

I parked the pickup on the main street. As I was walking towards the hotel, I heard someone call my name.

It was Ellie. She made a pretty picture, hair hanging loose around her shoulders, the sparkling green eyes making her smile even brighter. She wore a summery dress matching the color of her eyes. Ellie was one of those people who are born cheerful and remain that way all their lives.

"Hey, Axel. I thought you were going to call me this morning. Not nice to keep a girl waiting," she said.

"Hey, Ellie. A lot's happened after I dropped you last night... I've been on the road almost the whole time."

"Really? In Little Butte? You must be the only busy man in town. Leisurely doesn't even begin to describe the pace of life around here. Mable, my friend, was leaving for work. She works in that salon," she said, pointing to a salon behind us. "She's the one giving me a ride the last few days. I decided to tag along and grab a coffee. It was boring staying at home. And you know what..."

I was worried about Ellie being seen with me. I was making too many enemies in town. I could be bad news for anyone seen as my friend. We were standing outside the coffee shop, which was less than 30 yards from the Dawson hotel. It was safer to talk in there than on the street.

"How about we grab that coffee you're after? Shall we head inside the coffee shop and talk?"

"Sounds good," she said, leading the way in.

"You know what," she began talking before we had taken our seats, "you were right when you said the bar would be closed for a while. Actually, it's the end of the road for that place. The new bar at the hotel is being opened tomorrow. Just like that. It was supposed to be a week later. But I got a call. I'm supposed to head there in the evening."

"Really? They're opening the new place tomorrow? Interesting."

First the motel closing, then the bar. The Dawsons were surely feeling the pressure. My constant interference was not giving them time to catch their breath. I needed to keep up the pressure.

"Interesting? That's a funny way to put it," Ellie replied.

"Well, I'm not surprised about the old bar, after what happened there last night..."

"You mean when you bashed up those bikers and Tats?"

"Tats?" I asked.

"The bartender, remember?"

"Oh, yes. The guy with the weird name."

"It wasn't just his name that was weird. He wasn't a friendly guy."

"I did get that feeling when he and his pals decided to jump me."

Ellie laughed.

"So, what have you been up to? Why were you on the road all night? We have a nice hotel in town, in case you didn't notice. And there's a motel, which is a bit of a dump, but no worse than most motels you find."

"I know the motel. It's not in good shape right now," I told her.

"Why? What happened? Did you beat up a bunch of guys over there as well?"

"No, nothing like that. It's closed for repairs. So, how have things been with you? I hope nothing worrying happened."

"Since last night? No. It was fun. It's always party time when I get together with Mable. But why do you ask? What's up?"

"There's a lot up. I'll tell you. But first, who told you the new bar was going to open tomorrow?"

"Daphne. She called me this morning. Asked me to come over in the evening. It's going to be a formal launch tomorrow. Some Senator is coming to town."

"Senator? For opening a bar?"

"I don't know. I guess there must be other stuff as well. The Dawsons do have connections."

"I guess. Does Daphne usually call you for these things, stuff like when to come in?"

"No. Actually, I was a bit surprised. I guess it must've been because it's opening earlier than planned. We've talked a few times. At the bar, and once at the hotel, when she showed me the new bar a couple of weeks ago."

"Who used to call you otherwise, for stuff like bar shifts?"

"Tats."

"You know why he didn't call today?"

"I don't know. Is it because of what you did? He's not in a state to call?"

"Yes, he's not in a state to work. But that's not because of me. I did knock him out, but not so badly that he couldn't make a call."

"Then I guess he took off with the bikers. The way you were saying... you said you'd ask them nicely and they'd take the hint."

"It's much worse."

"What? How?"

"I don't want to scare you, but this business is more serious than I thought. Much more serious than last night, when I asked you not to stay at your own place."

"What do you mean?"

"Dawsons are into serious crime. They're going to go down. That casino you've been waiting for isn't going to happen. I want you to know that."

Her face lost some color.

"I did know the Dawsons aren't completely legit."

"Completely legit? They're crooks, Ellie. Mixed up in hardcore gangster stuff."

"But... Daphne... she's nice. Always looked out for me."

"Maybe. I don't know. Maybe she isn't as mixed up. But Baxter, Jasper and Grady, they're big time into drugs. Even murder. People going missing."

"God," she said, and was silent for a few seconds. Then spoke up again. "That's what Mable told me yesterday... people going missing. There's this girl, works with her at the salon. Clarise. Her boyfriend has disappeared, and no one has a clue. She went to the cops. But... nothing."

"Do you know what happened?"

"I don't know. I just know what Mabel told me. You better talk to Clarise if you want the details."

"Where can I find her?"

"At the salon."

"Oh. Can you bring her here for a while?"

"Yeah, sure… but… you're a cop, aren't you? You told me you were an investigator. I think you're more than just a private eye."

"Yes, I'm more than that. But technically, not a cop. I'm a US Marshal. Looking for a friend who's gone missing."

"Marshal? That's why you wear those cowboy boots?"

"You think all Marshals wear cowboy boots?"

"I don't know any Marshals. And I don't know anyone else who wears those boots either."

"I have always worn them. I grew up on a ranch."

"Ah, that makes sense. Where did your friend go missing? In Little Butte?"

"Yes. I know the Dawsons are involved in that. I just haven't been able to get to the bottom of it yet. Will you help me?"

"Of course. You want to talk to Clarise, right?"

"I've been gathering lots of information. She might know things that'll help put some of the pieces into place."

"You stay here. I'll pop over to the salon and get Clarise. If I tell her it's about Charlie, she'll come running."

"Thanks. I'll wait."

The salon was almost across the road from the coffee house. Ellie crossed the road and went in. A minute later, she walked out with another woman—taller than Ellie, attractive face, dark eyes, dark shoulder length hair in perms, crossing the road at a brisk pace, a determined expression on her face.

They walked in through the double doors and headed straight towards me. Ellie had barely opened her mouth to speak when Clarise sat on a chair in front of me and addressed me directly.

"Marshal, I'm here for you. Pick my brains. Ask me anything. Just help me find Charlie?"

"Uh, this is Clarise," Ellie piped in the second she got a chance, waving her hand towards Clarise. She waved the other hand towards me and said, "Axel."

"Oh, Hi Axel," Clarise said, extending one hand to me, while taking Ellie's arm with her other hand and guiding her down into a seat, without breaking eye contact with me.

I took her hand, careful not to get entangled in the long black-painted nails. She was a direct woman, clear on what she wanted. No beating about the bush. I liked her. I could also feel the pain and frustration behind her words.

"Hi Clarise. I'm here to get to the bottom of this. I promise I'll find out what's happened to Charlie."

"Thank you. No one has had the decency to say that to me until now."

Her voice quavered slightly as she said that.

"I've been told you've been to the cops. Nothing came out of that?"

"You know what, I never thought Little Butte's cops were an elite bunch, but they have turned out to be even worse. Half of them are crooks, the other half a bunch of pussies."

"Tell me about the day. What happened? Think back, take me through everything that happened."

"That's the problem. Nothing happened. Charlie went to work. And never came back."

"What day was it? You remember the date?"

"March 25th. Two days before that, the 23rd, we celebrated two years of going out together. Charlie was good at that kind of stuff, you know, remembering silly dates and all. Two days later, he was gone."

"Do you know it wasn't just Charlie that went missing? Another man disappeared the same day."

"I heard about it yesterday. Mechanic at that repair shop. I didn't know him. I'm not sure about Charlie, but I don't think he knew him either. Well, maybe, he might have talked to him if he'd taken his car there for repairs. Charlie bought a second-hand car a few months back. But that's not really knowing someone, is it?"

"I know. Did Charlie appear worried that day? Was he nervous about anything?"

"Well, he was sometimes like that. Getting all worked up, thinking there were people watching him... But now that you mention it, he wasn't happy about that gathering of creepos the Dawsons had organized. Lots of creepy guys came to town. You could tell by looking at them. But then, I don't think anyone was especially happy about them. The Dawsons strutting around with that bunch all over town, huh, Ellie?"

"Um... yes," the talkative Ellie was stuck for words for once.

"Go back to that day again. What happened? What time did he leave for work?"

"The usual. He always left home at 7.30, for the 8 o'clock shift. Used to take the bus, but ever since he bought a car, he'd been driving to work."

"And that was your last contact? Any phone calls later that day?"

"He called around 12, said Rixon was sending him out for some work. He would be late coming home."

"Rixon? Is that Peter Rixon?"

"Yes."

"What happened then?"

"Nothing. He never came home. I kept calling. Kept getting voicemail. Phone switched off."

"What did Rixon say?"

"Nothing. Said he doesn't know a thing. He said Charlie wanted to leave early that day, so he sent him to the truck depot to sort out a delivery, and head on home from there."

"You believe him?"

"I guess. Why would he lie?"

"I don't know. Just checking. Think about the call with Charlie. What did he say exactly?"

"What I told you, he said Rixon was sending him for some work. Said he would be late. Then told me how much he loved me... and, that's it."

"So, Charlie said he'd be late, but Rixon said he wanted to get off early, right?"

"Hmm... I don't know... maybe I'm confused. Does it matter?"

"Maybe it does. If Charlie and Rixon told you two different things..."

"I don't know... shall I call Rixon again and confirm?"

"No, we don't want to alert him."

"But why would he do that? He's a nice guy, I never saw him say a harsh word to anyone..."

"The thing is, we don't know for sure. I'll follow it up with him. Don't contact him again until you've heard from me. You get that, Clarise? We don't have much to follow on, so whatever we have, we need to be careful."

"I can't believe it, but, yeah, I get it... Jesus! It can't be... but if he's involved, then God save him from me."

"I'll get to the bottom of it. Give it another day."

"Yeah, OK," she nodded.

"Do you know what kind of car Rixon drives?"

"It's one of those expensive European cars. A dark blue Merc. You want me to get you the license number?"

"No, it's fine. I'll get it from the repair shop. But, tell me, what did the cops say? Did they find anything useful?"

"They found zilch. Graves kept putting me off for a couple of days. Then all they did was talk to Rixon, put out a search alert for Charlie's car. And that's it."

"Have you talked to anyone else?"

"Just about everyone I meet on the road. That's all I talk about."

"No, I mean, anyone official? Did a man called Carter contact you?"

"Yes, said he was a private investigator. Working for the insurance company. Said his guys were better at tracking down people than the cops. I could easily believe that."

"Did you tell him everything you told me? About Rixon's conversation?"

"I'm not sure... maybe."

The entrance door opened at that moment and a man walked in. It was Baxter's bodyguard, the one who stood behind him when he got out of his car at Chico's diner. Built like a linebacker, around six feet four, weighing at least 250 pounds, a gun in a shoulder holster under his jacket.

He was walking towards the counter when he saw me. He stopped for a second, looked at me, then walked on towards the counter. He must have ordered earlier as a couple of takeaway coffees were ready for him. He picked them, looked again in our direction, and walked out. Clarise and Ellie had their backs to him and didn't see him come and go. The moment he was out the door, I pointed him to them.

"Who's that guy?"

They turned and looked at him walking down the sidewalk.

"Baxter's bodyguard. Hank," Clarise replied. "There are three of them—Hank, Percy and Spencer. All look the same."

I made a mental note—two of the three bodyguards remained a threat. I had already taken out Spencer at the abandoned gas station.

"He saw you with me. That wasn't good," I said.

"Why? How's it any of his business?" Clarise asked me.

"I've been ruffling the Dawsons' feathers all day. They aren't very fond of me right now. I don't want you two getting any heat in the middle of this."

"I'm not scared of them," Clarise said.

"It's not about being scared. These guys are crooks. It's good to be careful. I'll get moving now. If either of you girls bump into me on the street, don't act too friendly. OK?"

"OK. Are you going to be alright?" Ellie asked me, sounding worried.

"I'll be fine. Let's just talk on the phone from now on. It's not going to last long. It'll all be over by tomorrow."

"Thanks," Clarise said.

"I'll get to the bottom of this," I replied, touching her hand as she got up.

She nodded.

I watched them leave. Then got up, went out, and walked towards Dawson Hotel. It was time to lay my stake inside the devil's lair.

CHAPTER 13

I pushed open the hotel's heavy glass doors and entered its lobby. The doors shut out the outside world as they closed behind me. All external sounds were muted. The bright light of the day was left outside as well. The interiors were plush but dark. Muted lighting along the periphery of the ceiling was accentuated by clusters of floor lanterns. When I looked out, it felt as if I was watching a silent but vividly colored movie playing outside.

The leather sofas with shiny gilded trim looked like you could completely sink into them. The lobby didn't seem large enough for the crystal chandelier hanging on the ceiling, but it did provide a further dose of lavishness.

There was no one behind the reception desk. I looked around. A glass partition divided the reception from the larger area of the bar.

There was a single occupant in the bar—a strikingly attractive woman, sitting comfortably on a couch, curls of honey blonde hair tumbling onto her shoulders, the sun-kissed tones caressing a finely-chiseled face. Arched eyebrows above sweeping eyelashes gave the blue eyes a deep, mysterious quality. There was a smoky kind of sensuousness about her.

It was Daphne—the woman I had seen sitting in the back of Baxter's Cadillac.

She must have been around thirty, dressed in a close-fitting black dress, showing off a toned body underneath. She was lounging on the couch, but there wasn't any slackness in her body, as if she had positioned herself carefully in that comfortable posture. This was a woman who knew she was beautiful. And used to enhancing the effect that had on others. It was difficult to picture her as coming from the same stock as the other three Dawsons. She seemed to be in deep thought, staring intently into a golden-brown liquid in the glass in her delicate hand. It was almost the same color as her hair.

Daphne's eyes finally moved from the glass, swept around the bar, and rested on me. We kept staring at each other for a few seconds. She waved me over. I walked into the bar.

The layout of the bar was as plush as the lobby. Mahogany tables, leather seats and couches. The ceiling length windows, although slightly tinted, gave a clear view of the street.

"You look lost," she said in a melodious voice, sounding slightly amused.

"Kind of. I'm looking for whoever is supposed to be behind that reception counter."

"That will be Billy. I'm afraid he's out doing a little chore for me. Should be back in a few minutes. What did you want from him? Can I help you?"

"I wasn't particularly looking for Billy. It was more a place to stay I'm in need of."

"Are you sure you want to be staying here, Blaze? At the Dawson hotel?"

That took me by surprise. She was sharp. I couldn't resist smiling.

"You happen to be psychic, Daphne?"

A smile began spreading across her fine features.

"So you've figured out who I am? Not bad for a stranger who just wandered into town this morning."

"It wasn't that hard. There can't be too many attractive women in town lounging in the Dawson hotel's bar as if they own the place."

She laughed.

"How did you manage to figure out my name?" I asked her.

"You made quite an impression on my brothers. They couldn't stop talking about you."

"Oh, that lovely duo?"

"Yes, those two."

"Did they describe me in such detail? That you could make me out at a glance?"

"Cowboy boots came into the description a couple of times. And I did get a glimpse at the diner. But are you sure you want to be staying in a place they own?"

"So long as they remain as nice and friendly as they were this morning... But it doesn't feel like they run this place. It would have been a dump if they did. I think this place is more your style."

She laughed.

"I didn't take you for a charmer. Now you're making me curious. You didn't just wander into town, did you?" she asked.

"Well, I've been on a road trip. And the name Little Butte sounded nice."

"And you decided to stop and discover the joys of life in Little Butte? Just like that?"

"The joys of life in Little Butte? I bet those are worth discovering. But it was your old man and brothers who made up my mind for me. They sounded keen I hang around—I couldn't disappoint them. Staying at their own joint makes it easier for all of us."

"Do you have some kind of a death wish?" she asked, not in an offensive way.

"Funny, someone asked me the same thing this morning."

She looked at me closely. I had clearly piqued her interest.

"You don't know those three. And what they're capable of doing."

"It's only fair, I'd say. They don't know me and what I'm capable of."

"Figuring you out might not be as simple as I thought," she said, looking at me thoughtfully. "But while I try figuring you out, and until young Billy makes an entrance, can I get a drink for you?" she asked me.

"Looks like fine bourbon. Can't let a lady drink alone."

Daphne took a sip, got up and walked towards the bar. I couldn't keep my eyes away as she slunk sensuously towards the bar counter. She went behind the counter, put her glass on it, picked a bottle, and was reaching for a glass, when she looked out the window and kind of froze.

I turned to look at what had caught her attention. There was a commotion going on outside the salon. It was Hank, the bodyguard. Involved in an argument with Clarise. The hulk of a man suddenly hit the defenseless woman. Clarise fell to the ground.

Without a word, I rushed out of the bar and the hotel. By the time I got out, Hank was lifting

Clarise up by her hair. Ellie was trying to get him to let her go, but he easily shrugged her away.

"Hey," I shouted from across the street.

Hank froze, looking a bit confused. My body was on autopilot. All I could see was Hank. The only thing that mattered to me at that instant was inflicting pain on him. I strode purposefully across the road. I heard the honking of a car coming down the road, but it barely registered on me. I raised one arm up sideways, faintly heard a car braking to a stop, but my sights were set on Hank.

He let go of Clarise. A nervous look appeared on his face as he watched me advancing. He was a big guy, taller than me, heavier by at least 50 pounds, most of it muscle. But muscle doesn't help if you don't know how to use it the right way, or lose your nerve. In Hank's case, it turned out to be a combination of both.

He moved his hand towards his shoulder holster just as I crossed the road. Wrong move. Trapped his hand, which he could have used to fend me off. I took one step onto the sidewalk and headbutted him, the entire momentum of my rising body behind it. I was moving up and forward when the hard part of my skull, just around the hairline, smashed into his nose, turning it into a bloody pulp. Hank's head jerked back, his legs gave out under him, and he fell flat on his back, barely conscious.

I grabbed the gun from his shoulder holster and field stripped it. Dumped the remains of the gun—the frame, slide, barrel and recoil spring—into a bin. Put the magazine in my pocket.

Another guy, almost the same size and build as Hank, rushed out of the bank, which was a couple of shops away. I guessed it was Percy, the third bodyguard. He looked at the fallen Hank, and me standing over him, and rushed at me.

My blood was up. I moved to meet him, ready to pound the living daylights out of this next adversary. The wail of a police siren stopped us in our tracks.

A cop got out of the car, one hand at his side, on his holstered gun. He was young, not more than thirty, a stern look on his face. The name tag said Hunter Nash.

"What's going on here?" Nash asked in a stern but calm voice.

I turned to check on Clarise. She was shaken, had a split lip, but wasn't in bad shape.

Nash looked at the fallen Hank, went back to his car, and reached inside the car for his radio, his eyes still focused on me.

"No need for backup, Hunter. Nothing happened here."

It was Daphne. I hadn't noticed her walk over.

"Are you kidding me, Daphne? There's a man lying knocked out on the sidewalk."

"He isn't knocked out. Just dazed."

"Doesn't matter. I can't close my eyes to public disorder," Nash replied. "What happened here?" he addressed the people around in general.

"Hank hit Clarise. She got mad and knocked him out," Daphne said.

A giggle escaped Clarise's mouth, despite her split lip. Ellie had the same reaction. No one else among those gathered around, except for the fallen Hank and his sour-faced colleague Percy, could suppress a smile. Even Nash had to struggle to maintain his stern demeanor.

"I'll need to take Hank's statement. And get him to a doctor," Nash replied.

"Don't bother," Daphne cut in again. "Hank was being an idiot. Should have known better. He won't make a statement. Percy will take him to a doc. Right, Hank?" she looked at Hank, who had regained some sense by then and was trying to get himself to a sitting position.

Hank nodded as Percy helped him get on his feet. Both glared at me before walking away, Hank hanging onto Percy.

Nash went up to Clarise.

"Are you alright?" he asked.

"Yes, I'm fine now."

"I suppose you won't be filing charges against Hank, seeing as how it was you that knocked him out," Nash said, a touch of sarcasm in his voice.

"Yeah, right, so it's all settled, fair and square, I guess," Clarise replied, looking at him and then at me.

"I guess so," Nash replied, shrugging. Then, looking at me, he said, "I'll need to take down your details."

"Sure," I replied.

Nash walked to his car to grab a pen and notepad.

Daphne looked at me, her expression suggesting she wanted to say something. I looked at her, then towards the hotel, and back to her. She gave a barely perceptible nod, which I returned. Then she turned and walked towards the hotel.

I turned towards Clarise.

"What happened?"

"It was as you warned earlier—he asked me to keep my mouth shut, not talk to anyone about

Charlie. I told him to go to hell. The rest you saw, I guess. He punched me," she said, hurt and anger in her voice. But then a smile appeared on her face as she added, "and I knocked him out."

I smiled.

"I don't think they're going to bother you again, but take care. Don't be alone, at least for today," I said, giving her shoulder a slight squeeze.

She nodded.

"And tonight, it will be best if both of you stayed at Mabel's place. Could you do that? I wouldn't be asking if I didn't think it was important."

"Yes, no problem," Ellie replied.

"Good. I'll talk to you girls later."

"Thanks, Axel," Clarise said, her tone reflecting the appreciation in her eyes. "I'm still not scared of them," she added.

"I know. Good for you."

The two of them went inside the salon. I turned and walked over to Hunter Nash.

"So, it was Clarise who head butted Hank and put him down?" Nash asked me.

"Is that a statement or a question?" I asked him.

He looked curiously at me.

"Let's make it a question," he said.

"Well, you heard what the lady said?"

"You're lucky she spoke for you. But don't count on that happening again. Messing with the Dawsons doesn't come cheap."

"A lawman asking me to be scared of those crooks. Bothered more with what happened to that thug than what he did to a woman. Really, Officer? Is that what you're about?"

The remark hit home. His face flushed.

"I'm simply asking you to be careful," he said defensively. Then, in a more aggressive tone, "Also, we don't want vigilantes roaming around town."

"Give me a simple answer. I've been told you're an honest cop, old southern values. What would you do if that thug punched a woman in your presence?"

"I'm a cop. I'll throw his ass in lockup. But punching him isn't the best way out."

"I didn't punch him."

"Ah, right, it was Clarise who punched him?" he replied sarcastically.

"It was a headbutt, not a punch."

He watched me, trying to think of a reply.

"I've been told you're one of the rare cops not in Baxter's pocket... but can't do much with Graves calling the shots. But the time has come for you to quit sitting on the fence."

"Who are you?" he asked in a curious tone.

"I'll tell you all about myself. But first, you need to make up your mind. If all you want are my details for your record, there you go," I replied, taking out my license and offering it to him.

He took it, looked at it, then asked me, "Make up my mind about what?"

"Ending the Dawsons' criminal empire. They're going to go down soon. I'm giving you the heads up so you can be part of that. I know you want that, just don't know how."

He was silent, trying to make up his mind.

"I know it's a lot to take in. You trust Quint?"

"Of course. How do you know him?"

"Go talk to him about me. See what he says. Meet me here in half an hour. We can do one of two things then. If you make up your mind about

173

what I'm proposing, I'll take you someplace, show you something. The other, easier option... take my details, do your paperwork, forget about what I said, and let the Dawsons carry on steamrolling this town."

His face displayed the turmoil going on in his mind. He finally made up his mind. Handed me back my license.

"I'll see you here in half an hour."

"OK. Two things before you go."

"Yes?"

"I stripped that bully's gun and threw everything in that bin... except this magazine," I said, handing it to him.

"And the second thing," he asked, taking the magazine.

"In case you agree with my proposal, grab a forensic kit on your way back."

He nodded, got in his car, took a sharp U-turn, and sped off in the direction of Quint's store.

I crossed the road and entered the hotel lobby again. A kid was standing beside the reception. Tall, thin, sporting a goatee.

"Billy?" I asked him.

He gave me a nervous smile.

"Ms. Dawson is waiting for you," he said, looking towards the bar.

I entered the bar. Found Daphne exactly where I left her. A bottle of bourbon in one hand. Two glasses in front of her. I walked over to the bar. She poured a shot into each glass. Picked one and held it out to me. She didn't let go when I put my hand on the glass to take it.

"That was a good thing... what you did for Clarise. It was brave. Foolish, but brave," she said, looking directly in my eyes, something close to admiration in her look.

"It was instinct. One of those things you do without thinking."

"Whatever the cost?"

"Whatever the cost."

She kept looking at me, trying to make up her mind about something. She finally took her hand off the glass.

"I thought chivalry didn't exist anymore," she said, almost to herself.

I picked the other glass and held it out to her.

"It does. You're just mixing with the wrong crowd."

She took the glass, saying nothing.

"Thanks," I said.

"What for?"

"Saving me from getting arrested."

"That's the only thing I can save you from."

"I don't need saving from anything else."

"You don't know them."

"Actually, I do. Don't worry about it."

"If you say so, Blaze."

"Axel. Blaze is for people I don't know well."

"You think you know me well?"

"I'm getting a fair idea."

We clinked our glasses together and took a sip.

"How did you come up with that—Clarise knocking out Hank? It was funny."

She laughed. It was melodious.

"It just popped out. I wasn't thinking. Shall we sit for a while?" she asked me.

It wasn't really a question. She walked out from behind the bar, touched my elbow, and led me towards a couch by the window. We sat looking out the window. Life appeared normal outside.

"That was a fine thing did you did, Axel. There isn't a man in town who's got the guts to do that."

"That's a real pity."

"It is. But seriously, I mean it, you have to be very careful," she said, touching my hand.

"I will be."

We were quiet for a while.

"You aren't just a casual visitor to town," she said.

It sounded more like a statement than a question.

"What do you think?"

"No one comes here as a tourist."

"The casino will change that, I've heard."

Daphne gave a cynical laugh.

"Yes, the casino. That's supposed to make everything alright," she said.

"Will it?"

She didn't answer. Just looked at me closely.

"You're not a gangster. Must be a cop."

"You just saved me from getting arrested, remember?"

"That's true. But it doesn't rule that out."

"Doesn't it?"

She looked at me, a touch of regret in her eyes.

"I wish you'd come to town a little while ago, when we hadn't sunk in so deep…"

I looked at her, waiting for her to go on.

"Talk to me, Daphne. Maybe I can help figure things out."

"It's too late, Axel."

We were quiet for a while.

"Are you determined you'll take a room in the hotel?" she asked me.

"There's no other place to stay in town."

"What if I arranged some other place for you?"

"I couldn't take that obligation."

"What if I refused you a room here?"

"I have a feeling you won't."

She looked at me, trying to make up her mind.

"I've asked Billy to reserve a room for you. Top floor corner room. It's the safest, under the circumstances."

"Thanks. I appreciate that."

I was surprised by the choice of the room. I would have picked the same one. Top floor, corner room. Difficult to approach from the outside for a surprise attack. Low possibility of an assault from above. A lateral attack could only come from one side rather than two.

"The Mexicans are on the second floor, below yours," she said meaningly.

I didn't reply. Just looked at her. She was warning me, doing all she could, without actually saying much, to keep her family and the Mexicans from getting to me. I couldn't really figure out why.

"Will this get you into trouble, sheltering the enemy?" I asked.

"I'll be fine. But... are you? The enemy?"

"The menfolk in your family might think that way. And the Mexicans."

"The Mexicans are killers. Not brawlers, not dumb, just cold-blooded killers. They don't play games."

"Then you too need to stay away from them."

She handed me her phone. "Give me your number. In case I need to get in touch urgently."

177

"A beautiful woman in a bar, asking for a guy's number... some men might start getting ideas...," I said, keying in the number and handing it back.

She smiled.

"Take care, Axel," she held out her hand.

Daphne was elegant. Beautiful. But there was sadness and regret in her eyes. It struck something within me. I wanted to somehow protect her.

"You take care, Daphne," I replied. "It's never too late."

I gave her hand a slight squeeze. She nodded.

We emptied our glasses and got up. Daphne escorted me to the reception counter and nodded to Billy. Then she walked out, crossed the street, and went inside the bank.

I filled out the details in the hotel register. Billy handed me the key card. I took the stairs up to the third floor. Made sure the room wasn't bugged. It had a good view of the exterior—I could observe the entire main street.

I locked the room and headed out. It was time to find out which side of the fence Nash would choose.

CHAPTER 14

When I exited the hotel lobby, I saw Nash's car parked outside the salon. He was sitting in the car.

"Made up your mind?" I asked him.

"Get in," he replied.

I got in.

"Where to?" he asked.

"Depends on what you've decided to do?"

He paused before replying.

"Can't say I condone vigilantism. And you seem to have a knack for it. Quint told me all about what you did."

"And?"

"I guess the town needed a vigilante when cops can't do what they should be doing."

He looked at me again and repeated his previous question.

"So, where to?"

"The motel."

"That's been suddenly closed for repairs. Anything to do with you?" he asked.

"You'll find out soon enough. But it'll be better if we don't go there together. Graves has been busy all night making evidence disappear. He's given it a rest during the day. I don't want him getting busy destroying more evidence. That might happen if he or any of the Dawsons' men see us heading for the motel together."

"I don't get it. For all they know, I'm detaining you for knocking out Hank. What's so special about the motel?"

"There was a war going on last night while the town slept. Heavy armory, Uzis, AR-15s. There were dead bodies lying all over the motel. Twelve bodies, to be exact. Six of them Mexican sicarios. Five were bikers they'd shot dead. The twelfth was the motel owner."

"I don't believe that. I know you think we're just local hicks, but we'd have known if something that big was going on right under our noses."

"It was Graves. He made sure none of you found out. He was there, helping get rid of the bodies."

Nash remained quiet, taking in what I said.

"Graves coordinated the whole thing. Jasper, Grady and the Mexicans cleared all the bodies. The plan was to make it appear as if nothing had happened. But I put a crimp in their plans. That's why they had to close the motel. They didn't get the time to clear all the evidence."

Nash looked at me thoughtfully. He had a calm temperament. Not a man who got ruffled easily. That inspired confidence. I liked him.

"You're clearly no casual visitor to town. Who are you? Highway trooper? Or a Fed?" Nash asked me.

"Marshal."

He nodded. That put me in a different light. Now we were colleagues. He dropped the cop routine with me.

I gave him a quick brief about what happened last night. He listened calmly. Didn't display much emotion when I told him about Graves' complicity in the affair. He did appear slightly ruffled when I showed him photos of Graves with the bodies. Nash identified the cop who escorted the vans to the construction site as Elliot Birdie, the cop who did much of Graves' dirty work.

"Who was on night duty yesterday?" I asked him.

"Birdie."

"No wonder none of you have a clue. Graves and Birdie made sure you'd be kept in the dark."

"Hmm... you're right."

"So, you see... not a good idea for us to drive together to the motel. Someone is bound to notice you're on to them."

"I get it. Where's your car?"

"Across the road. I'll see you at the motel in five minutes."

"Right," he said. I got out of the car and went to get my pickup.

As I drove towards the motel, I called Brick. Told him to stay in his room until I called him again. He was about to ask why when I told him the reason—I would have a cop with me. That was enough to convince Brick. There's something about bikers and cops—they don't go well together.

Nash was getting out of his car as I turned into the parking lot and stopped next to him. The motel looked desolate. I knew Brick would be watching from his room.

I showed Nash the spot beside the reception area. The dried blood and the spent shells from the Uzi told a clear story.

"I can't believe this..."

"There's a lot more blood inside there," I indicated the closed reception area. "That evidence isn't going anywhere. It'll take buckets of bleach to get rid of that."

Nash didn't need to hear more. He got to work, taking a sample of the blood, sealing it in an evidence bag. He took photos of the place, picked a few shells, and added them to a separate bag. He agreed not to disturb anything else in the motel. We let everything be as it was.

"Shall I call highway troopers? This thing is big. We have enough to haul the Dawsons in."

"We've got nothing until we find the bodies and their meth lab. All we have is blood and bullets in the motel, but nothing to match them with. If you call in the troopers, we'll never find any trace of the bodies."

"I'm worried about the cartel being in town. That's not good."

"Cartel is never good news. Let's wait until sundown. I'll be done by then. We'll need backup after that. You can call in the troopers. I bet DEA will want to be involved as well. And our own boys are on standby."

"Where?"

"Vegas."

"Hmm... two hours."

"Yeah, but they'll move in closer in the evening."

"Sounds like a plan."

"How about the other cops in town? Can you trust them?"

"After all you've told me, I'm not sure anymore. I knew Graves and Birdie weren't clean, but what you've told me... that's hardcore criminal action. I can vouch for Betsy—I've known her all my life. Johnson is the detective. He's been here for a couple of years. I think he's a straightshooter. I don't know Owens well enough."

"Don't confide in anyone you're not certain about. These are no petty criminals. We're dealing with killers."

"That's why you need to be careful. You've ruffled a lot of feathers. Your lone cowboy act could be dangerous."

"I'm running against a clock, can't slow down. I'm deliberately sticking a finger to the Dawsons every chance I get. They've got a deputy of ours. He disappeared two days ago. That's why I'm here. The more time passes, lesser the chance of my finding him."

I told Nash about Carter and the reason I was in town. He had no idea about Carter. Quint had mentioned that Carter did talk to a cop. That might have been Graves. Nash promised to keep his eyes open for any clues back at the station.

I next told him about Brick—how he managed to stay alive while the other bikers were murdered in cold blood. Nash was a meticulous cop. He urged me to bring Brick down to the station for an official statement. Eventually, it would be the state police investigating the charges against the town's chief. And given the cartel angle, the Feds would get involved as well. But now that Nash had committed to bring Graves and the Dawsons down, he wanted the case to be airtight. Brick's testimony would be a crucial part of it. So would mine, and the photos I had taken.

I didn't want to stick around the motel with Nash, in case someone came by. We agreed to make contact later to set up a meeting.

We were about to get into our vehicles to move off when we saw another cop car coming from the direction of the town. The car pulled in next to

Nash's. The cop who got out was Elliot Birdie—Graves' crooked subordinate.

Hunter casually reached inside his car, picked the evidence bags, and pocketed them before turning towards Birdie, who was just getting out.

"What're you up to, Nash? Guarding the closed-down motel?" Birdie said in his slightly high-pitched voice. He was trying to sound pally, but Nash's face retained its usual emotionless expression.

"What happened to the motel, Birdie? How come it's suddenly closed for repairs?" Nash asked Birdie.

"Lord knows what Tucker's up to. He did mention some cracks in a wall," Birdie replied.

"Oh, you spoke to him?"

"Yes, saw him this morning. Said he was going out of town to buy some stuff for repair work," Birdie lied through his teeth. I had seen Tucker's body dumped in the back of the van last night.

"Right, that explains it," Nash said, sounding convinced. Then, turning to me, he said, "It seems the motel's going to be closed for a while. The only other place in town is the Dawson Hotel. A bit expensive, if you can afford that."

"Right, thanks, Officer. I'll take a look. Or maybe, not stay in town at all."

"Visiting anyone particular?" Birdie asked me, trying to sound casual. I wasn't sure if Graves had told him about my pickup parked next to the motel last night, and our conversation this morning. I thought not, because otherwise, Birdie would have been watchful as hell.

"Nope. Just been on the road all night. Thought I'd take a rest, get some sleep."

Before he could ask another question, I got in my pickup. There was a message from Chico on my phone. He wanted to talk about something important.

In the meantime, Nash had got in his car and was pulling out. Birdie seemed unsure. He was standing by his car, unable to make up his mind. I could see he didn't want to leave me hanging around the motel.

"You need directions to the hotel?" he asked me, walking over.

"Sure," I replied, playing him on.

"Just take this road straight into town. You can't miss it. It's the only three-story building in town."

"Thanks," I said and turned on the ignition.

Birdie looked relieved and walked back to his car. I pulled out and headed straight towards town. I didn't want Birdie to see me stopping at Chico's until I was sure what was happening there. I pulled over to the side of the road, just past the auto repair shop, and called Chico. Birdie gave me a nod as he passed me by on his way to town.

Chico began talking the second he picked the phone.

"Hey, Marshal, I've been doing my private eye shit all morning. And man, I've got some crazy intelligence for you. These cartel dudes are planning a lot of gangster shit with the Dawsons. And they've got a thing for you, Marshal. You've got to watch out, bro. But I can't talk right now. Those cartel dudes are still out there talking. I'm listening to every word they're saying. I'll call as soon as they split. You hang in there, bro."

He ended the call. I hadn't managed to put in a single word.

I decided to head back to the motel to check out Brick. But before that, I needed to have a word with Aldon. I got out of the pickup and walked over.

Aldon was about to take a lunch break.

"Can I offer you a bite?" he asked.

"No, thanks. I won't keep you long. Just need one detail. Would you know the license number and make of Peter Rixon's car?"

"Why don't you see for yourself. It's in the repair shop. Rixon dropped it this morning. Said he's going out of town tomorrow. Asked me to give it a complete check. He'll be over in a couple of hours to pick it."

Aldon led me inside. It was an E-class Merc.

"What's it about?" Aldon asked me. "Is he mixed up with them Dawsons?"

"I think so. That's why I need to run a check."

"God almighty. He looks like such a decent man."

"You never can tell. I'll grab a pen and paper from my pickup. You mind if I note a few things."

"No, go ahead. Need anything from me?"

"No, thanks, that's it for now. Why don't you carry on, have your lunch? I'll make a note and be on my way."

"If you say so. Give me a holler if you need anything."

"Sure thing."

I went to my pickup and grabbed a tracker. Installed it in the car's tire well. Time was short. I had decided to grab Rixon that evening. The tracker would help me pick a good spot.

Then I headed to the motel to pick up Brick.

CHAPTER 15

I pulled into the motel's parking lot and called Brick. The man who walked out of one of the rooms barely had any resemblance to the one I had left behind a couple of hours ago.

Brick had been transformed. Had I not been expecting a man of his size to come out of the rooms, I wouldn't have recognized him. The long hair and beard were gone—the man in front of me was cleanshaven. He had also managed to give himself a good enough haircut. His biker's all-black leather attire was gone as well. He wore a loose T-shirt over somewhat baggy jeans. He looked more like a heavyset middle-aged tourist than a biker.

When he came closer, I noticed a lumpy bruise peeping out from under his hair on one side of his head—the one I had given him when I banged his head against the door jamb.

"That was you, man," he said, when he saw me looking at it.

"Oh man, that looks painful."

"Not as bad as it was last night. I'll survive."

"No hard feelings?" I said, holding out my hand.

"Water under the bridge," he said, grabbing it.

"Get in, let's get moving."

"Tell me, what do you want me to do next? I'm ready and raring to have a go at the bastards," he said, the moment he got in.

"You sure look ready. I don't think anyone will recognize you. That'll work in our favor. I'm fast becoming a marked man in town. You'll be our hidden ace in the hole."

"Sure thing," he said.

I handed him a baseball cap. His touristy getup looked complete once he put it on. Chico's message had already landed in my phone by that time—the Mexicans had gone.

"Time for some grub. We're heading to the diner. You must be hungry."

"You have no idea."

"I'll drop you a little way before the diner. Let's not be seen together for a while. Everyone knows by now that I'm up to something. But you're just a tourist. You can move around in a way I can't."

"Whatever you say, man. So long as we're taking the Dawsons down..."

"We will. That's a promise. Just tell me you won't fly off the handle if you see the Dawsons or any Mexicans in town. Keep your cool until it's time."

"You got it, man. No worries."

"Good."

I dropped Brick a short distance from the diner. Asked him to walk inside, have lunch, and then stick around the main street. Give me a heads up if he saw anything unusual.

I parked the pickup in the same place I did earlier, slightly hidden behind the crumbling boundary wall of the lot next to the diner. Then I went to the back exit of the diner. Chico was there to meet me, a plate with a burger in one hand. I was famished. That burger was exactly what I needed. I grabbed the plate and took a bite as he led me to his back office.

"Whoa, Marshal, you've created a real stir in town. The kind of gangster shit that's going on here, it reminds me of times back in Chicago. Remember the two Mexican dudes from the morning? They were back again for lunch. I don't know why the Dawsons don't feed them elsewhere."

"Your culinary skills, Chico. Man, this burger is good."

"I know, bro. I've got some serious skills, haven't I?" he said, without a hint of modesty. "But still, you know..."

"I guess they think you're their homie."

"No way, bro. I've been hiding back here all the time they were around. It got Anna May real mad, she's had to do all the cooking and waitressing. But man, it was good I hung out here, cause I caught every word they said. I've gathered some crazy intelligence, bro."

"Good. So what's up?"

"The cartel's going loco, dude. They've lost most of their men in town. We know why, bro, but they don't have a clue. They think it's some gang shit going on in town. Out-of-state gangs taking aim at the Dawsons, and their guys getting caught in the crossfire. But they also don't trust the Dawsons. They're not sure if it isn't the Dawsons trying to get them out of town. Right now, there are just five cartel dudes in town. Those two that you know. And you know how they're like, scary guys, sicarios and all. But the other three, they sound like they're full on psycho, bro."

"Who are they?"

"The cartel's top lieutenant, Hector Alvarez. A cold-blooded killer. He and his two bodyguards.

They're bad news, Marshal. They aren't really sure about you… if you're just a tourist or involved in all the gang shit. I think they're going to confront you sooner or later. There are more of them coming in tonight. They're going to take over the town. You really need to watch your back, bro."

"I know. I got some intel on them. They're all ex-Mexican army."

"No shit. Ex-army? Marshal, I know you can be a real badass, but, dude, are you sure you can take them all alone? I'm worried about you, bro.

"I'll be careful."

"Maybe it's time for some backup?"

"The boys from my old SOG team are in Vegas. Waiting for my signal. They'll be here in full force within a couple of hours any time I give them the signal."

"That's good to hear, bro. Although two hours can be a long time when bullets start flying. What's SOG, Marshal?"

"The Marshals' Special Operations Group. Those boys can be deadly."

"And they're your boys?"

"Kind of. I headed them until I left six months ago."

"So that's how you've got your badass skills."

"I guess. But you need to stay clear of those guys. Don't go overboard with your snooping. This Hector is a smart guy. And dangerous. Won't think twice before killing anyone. The Dawsons are small fry in comparison."

"You said it, Marshal, I'm going to be a mile away from them. Not a chance in hell me playing hero."

"Good plan. Did you get anything else?"

"Hmm... let me think... yeah, right, the Dawsons took this Hector dude around to their factory and casino site today. I think they were trying to impress him, cause he's really not a happy man, bro, losing his men and all. They're going to be moving all their crystal shit to some place in Arizona..."

"Las Hermosas?"

"Yeah, right. How do you know that? I've never heard of the place."

"Mitch told me. It's a small place near Tucson."

"Yeah, right, so that's what's going on, bro. They'll be shifting the lab and all the meth stored here to that place."

"Did they mention where it was stored?"

"No, but it's going to happen tonight. And, there was one more thing... lemme think, lemme think... yeah, right, there's some Senator coming to town tomorrow. He'll be opening the new bar, and visiting the casino site.

"That makes sense. That's why the Dawsons have been trying to clear up all their shit. Their future depends on the casino. They can't let anything mess it up. That's why they hid all the bodies, sealed the motel. Well, that makes it easier to mess with them."

"All that shit's happened to them ever since you came to town."

"That's the idea. Keep them running until they stumble. That's all I need to get to Carter."

"Fingers crossed, bro."

"That was some fine detective work, Chico. You'd make a fine Deputy."

"Don't mess with me, bro. You'll break my heart. You know I'll do anything to leave all my gangster shit behind, do some good stuff. This diner is good, man, and I've got Anna May looking after me. But really bro, Little Butte's hardly a rocking place..."

"Let's find Carter first. Once the dust settles, who knows what'll be left at the end of it."

"That's true, bro. We've got to find Carter. I'm with you, Marshal. Tell me what to do."

"You're doing well. Carry on. Let me know the moment you hear anything. And one more thing... I've got some backup," I said, pointing to Brick, who was visible in one of the monitors.

"Who's that? I don't think I've seen him around before. One of your Deputies?"

"Go on in, take a look. There's no one there you're hiding from right now, is there?"

"No, bro. I'm the king of this place right now. I'll go check out your deputy."

I watched the monitors as Chico went into the diner. He peered from the kitchen area, then walked to the counter, then towards the entrance, and finally walked the length of the diner. When he came back in, he looked confused.

"Who's that, Marshal? I looked at him from all angles. And then it struck me. I was like, damn, that must be one of the biker dudes. Is he the biker?"

"Yes."

"For real? That's one hell of a disguise, bro."

"I could barely recognize him myself. He's on our team now. Itching to make the Dawsons pay for what they did to the other bikers."

"No shit, bro. The way they set those sicarios on them, they should rot in hell."

192

"They're not getting away. Carry on Chico. I'll be in touch later."

I got out the back exit.

If the Dawsons were planning to move their meth stash and lab tonight, I didn't have much time to locate it. Mitch had told me the lab was in the casino site. The stash had to be there as well.

The site was heavily guarded, almost impossible to access, with its impenetrable perimeter wall, monitored 24/7 through security cameras. No way to enter from the front apart from ramming your way in. But I had a different route planed. From the butte. I would climb the butte, fix a rope at the top and rappel down, leaving it ready for the next climb in the dark.

CHAPTER 16

I drove south on the main street, past the police station, Dawson factory, water tower and the Dawson residences, before turning right, on to the road running towards the butte. I was approaching it from a direction opposite the one I had taken earlier. I reached the back of the butte, well hidden from anyone monitoring the perimeter of the casino site. I parked the pickup slightly away from the road.

I went over all the steps in my mind. I would free climb to the top, carrying a rope. Fix the rope at the top. Do a quick recon of the site. Rappel down. Get away from the place within an hour.

I took off my cowboy boots, got into climbing shoes, stepped into a climbing harness, and slung my backpack and two lengths of 60-meter rope across my body. I was ready.

I already had a clear idea about the starting point. The thing about climbing, or any other complex problem for that matter, is to break it down into specific tasks. Focus on the individual tasks, forget about the whole. While going up, focus on not more than the next few moves, forget about how far the peak happens to be. It's the same while coming down—don't fixate on the bottom, or how many bones you'll end up breaking if you were to fall.

There's a striking similarity between climbing and combat—it's good to have muscle, but that alone doesn't quite cut it. You need to know how to use the muscle the right way. Powering your way up a steep rock face doesn't usually work. You need finesse.

I made fast progress up the steep face, zigzagging my way up the almost vertical wall, taking minimal breaks for a breather. I was kind of soaked in sweat by the time I reached the top 45 minutes later. The town lay spread out before me as I stood on top of the butte and scanned the horizon. The spanking new part of town gleamed. The mirrored façade of the hotel reflected the sunlight. The old part of town appeared even more decaying and crumbly in comparison.

But there wasn't time to sit back and enjoy the view. I took the two 60-meter ropes off my shoulders and tied them together using a double fisherman's knot, turning them into a single rope 120 meters long. I walked over to the far edge of the butte, found a solid piece of rock jutting out, and secured the rope around it. I would throw it down when it was time to descend. The rope would be hidden by the natural curvature of the butte, so it couldn't be seen by any vehicle passing on the road below.

Descending the butte would be a breeze, now that the rope was in place. But before descending, I wanted to get a good look at the layout of the casino site. The top of the butte was rectangular in shape, around 50 yards wide by 35 yards, and fairly flat. I walked across the rocky top to the other end, took out the binoculars from my backpack, lay down near the edge, and looked down. I had a clear view of the site, which was spread out directly below me.

I saw some workers moving around in hard hats and fluorescent jackets. The dominating structure within the site was a large square-shaped hall in the center. The ground around the hall looked freshly excavated. An excavator was busy digging a new cavity.

A couple of big trucks were parked along one side of the perimeter. There wasn't any activity around the trucks. I guessed they would be loaded in the evening, once the construction staff left the site.

There was no sign of any van. The tracker I had put on one of the vans showed that it was still parked on the site. It must be the van packed with the bodies of the bikers and the sicarios. It could be either inside the hall, not visible from my position, or inside one of the trucks. I would only get to know for sure once I descended into the site in the evening.

There was a long rectangular building in one corner of the site, almost directly below me. An armed guard was sitting outside what I guessed was its entrance. The main gate of the construction site consisted of two sliding doors, which were controlled by two guards sitting inside a cabin beside it.

As I watched, a man walked out of the rectangular building and moved towards the gate. He went inside the guard's cabin. At the same time, I saw a pickup speeding towards the site, coming from town. There were two men inside it. The pickup stopped beside the gate. The driver talked to the guard for a couple of minutes. I expected him to either enter the site or turn around and head back to town. But what he did next caught me by surprise. The pickup began moving around the periphery of the site towards the back of the butte. Straight towards where my truck was parked.

I cursed inwardly. I didn't think anyone used that back road.

There was no way the two men would miss my pickup. They would surely stop and investigate. Finding no one there, they were sure to alert others. I was in a fix. I couldn't risk rappelling down while a couple of armed guys were wandering around. I would be a sitting duck if they saw me. I didn't think anyone would imagine the driver of the pickup would have gone up the butte. So, the only option was to keep waiting at the top of the butte until it got dark. That would mean a wait of at least three hours.

I didn't want to peer down, in case someone looking up caught sight of me. I was still weighing my options when my phone buzzed. It was Adriel. He had planned to drive out from the ranch early that morning.

"Adriel? Have you arrived?"

"Yes, kid. Told you I'd be here in the afternoon."

"Great timing. You won't believe where I'm stuck right now."

"Tell me about it when you come down. Or do you plan to stay up and enjoy the view?"

"What? Where are you?"

"Come down, kid. I'm parked next to your pickup. It's all under control."

I peered over the edge. I saw two more pickups apart from mine. The one that had just arrived, and Adriel's blue Ford Ranger. Adriel was sitting on the hood. All I could see from the top was his black cowboy hat. Two men were lying beside the pickup. Looked like they were knocked out cold.

I picked the rope I had already anchored to a rock and threw it down. Pushing a loop of rope through my rappel device, I locked it with my carabiner, and was good to go. It took me less than a minute to touch ground. Detaching myself from the rope, I walked around a bend in the butte to where Adriel was waiting.

He looked relaxed, as if enjoying the view on a nice day out. His long, grey-streaked hair flowed out from under his cowboy hat. His boots were identical to mine. Both pairs made by his guy up in Montrose.

There was a hint of a smile on Adriel's face as he watched me walk over. More in his eyes than his face. He wasn't a man given to broad smiles. Or to laughing. The kind of guy who's a stand-up comedian's nightmare.

"You should have come up, Adriel. Nice view from up there."

"Too busy watching your back, kid. And too old for these vertical free climbs," Adriel replied.

"You sure got my back today. I was stuck. But how did you know I was up there?"

"An empty pickup standing in the middle of nowhere. Your cowboy boots lying inside. You could either be hiking around barefoot or, more likely, scaling yet another vertical face."

"Good thinking."

"You too, turning on the location finder on your phone."

"What happened to them?" I asked, looking at the two men lying unconscious.

They were Hank and Percy—Baxter's bodyguards. I had already put the third one, Spencer, out of action. That took care of all three bodyguards.

"Angry kids. Rude. I hope they reflect upon their life's choices when they wake up," Adriel replied.

It wouldn't have taken Adriel much effort to put down the beefed-up bodyguards. I noticed both of them had their right arms turned at a crooked angle.

"Broken arms. They tried drawing on you, Adriel?"

"Yes, kid," he replied, letting out a sigh. "I didn't really want to hurt them. But what can an old man do when young punks draw on him? Too much rage in these boys. I don't understand why."

"Maybe rage, maybe fear... too scared of the bad people they work for."

"You may have a point there. They must have decided to follow me here when I came through town. There were some guys, including a couple of cartel types, tattooed necks and faces, watching me as I drove through town."

"That's my fault. They must be getting wary of strangers driving into town."

"One of them already had a broken nose. Was that you?"

"Yup."

"Hmm... What's the plan now?"

"I've set up a rope up there. We'll have to come back in darkness. But before that, we have to grab a guy. He's a chemist. And head cook for the meth operation."

"OK. After that?"

"In the evening, I'll descend into the site. You stay up top, keep an eye out, in case things get out of hand. I'm guessing you've got a long-range rifle in the pickup?"

"Yes. A long-range Ruger. You told me to come armed."

"That'll come in handy. Things are going to heat up tonight."

"Yeah, I'm getting that feeling. What do we do with them?" he asked, looking at the men on the ground.

"I know exactly where to take them. There's this motel. We'll dump them there. Give me a minute."

I called Brick, asked him to meet me near Chico's.

"I'll dump their pickup behind that curve around the butte. It won't be visible from the road."

I got in the pickup and drove it off the road, over rough ground, and left it in a place around a bend. It was no longer visible from the road.

Adriel helped me to pick up the two men and dump them into the back of my pickup. I cuffed their hands, tied their feet, and tied bandanas over their mouths, just in case they woke up before we reached the motel. Then pulled the tonneau cover over them.

"The motel is at the north end of town. You must have passed by it. Let's meet there."

He nodded. Both of us got into our pickups.

Brick was waiting near the diner. He jumped in and we drove to the motel. Brick forced open one of the rooms. We dumped the two bodyguards onto the bed.

One of them was beginning to come around. Brick put him out again. I got a rope from the pickup, tied it to one man's feet, threw it under the bed to the other end, tied it to the second man's feet, and finally to the bed post. Neither of them would be going anywhere when they got up.

We were heading back to the pickup when I received a call from Daphne. She wanted to meet me. I told her I would come see her at the hotel.

I asked Adriel to take Brick to the coffee shop close to the hotel. Wait for me there. Then I drove on to the hotel.

CHAPTER 17

When I entered the hotel, Billy, the kid behind the reception counter, was talking to a couple of guys. The bar was empty. When Billy saw me walk in, he told the guys to hang on, and asked me to follow him inside the hotel to a conference room.

The room had a large, rectangular table in the center, with over a dozen chairs arranged around it. The wall at the far end was made up of ceiling length windows, overlooking a garden at the back of the hotel. Daphne was standing by the window, looking out.

She turned when we entered. There was a troubled expression on her face, which her unsure smile couldn't really hide. Billy closed the door as he left the room. I walked towards Daphne, leaned back slightly against the table, and crossed my hands.

"Miss me already?" I asked her.

She smiled. But it didn't last.

"It's about the room. I think it'll be best if you checked out. No charge," she said.

"What happened? Jasper convinced you otherwise? Or was it Baxter?"

"It's not that. It's not even about the hotel. You need to get away from town."

"We had this conversation earlier. Maybe it's time to lay our cards on the table."

"Alright. They know you were a Marshal. Ex-army. Special Forces. You're no random visitor to town."

"I see. Graves been busy?"

She nodded.

"You know why I'm here?"

"No," she replied. Didn't sound very convincing.

"I'm a civilian now. Ex-Marshal. Ex-army. Why can't I be a random visitor?"

"It's not about what I think. These men are killers. They don't need much of a reason to kill. I don't know how but you've given them quite a few."

"I know they're killers. They killed that kid in this room. Where was it, this corner? Or was it the other end?"

"What? What kid? What are you talking about?"

"Rollie, the kid who used to work with Mitch. That psycho, Hector Alvarez, shot him. Point blank. No reason, except proving how tough he was. That impressed you, Daphne?"

"No!" the look of shock on her face seemed genuine. "I have no idea what you're talking about. I swear. You've got to believe me."

"And I guess you have no idea about Charlie? No clue about why Clarise is going crazy running around town, trying to find out what happened."

This time her face revealed she knew something. It felt like she was on the verge of revealing some secrets. I decided to dial up the pressure a notch. Time to lay my cards on the table.

"And what about Carter, Daphne? No idea at all, right? Why was he here? What happened to him?"

She was silent for a while.

"So that's why you're here," she whispered, almost to herself.

Daphne turned her back to me, looking out the window, trying to make up her mind. Then turned again to face me.

"I'll answer all your questions, Axel," she said, moving to a chair and sitting down. "Have a seat."

"I'm fine. Carry on."

"Have a seat, Axel," she insisted. "Please."

I took a chair opposite her.

"I'll start with Rollie. I don't pretend to be an angel, but I had no idea about him until you just told me. I've seen him with Mitch, but I didn't really know him. I haven't even seen either of them for a few days. I can't imagine why anyone would want to kill a kid."

"I told you why."

"It still doesn't make sense. I also didn't know about Charlie until Carter came to town asking about him. That's when I saw Jasper getting scared. I asked Baxter. He didn't give me a straight answer. All I could make out was Jasper had something to do with Charlie's disappearance."

"And Carter? Is he alive?" I asked her. My voice was steady, but I had stopped breathing.

"I believe he is, but I'm not hundred percent sure," she replied.

"I'm not trying to play you," she added, when she saw the unconvinced expression on my face.

"Go on. I'm listening."

"Where should I start..." she said, almost to herself. Then took a deep breath and began speaking.

"I'm not part of the Dawson family. More like a distant cousin to Jasper and Grady. When they moved to Little Butte from Tennessee, Baxter asked me to help him set up the pharmaceutical business. I was working in a bank in Nashville. I owed Baxter, gave up my job and came here. Set up a professional pharma company. Then he also wanted a bank, so I got him permission for that. Then the casino project came up... I began realizing they were just setting up a front for their illegal activities. But by then I was stuck... But long story short, I closed my eyes to their meth business, choosing to ignore it. But everything changed after the gangster meet they organized last week."

"That's when that psycho shot Rollie."

"I had no idea. I stayed away from them. I didn't want anything to do with those gangsters. So I just left town, went to Nashville for a couple of days."

"Hmm... go on."

"It was only when Carter came to town that I realized Jasper was responsible for the disappearance of Charlie and that mechanic, Lou. He was also planning to kill Carter as he was getting too close to the truth. Jasper wouldn't have listened to me, but I convinced Baxter that killing a federal agent would take him to a place of no return. There would be Feds swarming the place. That would be the end of all his legal businesses as well. That made sense to him. Jasper had already kidnapped Carter by the time Baxter intervened. They have him somewhere. I don't know where. But Baxter told me they haven't killed him, and I believe that."

She went silent for a while. I was bursting with questions. But wanted to give her time to come up with everything on her own. I didn't want to put her on the defensive.

"Do you believe me?" she asked me, her eyes looking directly into mine.

I held her stare.

"Yes. You've given me no reason not to."

She got up and stood by the window, looking out for a few seconds.

"Can I ask you some questions?" I asked her.

"Go on," she replied, walking back, and sitting down facing me again.

"Do you know how they kidnapped Carter?"

"I'm not exactly sure, but Graves and Birdie were involved."

"But that means they're banking on his being killed. If Carter gets away, it's the end of the road for them."

"They have it all planned. Jasper wasn't involved in the kidnapping. So, he can't be implicated. Graves and Birdie will be getting a big pay out and skip town. In fact, skip the country. Go to Mexico, or wherever fugitives with money go."

"But if Carter gets away, it's the end of the road for the Dawsons."

"Their plan is to get all the illegal business out of town. Make the entire operation in town completely legit. It will just be the businesses and the casino. There won't be anything left after tomorrow to implicate Jasper or Baxter. A Senator is coming for a visit. It's the last formality before they get a casino license. They'll release Carter after that."

"Or they might not. They might decide it's easier to kill him."

"I think I convinced Baxter the business will not survive close scrutiny if the Feds came to town. I can only hope he sticks to his decision."

"And what about you, Daphne? Are you happy running those businesses in town?"

"I have no illusions about the business. They're going to go down eventually. Everything has been built on drug money. They think they're smart and have cooked the books... But not smart enough."

"What do you want to do?"

"What I want to do? Get away from here. I never liked this place. I owed Baxter. I think I've done more than enough... But there's a big difference between what you want, and what you get."

"What does Baxter have on you?"

"He doesn't have anything on me. Helped me at a bad time. He was a distant cousin of my mom. She wasn't what you'd call a great mother. We'd have a new guy living with us every few months. Most of them wanting to get their paws on me as well. I never even knew Baxter until he turned up one day, just by chance, saw what was going on, beat the shit out of mom's boyfriend, helped me get out, make my way through business school. I owed him."

"What about Jasper and Grady?"

"They don't like me. And the feeling is mutual. A woman running their businesses, at least the legal ones, makes them feel dumb. But they can't do much—too scared of Baxter. We just about tolerate each other. I never let them into my place and well, neither do I care to visit theirs."

"Get out of all this, Daphne. They're going to go down... you don't need to sink with them."

"Who knows where this'll lead to. But you need to watch your back. The Mexicans are after you. There are more of them coming in tonight. You can't handle all of them alone. Leave town, Axel.

Come back later if you have to. But leave before the night."

"Thanks for the heads up. I know you've taken a risk talking to me. You trust the kid out there won't squeal you out?"

"Billy? No, he won't. He's a good boy. He wouldn't rat me out, not to Jasper. And he's too scared of Baxter to even look him in the eye."

"But they could still find out. You could be in trouble."

"I'll be fine. You take care of yourself. Seriously, leave town."

"I can't. Not without Carter. But don't worry about that. What's important is you delete my check in details from the reception computer right now. No point the Mexicans getting to know you gave me a room. I wasn't planning on staying in the room anyway."

"OK. I'll do that."

"I better leave now, I don't want you getting any heat cause of me. Just one last thing, do you have even a vague idea about where Carter could be?"

"They could've hidden him anywhere, Axel. I honestly don't know. Believe me, I'd have told you. I'll let you know if I get a hint."

"OK, you take care," I said, taking her hand. "Stay alert and don't get involved any further. When all this is over... I'd like to buy you a drink."

"I'd love that, Axel, but..."

"No buts. I'll be seeing you, Daphne. Take care," I said, gave her a peck on the cheek, and got up.

"Take care, Axel," she replied, stood up, and walked me towards the door. She was reaching for the door handle to open it when she stopped, turned and looked at me. She was beautiful. Her perfume took hold of my senses as she gave me a hug. I didn't realize when our lips met. We had to separate when someone knocked on the door.

It was Billy. He had come to tell us the Mexicans were outside, about to come inside the hotel.

It was no time to be lax. I couldn't let the Mexicans suspect I was friendly with anyone within the hotel.

"Delete all my details from your computer immediately. I came in enquiring about room vacancy, but you sent me packing. Got it?"

"Yes," Daphne replied.

We walked to the reception. She went behind the counter. I didn't stop. Walked out of the hotel.

CHAPTER 18

A black Hummer was parked next to the hotel entrance. Two Hispanic guys were standing on the sidewalk beside it. Mean-looking characters, used to wearing surly expressions all the time.

Apart from the expressions, there wasn't much similarity between the two. One guy was tall, well-built. Looked tough, not in an overly beefed-up gym buff kind of way. Thick veins crisscrossed his forearms as he stood with arms folded. No tattoos on the face, but lots of ink on the neck. I noticed a coiled rattlesnake among the tattoos.

The second guy was medium-height and wiry. Not much ink on his neck, except for the rattler tattoo. But his forearms had a lot of ink. Not the usual animal figures or exotic letters most people carry. This man was a killer. His arms were scorecards of his kills. Straight lines running along both forearms, with notches at regular intervals. He wanted the world to take note of his killer status, maybe overcompensating for his somewhat insignificant stature.

Each man had an MP5 slung around his body on a strap. The Heckler & Koch 9x19mm parabellum submachine guns weren't the civilian version—the ones with only a semi-automatic option. They were army issue versions, with a dual automatic/semi-automatic option. In automatic mode, they fire 800 rounds per minute. Empty the 30-round magazine in just over two seconds. Illegal for civilians to carry.

The two men were not making even a minimal attempt to conceal the guns. The MP5s were meant to be seen. The cartel was getting brazen about flexing its muscles.

There was a third guy sitting inside the Hummer. Talking into a phone held in his right hand. His left hand was rubbing his ear, or what was left of it. The man had only half of his left ear, the top half was missing. Lucky escape from a bullet, Mitch had told me. I didn't need to be told who it was. This was the cartel's top lieutenant. Hector Alvarez. The two men outside the Hummer were his bodyguards. Chico had warned me about the three.

Hector looked in my direction. Our eyes locked briefly. I saw a hint of recognition in them. He might have seen a photo of me—I was pretty sure Graves must have compiled some kind of dossier on me. I stepped onto the sidewalk and began walking toward the coffee house, which was not more than 30 yards from the hotel entrance.

I had covered half the distance when I heard a voice say loudly, "Hey, you". I thought it might be one of the Mexicans. Possibly hailing me. I decided to ignore it. Continued walking without breaking stride. The coffee shop was less than ten paces away. I could see Adriel sitting by the window, craning his neck to look at me.

"Hey... Blaze," the voice hailed me again.

This time I stopped and turned around. It was Hector. He had gotten out of the Hummer and was standing beside it. He beckoned me to come over to where he was standing. An air of authority in the gesture, expecting immediate compliance.

I didn't move. Beckoned him over with the same gesture, with the same arrogant air of dominance. That was something he didn't expect. His expression changed. So did that of the two bodyguards—they looked surlier.

The big one began moving towards me. He came up to me and was reaching out to grab my elbow when I flicked his arm away, shaking my head in an exaggerated motion.

"You don't want to be doing that, amigo," I warned him.

I looked at Hector, turned, and began walking away. I knew Adriel would have my back if guns were drawn; if it really came to a showdown. I decided to act even more brashly. I knew I had insulted the man by flicking his arm—he wouldn't just let me walk away.

The man grabbed my wrist from behind to pull me back. Bad move. Taking down criminals trying to grab you from behind is routine stuff for Marshals. You don't have to think about it. It becomes part of your muscle memory. Practiced over and over until it becomes embedded in your subconscious. Until you develop a reflex of just putting them down on the ground, ready to be cuffed.

My body was on autopilot. I turned and put my hand on top of the hand with which he had grabbed my wrist. That locked his hand, making it immobile. I rotated my wrist that he was holding, so that my hand was now on his forearm, clutching it tightly. I moved back a step so that the forearm of my other arm ran parallel with his, my elbow directly behind his. I pushed his elbow forward, overextending it. The only way for him to prevent his elbow from getting broken was to lean forward and down.

The entire sequence had taken less than two seconds. A further push from me on his elbow would have him face down on the ground.

Holding him in the bent over position, I looked at Hector.

"Better ask him to behave," I said. "He won't look good lying face down on the ground."

A flash of anger appeared on Hector's face, but he checked it. He was a cold-blooded killer, knew how to keep his emotions in check. If he got the chance, he would kill me with the same expressionless look on his face.

The other bodyguard had grabbed his gun and had begun lining it on me, hoping to add another notch on his forearm. Hector reached out and pushed the gun down towards the ground. He was not the kind to have any qualms about shooting an unarmed man, but he couldn't do it in the middle of town.

Hector nodded, indicating compliance. I let go of his bodyguard. The man's eyes were filled with hate at the humiliation I had just put him through. He took a step back and reached for his gun, not even bothering to look at Hector for approval. The only thing that mattered to him at that moment was putting a bullet in me. But his reactions were slow—his elbow was still too stiff. I knew he wouldn't stop until I put him down, either physically or with a bullet. Drawing a gun would draw a similar reaction from Hector and the other bodyguard. It wouldn't go down well for me. I decided to knock him out.

I was beginning to step forward when I saw the man freeze. A huge gun was pointed at his head, from behind my left shoulder. A Desert Eagle—that cannon of a handgun, filled with seven .50 AE hollow point bullets. Each of those with enough power to kill four of him standing back-to-back, and then carry on and get embedded in a wall across the street. No wonder the man froze.

It wasn't just the gun that was deadly. The man holding it was equally lethal. Adriel. "Don't mess with me" almost written in large letters across his face. He had quietly stepped out of the coffee shop when everyone else was busy.

Adriel didn't say a word. He didn't need to. The gun was doing the talking, loud and clear.

"Luca," Hector snapped at the bodyguard.

The man let go of the gun and backed off a couple of steps. Hector walked over. Stopped a couple of paces away from me. Didn't attempt to extend a hand—either to grab me or to shake. He turned out to be smart that way. Going by my actions with the bodyguard, both moves could end in embarrassment for him. Grabbing me wasn't likely to end well. Extending a hand and getting rebuffed in the middle of the high street would also be humiliating for the cartel boss. I had no illusions about his ability to kill. But I didn't think he was prepared for that yet. There was too much at stake for the cartel until the meth transfer was completed that evening.

"You know who I am?" he asked me.

"Nope. But looks like you know me."

"My name is Hector Alvarez. You've heard of me?"

"Nope."

"Hmm…" he almost sounded disappointed, before continuing, "I've been hearing things about you."

"Good for you."

"Can we sit somewhere and talk? The hotel maybe?"

"There's the coffee shop next door. We can sit there. But you'll have to ask those two to dump the MP5s, or wait for you in the Hummer."

"OK," he agreed.

He spoke to the other two in Spanish. The two bodyguards walked over to the Hummer, put their MP5s inside it, locked it and walked back.

"Hotel would be comfortable. You've taken a room there?" Hector said.

"No. I planned to, but didn't like it. Let's go to the coffee shop," I replied.

"OK," he said, shrugging.

Hector nodded to his guys and began walking towards the coffee shop. I followed him. His guys were behind me. I would normally have been super wary in such a situation. I knew I was on top of their target list, both were so pissed off with me they would put a bullet in me at the first chance.

But Adriel was walking behind the two guys. He had my back.

When I entered the coffee shop, I saw Brick sitting at a table by the window, on the same seat Adriel was occupying when he was watching me from inside the shop. He kept looking outside, completely uninterested in me or the Mexicans. He had street smarts. I knew he was packing at least one Glock, the one I had seen before, and maybe more. He would jump into the fray at the slightest provocation. He had a personal score to settle.

Hector stopped by a table in the center of the coffee shop and looked at me. When I nodded in the affirmative, he took a seat. He was smart—he quickly understood he couldn't mess with me the way he was used to with most guys.

Hector's bodyguards sat at a table behind him. Adriel took a seat at the counter. A couple sitting at a corner table decided they didn't feel comfortable sticking around. They walked out. Smart move.

"I was curious. What's an ex-Marshal, ex-army man doing in Little Butte?" Hector asked me.

"Who told you I'm all those things?"

"A reliable source."

"Right. You're pally with the police chief?"

"You could say that."

"How come you're so interested in me?"

"I'm curious why you're snooping around in Little Butte?"

"What makes you think I'm snooping around?"

"Strange things have been happening ever since you came to town. I'm trying to understand why?"

"What things? You're getting me curious."

"Well, strange things."

"What, some UFOs landed in town?"

"Funny man," he gave a sarcastic laugh, looking back at his men. "No UFOs. Other strange things. Like people dying."

"Really? Who? It's a small town. I'm sure I'd have heard about it."

"I mean people have been going missing."

"Really? Interesting."

He was beginning to look frustrated. The conversation wasn't going anywhere. He wasn't used to people not taking him seriously.

"Were you in town last night?" Hector asked.

"Why's everyone so interested in where I was last night? Jasper asked me the same question this morning."

"Were you?"

"No."

"One of my men says he saw you in town."

"I think your man is on drugs. They make you see things."

He was silent for a while, looking at me intently, trying to gauge me. He must have been under pressure—he lost six men the previous night. It wouldn't look good for a cartel lieutenant if he couldn't get the killer. At this point, he wasn't even sure where to begin looking.

"If there's anything particular you're looking for, I can maybe help you," he said.

"That's very nice of you. What kind of help are you talking about?"

"I'm a businessman. I make things happen. What's the word for it... um... it's *facilitador* in Spanish... ah, yes, a facilitator."

"What can you facilitate?"

"You tell me what you need. I'll try to make that happen."

I decided to test him.

"Have you heard of the Nevada Devils?" I asked him.

Brick was still pretending to be casually looking out, but I noticed a subtle change in his body language.

"No."

"It's a motorcycle club. You know I'm an ex-Marshal. What you don't know is I joined the club after leaving the Marshals. Six of my club brothers went missing yesterday. Without a trace. Strange that you mentioned people going missing. Did you mean the bikers when you said that?"

"No."

"Well, if you can do your facilitation and tell me where my brothers are, my business in town will be done. I'm here to find them."

Hector's face remained expressionless. But I could see I had put him in a fix. It was clear he wanted me out of town. But he also wanted the day to go incident-free, so the meth transfer to Arizona could go on unhindered. The door opened at that moment. Three men walked in. Baxter, Jasper and Grady.

"Howdy," Baxter said, looking at me.

"Howdy," I replied.

"I hope I'm not interrupting," he said, looking at me and Hector.

"I guess not. Hector here was meaning to get better acquainted with me. I think we're close to understanding each other," I replied.

"That's timely. I too meant to get better acquainted with the mysterious strangers in town," he replied, looking at me and Adriel.

"Join the party," I said.

Baxter looked at Hector, nodded and took a chair at the table. Jasper and Grady sat at a table behind him. I could see Jasper was dying to take a dig at me.

I looked towards Brick. His face wasn't as expressionless as it was before the Dawsons entered the café. He looked at me, gave me a slight nod, and looked out the window again. I could rest easy—Brick wasn't about to pounce on them.

"You better run out of town quick, if you want to get out in one piece," Jasper suddenly blurted out, unable to contain himself.

Baxter turned to Jasper, giving him an admonishing look.

"Well, if it ain't the friendly gentleman from this morning," I replied to Jasper.

"If Pops weren't here, I'd..." he left the sentence unfinished.

"You'd what? Go on...," I challenged him.

Baxter raised his hand to shut up Jasper.

"We're meaning to have a civilized conversation, Jasper," he said. Then, turning to me, "What brings you to town? Blaze, isn't it?"

"I'm sure you know much more than just my name. I've heard Graves has been digging up my past."

Baxter exchanged a glance with Hector before replying, "You're right. Graves did mention you used to be a Marshal. Ex-army before that, Special Forces. As town council president, I get to know things. It's Graves' duty to inform me about things like that."

"I'm sure he's really good at taking orders from you."

"What we couldn't figure out was, what brings you to town," Baxter replied, ignoring my remark.

"I was just having the same conversation with Hector here. And he turned out to be a helpful soul, offered to be a facilitator for things I was looking for."

"And what might that be?" Baxter asked.

"Nevada Devils."

"I don't follow."

"My friends from the biker club. They work with Jasper, I've heard. They disappeared last night. I'm here to find them."

"Mitch sent you here, didn't he?" Jasper interjected.

"Hush, it's bad manners to interrupt when two adults are having a conversation," I scolded him.

Jasper and Grady stood up simultaneously, bristling. Baxter was losing his cool as well, with me to some extent, but more with those two for being openly insubordinate.

"Sit," he hissed at them.

"You say they went missing last night. How do you know they didn't just take off somewhere? Isn't that what bikers do?" Baxter asked me.

"No, not when there was a plan for us to meet and ride together. They've gone missing. Hector agrees. Don't you, Hector, that people have been going missing since last night."

All three Dawsons looked at him, a bit incredulously.

"I meant other people, not the bikers."

"What other people?" I asked him.

"I think you better talk to Graves," Baxter intervened.

"I was meaning to, until you and Hector asked me to share my problems with you."

"Yes, of course. So, that's why you're here. And once you find out where they are, you're planning to leave?"

"Yes."

"And what about chief over there, he'll be splitting town with you?" Jasper butted in, his tone mocking, looking towards Adriel as he spoke.

"Try calling him chief one more time... you'll be out on the sidewalk, and not through the door," I said, turning in my chair to face him, my tone laced with menace.

Adriel's face remained expressionless. Jasper misunderstood his silence. He stood up slowly, with Grady following him.

"Will that be you or him who'll try it?" he said, his hand at his side, ready to draw what I knew was a gun tucked in the back of his jeans.

"We might draw straws. Why don't you try finding out?" I challenged him.

Jasper looked at me, then at Adriel, then at the Mexicans, trying to gather the nerve to take a stand.

"I know what's going on in that tiny brain of yours," I said. "You're thinking, we're six guys, they're only two. Maybe I could take a shot... But are things as simple as that, Jasper boy? Can that pea brain get all the variables involved? Do you have any idea of the hand cannon my friend is carrying? That would take out more than one with a single bullet. Are you sure Hector and his guys will have your back? And are there just two of us? What about him, the kid behind the counter? Could he be on our side? Could he have a shotgun under his counter? How about that guy by the window? Is he just a random stranger?"

"He's bluffing," Grady talked this time.

Jasper looked unsure, as he stood licking his lips.

"You believe him? Think I'm bluffing? Willing to take a chance?"

Baxter stood up and turned towards the two. "Both of you will sit down now. That'll be the end of it," he spoke to the two in an authoritative tone.

The two complied without a whimper. I kept staring at Jasper until he looked away.

"My apologies. I'll ask Graves to look into it right now," Baxter addressed me.

"I'll be interested in what he says," I replied.

"But until then, I'd advise you to tread carefully. You're rubbing too many people the wrong way. You might end up getting hurt. Or worse."

"And who might those people be?" I asked him.

"You have roughed up my men. One of them right here in the middle of town. We can't have that going on."

Unlike his sons, Baxter was quite the manipulator. He stepped in to defuse the situation, but in the next breath, tried reasserting his dominance. Hector took the cue from him.

"I'm warning you as well," Hector spoke up. "What you did to Luca, people don't stay alive after doing that. Carlos there would have added another notch on his forearm if I hadn't stopped him."

"Carlos better worry about not becoming a notch himself."

"You don't know who you're messing with. Do you know the meaning of '*serpientes de cascabel*'?"

"Yeah. Some have tried biting me. All of them ended up dead."

"If we'd been in Mexico..." he muttered.

"Well, we aren't, pal. In case you didn't notice, this is America. But no point discussing what could have been," I said, and addressed Baxter again.

"Baxter, you've been civil with me and I'll do the same. I don't believe in causing trouble unless someone messes with me. Your guys were rude and obnoxious. It was the same thing with Hector's guy. Let's just decide to stay clear of each other. Get Graves to find my friends and I'll be gone. Or else, I'm not leaving town."

"Fair enough. I'll come with you to the station. Ask Graves to take it up as top priority."

Baxter looked almost relieved. Like a man who found a solution for a problem that was really bugging him.

"Why don't you have a word with Graves? I'll make my way down to the station in a while."

"I'll do that. Do come by the hotel for a drink on us before you leave town," he made the pointed remark.

"If Graves convinces me and we decide to leave, I just might," I replied.

Baxter didn't like the reply, but there wasn't anything else to be said at that point.

"Come on boys," Baxter said to Jasper and Grady, getting up.

The two got up grudgingly, unwilling to move even when Baxter began walking towards the exit door. I could see from their faces that our little meeting wasn't really over so far as they were concerned. Jasper's injured ego wouldn't let him leave just like that. And Grady had a habit of mirroring whatever his brother did.

But they were amateurs. Their faces and body language declared their intentions loud and clear way before either man's hand began moving towards the back of his jeans to grab a gun. It was so obvious that even Hector straightened up in his chair.

There are multiple ways of disarming someone with a gun. Some of those ways are relatively painless. I decided to go for a painful option.

I waited for Jasper to grab his gun before reacting. He grabbed the gun tucked in the back of his jeans and was beginning to move his hand forward when I leaped out of my chair. I grabbed his hand with the gun in it, and twisted it outwards and away from the line of fire in a sudden jerk, breaking his trigger finger before pulling the gun away. Jasper yelped in pain. I pushed him back onto Grady.

Grady was raising his own gun, but Jasper got in the way. I had drawn my own gun by that time. I moved a step and pushed the muzzle into the center of Grady's chest. Adriel's gun was already pointing at his head by that time. Grady let his gun clatter onto the floor.

I looked at the Mexicans, the second gun in my hand was pointing to the ground. I didn't want to force them into a firefight in that closed space.

Hector and his guys were on their feet by that time, guns in their hands, but pointed down. Adriel was covering them with the Desert Eagle from the front. Brick had his Glock out, but remained at the window, watching the scene with alert eyes.

Baxter was silently watching the scene all this time. I holstered my gun. The Mexicans followed suit.

I picked Grady's gun, took out the magazines of both guns and the extra bullet in the chamber, and handed them the empty guns.

"Time to get moving boys. Next time you try pointing a gun on me, it won't go well," I said to them, then addressed Baxter, "I'll stick to the plan and go see Graves in some time."

He nodded and went out. His sons followed him meekly, Jasper clearly in pain.

"You broke my finger," he said in a complaining tone as he left.

"Don't give me cause to break anything else," I replied.

Hector turned to leave as well.

"You be careful, Marshal. I hope you leave town soon. Next time we meet, we won't be talking."

"You too, Hector. Hope our paths don't cross again."

A mirthless smile appeared on Hector's face as he walked out. The two bodyguards gave me murderous looks as they followed him. I knew I would have to be extra vigilant. Those killers would put a bullet in me the moment they got a chance.

Adriel came up to me and we moved to Brick's table by the window.

"You'll have to be careful. They mean business," he said.

"I know."

"Are you going to be meeting Graves? You think he can do something?" Adriel asked me as we were sitting down.

"He can't do a thing. We know exactly what happened. They've killed all of Brick's bikers. I just mentioned Graves to Baxter to tie them up in knots. Keep them guessing about my intentions. Get them to let their guard down."

"Good move. So, what's the plan now?" Adriel asked me.

"A couple of things. We kidnap a guy."

Adriel raised an eyebrow.

"And we leave town," I added.

"What? Just like that?" Brick asked, his voice incredulous.

"Not really. Just pretend to do so."

I took out my phone and showed them a text.

"While Baxter and Hector were busy chatting with me, I got this text on my phone. Someone has installed a tracker on my pickup. Must be one of them, or maybe Graves."

"Your phone can tell you when someone puts a tracker on your pickup?" Brick asked, sounding skeptical.

"It's not about the phone. It's the truck. That's a special recon vehicle. You install any external object on it, be it a tracker or an explosive device, I get a message on my phone."

"What if it's a bomb or something?"

"It's not sizeable enough. It will be a tracker. So, the plan is to meet Graves, let him convince me he's on the case, that his guys will soon find our guys, and there's no point hanging around. We'll install the tracker on another vehicle and send that out of town. I'll hide my pickup somewhere they can't find it. And then go kidnap a guy, get some info from him, before raising hell at the casino site."

"Interesting," Adriel said. "And who are we kidnapping?"

"Peter Rixon. The Dawsons' head chemist and meth cook."

"Why him?"

"He was involved in the disappearance of Charlie. He might have an idea about Carter and Lou as well. I think that Carter is still alive and being held somewhere. Rixon might know where.

226

In the very least, he'll know what's going on at the construction site. When I was up on the butte earlier, everything seemed normal. It didn't look like there was anything illegal going on there."

"Sounds useful. What's the plan?"

"The cartel's bundling him off to Arizona to be their meth cook. He went to the construction site an hour ago. Probably making sure the entire lab apparatus gets packed properly in the trucks. We'll grab him as soon as he leaves the site."

"I'm guessing you know his vehicle."

"Better. I've got a tracker on his car. We'll know as soon as he leaves the site. Meanwhile, I'll go arrange for the tracker on my pickup to leave town... after I have met Graves."

"Want us to go with you?"

"I'll head out alone for now. I'll give you a call as soon as I've hidden my pickup. Come pick me then. Adriel, we'll use your pickup to move around. I'll call in less than an hour."

"Got it."

I was soon headed for Quint's place.

CHAPTER 19

I drove my pickup to the back of Quint's hardware store. I needed a little seclusion to search for the tracker device. It was the same spot I had chosen in the morning to take out the four bullies, away from prying eyes.

It didn't take long to find the device. It was hidden in the rear right tire well. I continued checking the rest of the vehicle, in case there was a second one. There wasn't.

I took the pickup back to the front of the store, parked and went inside. Quint was explaining the features of a chainsaw to a customer. Dewey, the kid behind the counter, gave me a friendly wave. Quint walked over as soon as he saw me and took me to the back office.

"Sounds like you've been having a busy day, Marshal? Nash told me what happened with Hank?"

"One less in the Dawsons' army of bullies."

"Good for you. I bet Baxter didn't figure on a one-man army coming to town. What you did coming to the aid of that girl, everyone in town knows it. I'll be mighty glad to be of any help."

"Thanks. That's why I came to you. Are you familiar with tracking devices on vehicles?"

"You know what... I am. Dewey has been teaching me about new technology. I actually sold a few of them."

"Maybe they bought it from you. The Dawsons have put a tracker on my pickup. I could take it off, but I want them to think they've got me fooled."

"I like where this is going. Go on."

"Would you know someone who's going towards Vegas tonight? If they can carry the tracker part of the way, dump it somewhere along the way to Vegas..."

"The Dawsons will think it's you who's left town and gone to Vegas..."

"Exactly."

"Grand plan. You really must have rocked their boat if they're so desperate to see you leave."

"They'll surely be happy to see me go."

"But you'll be in town doing your Charlie Bronson act while they think you're gone?"

"That's the idea."

"No problem. Give me a minute," Quint said and walked out of the office.

He was back a minute later.

"All sorted. Dewey will carry the tracker to Vegas."

"Dewey? I hope you aren't making him go just for me?"

"The kid jumped at it when I asked him. You have no idea about the fanbase you're creating in town. After what you did this morning, Dewey would walk all the way to Vegas if you asked him. He's calling this his undercover mission."

I couldn't help smiling.

"That's very helpful, Quint."

"No problem at all. Happy to help any way I can. After what you did this morning, I can't do enough to make it square."

"Don't even think about that."

"I won't. So, what's the plan? When do you want him to head out?"

"In about half an hour. I'm heading to the police station. Give Graves a chance to convince me he's taking care of things and I needn't stick around in town. I'll get convinced. Then leave town," I said, as I stood up to leave.

"Good plan. We'll be ready for you as soon as you're back," Quint replied.

"I'll also need to park my pickup out of sight somewhere."

"No problem. I've got a garage back there. You can park it there. No one will be the wiser. How will you travel? Do you need a car?"

"No, thanks. I'll have someone pick me up. I have a couple of friends helping me. This town will see some action tonight. The Dawsons' game will be over long before sunup."

"Let me know if you need a hand. I may be old, but strong enough to pull a trigger. There are many people in town who feel that way."

"Thanks. I'll keep that in mind."

I got in my pickup and headed for the police station, which was about half a mile towards the town. As with most buildings in the new part of town, except for the Dawson hotel, it was a single-story structure. But as with all buildings in that part of town, it too must have been built using Baxter's drug money. The words Little Butte Police Headquarters were written in big, block letters above the entrance.

Baxter's Cadillac was pulling out of the parking lot as I pulled in. It was good timing. I wanted him to notice that I took his word seriously and expected Graves to help me search for the bikers.

The only other vehicles in the parking lot were a couple of cruisers.

When I entered the station house, the first person I encountered was a pleasant-faced woman behind the reception counter. Betsy Adams, I guessed. Her name tag confirmed it.

Behind her, there was an open space with desks. Birdie was sitting on one of them. Nash was nowhere to be seen.

"I'm here to meet chief Graves," I said to Officer Betsy.

"Are you Axel Blaze?" she asked.

"Good guess," I replied.

"You're becoming famous in town," she said, without any hint of an accusation.

"I didn't intend to be."

"Well, Earl asked me to expect you. Get you right in," she said, coming out from behind the counter.

"Follow me," she said, as she led me towards a room.

She knocked, opened the door a bit and put her head in, and then led me inside.

Graves was sitting behind a large wooden desk. A couple of flags behind him. The Stars and Stripes on the left. The dark blue Nevada flag on the right, carrying the words "Battle Born" and "Nevada" on the top left corner, above a wreath, with a star in between.

"Looks like there's been some misunderstanding," Graves offered me his hand as he came around the desk. "I didn't know when I stopped you this morning that you were looking for your friends."

We shook hands and I sat down.

"I did tell you people had gone missing. Baxter must have filled you in on the rest. I just saw him leave."

"Yes, he did. Tell me about it. I'll personally look into it."

"As Baxter must have told you, it's about my biker buddies. They've been in town for a while but went missing last night."

"I see. And how do you know them?"

"Part of the same club."

"You're a biker yourself?"

"Yup."

"Have you always been a biker?"

"You know my history. There must be a file on me in one of those drawers."

"Yes, that's why I'm curious. Ex-Marshal, ex-Special Forces. Then a biker gang."

"Club," I corrected him.

"What?"

"Biker club, not a gang."

"Right. But still..."

"So, that's what makes you curious?"

"Yes."

"You know what puzzles me?"

"What?" he asked.

"Why a police chief shares confidential information with a gangster?"

"I don't understand."

"Hector Alvarez. He told me you showed him the information you had on me."

Graves' face flushed.

"I didn't do any such thing. Baxter must have done that. I only share information with him as he's the town council president," he replied defensively.

"I see. But I told you in the morning there were gangsters in town."

"I said there weren't any."

"What about Hector?"

"As far as I know, he's a business associate of Baxter."

"And that's all he is?"

"As far as I know."

"Right. That clarifies everything."

"Let's get back to the bikers. I don't think they're in town."

"I know that, that's why I'm looking for them around town."

"What I meant was, they're not in Little Butte. Must have ridden off somewhere. Doesn't mean they're missing."

"They didn't go riding. We were supposed to have gone together. They wouldn't just leave."

"I see. Well, Baxter has asked me to consider it a matter of utmost importance."

"Good of him."

"Yes, and I can assure you, we will treat this as top priority."

"How?" I asked.

"I'll ask all our Officers to keep an eye out."

"Eye out? I don't see any cruisers roaming around town looking for them."

"They will. In fact," he pressed a button on his intercom. "Is Nash in? And Birdie? Send both in," he said to the person at the other end, which I assumed was Betsy.

The door opened and the two came in. Nash gave me a curious look but didn't say anything.

"Nash, Birdie, we have a report of six bikers having gone missing. We need to investigate it on a priority basis."

"Gone missing? From where?" Nash asked.

"They should have been at the bar, or at the motel?" I replied.

"But both places are shut for repairs," Birdie chimed in.

"Obviously they aren't in either of those places. Forget them," Graves said. "Go around town, ask people. We can't have people going missing in town."

"Sure thing, boss," Birdie chimed in.

"That'll be all," Graves said. The two went out.

"We're on it. I'm sure we'll have something by tomorrow. In case you're leaving town, I can update you on the phone."

"Alright. I'll wait for an update tomorrow. I'll be leaving for Vegas tonight. But if nothing comes up by tomorrow, I'll be back."

"I'm sure it's nothing. We'll have solid information for you," he replied, sounding relieved.

I got up, shook hands, and exited the room. The moment I got out, Birdie rushed back in.

Nash met me near the entrance and walked out with me.

"What're you playing at?" he asked me.

"Making them believe I'm leaving town."

"How come?"

"I had a long chat with Baxter and Hector. You know him?"

"No."

"Top lieutenant of a Mexican cartel. Up to some nasty business with Baxter. They wanted me gone. I decided to oblige."

"I don't get it. Are you leaving?"

"Not a chance. Not until I've seen this thing through. But someone installed a tracker on my pickup," I nodded towards my truck in the parking lot. "I'm going to play their game. Make them believe I've left town."

"So, all this... was an act?"

"Yup. Graves must be kicking Birdie in there for mentioning the bar and motel. If any of you were to really investigate either of the places, it would create a mess Baxter doesn't want. He'll have Graves' hide for it."

Nash laughed. The first time I had seen him do that.

"Birdie's coming out," he said, assuming his stern expression.

"Right. You'll be hearing from me soon."

"I'll be ready. Be careful," he said and walked off towards his cruiser.

I got in my pickup and called Adriel. Asked him to get Brick along and meet me at Quint's.

When I pulled in at Quint's, there was a beat-up Chevy parked in front of the store. Dewey was standing next to it, trying his best to contain a big smile. I stopped near him, told him I would park my pickup at the back of the store, and carried on. I got out, took off the tracker from the tire well, and opened the weapons compartment. Picked all the guns and put them in a duffel bag. I grabbed the remaining trackers and flexicuffs as well. Then walked back to Dewey.

"Thanks for helping out, Dewey."

"No problem, Mr. Blaze. Glad to be of help."

"Axel. Call me Axel."

"Axel? Sure."

I handed him the tracker.

"Keep this beneath the passenger seat so it isn't visible. Stop at any motel once you're well clear of town, maybe 50 miles from here, dump it in a bin, and turn back. OK?"

"Are you sure you want me to dump it?"

"Yes, be very clear on that. Don't hang on to it when you're stationary. Dump it and turn back. You don't want anyone tracking and identifying you. There's going to be lots of traffic the moment you hit Route 93. So long as you're moving, no one can make out which car's got the tracker. But if you stop too long at an isolated spot, like a motel parking, you can be identified. Got it?"

"Yes," he nodded, taking in every word seriously.

"Just in case you have a breakdown or something, throw it far away. All that's important is that it gets out of town, so whoever's tracking me thinks I've left town. Don't keep it with you once you've stopped. OK?"

"Yes, got it, Mr. Blaze. I mean, Axel," he replied, looking more excited than scared.

"Good. See you later, tiger."

And he was off, a grin on his face. I went towards the back with Quint. Parked the pickup in his garage. He closed the door and locked it. When we walked back to the store, Adriel and Brick were waiting in Adriel's pickup in the parking lot.

I got into the back seat, flung the duffel bag in the space behind the seat, and slouched low. It was time to keep a low profile.

"Where to?" Adriel asked me.

"The butte. Rixon has been there a couple of hours. I don't think he'll hang around for much longer. Let's get ourselves in place, ready to grab him as soon as he comes out."

"What's the plan, where do we grab him?"

"The road between the casino and town. There's a bar on the way. No one's there today. We'll park the pickup at the back and wait. We'll grab him when he leaves the site. Adriel, you go take up position on top of the butte, keep an eye on what's happening at the site."

"You're going to make me climb up there? I told you these joints are getting old, kid."

"Stop whining, old man. I already put the rope in place. Not that you needed it. But with the rope, you won't even need to get out of your cowboy boots."

"Well, alright," he replied with a sigh.

"Brick and I will hide near the bar. Let us know the moment you see him getting ready to leave the site."

"What's he driving? Car or pickup?"

"A dark blue Merc. No confusion on that point. It'll be the only car on site."

"OK. Lie low. You don't want anyone catching sight of you."

"We won't drive through town. Turn right when you hit the road. We move out of town and take a road that'll take us to the back of the butte."

"Roger that," Adriel replied, pulling onto the road.

It was time to grab Rixon.

CHAPTER 20

Adriel didn't really need a hand to go up the butte. He was an old pro at high altitude reconnaissance.

Adriel had been a MOS 19D armored reconnaissance specialist in the Bosnian war in the 1990s. For that, you needed to be the best in covert and direct force operations. If you were a cavalry scout in Task Force Eagle, the deployment of the 1st Armored Division in the largely mountainous terrain in Bosnia, you were simply the best at what you did—just being good didn't quite cut it. And if you've been the eyes and ears of the US army in the middle of a war against genocide, you're surely good enough to take on a routine scouting mission in Little Butte.

As soon as Adriel stopped the pickup behind the butte, he got out, picked a Ruger long-range precision rifle, the 6.5mm Creedmoor version, from the back and slung it over his shoulder. Adriel was one of those guys who could shoot back-to-back 1-inch targets at 500 yards, consistently shooting under 0.25 MOA.

In less than a minute, he was in his climbing harness and ready to go. He fixed his mechanical ascender to the rope and was on his way up.

The fixed rope made the climb relatively simple. Adriel was at the top of the 300 feet butte within ten minutes. The moment he signaled from the top, I rushed back to the pickup. Brick was already in the driver's seat. I got in the back seat and slouched real low. We would need to take a long detour to reach the bar; taking the road going past the casino site was likely to bring too much scrutiny.

Brick drove back towards town and approached the bar from the main road coming from town. A drive of around ten minutes. I was lying low on the seat. We were passing through the middle of town—I couldn't afford to be seen. Adriel texted me saying Rixon's Merc was still at the construction site. No sign of any movement yet.

I decided to confirm the location of the other two vans. Last time I checked, one of the vans was at the site. That must have been the one with the bodies in it. The other van, which was being driven around by the two Mexicans, had been parked at the hotel.

The app was acting up a bit and working slower than usual. We had almost reached the bar when the location of the first van came up. It was still at the site. I clicked on the coordinates for the second one. We were almost at the bar before its location began getting loaded onto the screen. Brick was going around the bar to park the pickup at the back, hidden from anyone driving down the road. The location map got loaded onto the phone screen just as Brick made the final turn.

The phone showed me the van's location a second before we rammed into it. The van was parked with its back end facing us, doors open wide. One of the two killers from last night was just about to step out, an AR-15 rifle in his hand.

Brick made the turn just at that moment and, unable to brake in time, rammed into it. That turned out to be a good thing. Although Brick was slowing down while turning the corner, the impact was enough to fling the other man into the back of the van, his gun flying out of his hand. Had Brick braked on time, we would have been sitting ducks for the guy.

But the danger wasn't over. The second killer, the one with whom I had locked eyes the previous night, came out of the bar. He stood at the door, around 15 yards away, the stock of a suppressed AR-15 firmly placed on his shoulder. There were muffled sounds of three shots fired in succession as bullets pierced the windscreen, missing Brick's head by inches. Brick ducked beneath the windscreen.

The man's eyes were on Brick. I was slouched low in the seat and the impact had sent me further down into the space between the front and rear seats. The man began moving towards the pickup, letting off a shot with each advancing step. Neither I nor Brick had the slightest chance of raising our heads to fire a return shot.

I opened the rear door on the far side, hidden from the line of view of the advancing man, and slipped out. I slithered out of the back door, head first, landing flat on the ground. I rolled over to see the feet of the advancing man. A couple more steps and he would be beside the driver's door, shooting bullets into Brick. I grabbed the Glock tucked in the back of my jeans and fired off quick shots into the man's shins and ankles. He fell. Our eyes met as he saw me from under the vehicle. I was about to take a final shot, but Brick beat me to it.

"For my brothers, asshole," he said, as he shot a second bullet into the dying man, while exiting the pickup.

But the next second, he caught a bullet in his left shoulder as the other Mexican, who had fallen inside the van, got up and began firing with his rifle. In our bid to escape the onslaught of the other assassin, we had forgotten him. Luckily for Brick, he was partially covered by the windscreen's A-pillar. The second bullet got lodged in the pillar.

Before the man could fire off a third bullet, I fired five rapid shots. The man fell back into the van, dead before he hit the floor.

Before checking on Brick, I needed to make sure the inside of the bar was clear. I stood beside the open back door, fired a shot inside, and moved immediately to the other side, getting a view of the corridor inside. It was clear. I moved in, checked all the rooms, including the restrooms. There was no one else around.

A wide space had been cleared in the bar area, with all the tables and chairs pushed to one side. That was where the sicarios must have placed their plastic sheets, before murdering the bikers.

I rushed back to check on Brick. He was sitting in the driver's seat, clutching his shoulder.

"How're you doing, big man?" I asked him.

"Not too bad," he gasped. "Felt good to put a bullet in that psycho."

His luck had held out again. Well, kind of. He was shot, which is pretty unlucky so far as things go, but the bullet had gone clean through. No crucial organs or major artery hit. No complications of the bullet shattering a bone and getting lodged in it, requiring major surgery. But if you get shot, you lose blood, major arteries being hit or not.

I got pieces of heavy cotton gauze from a first aid box in the pickup and pressed them firmly on the wound to stem the blood.

Brick seemed more angry than hurt. "These guys are psychos, man," he exclaimed. "We could've been random visitors for all they knew. But they'd have killed us any way."

"They're mad dogs. Only stop when they're dead. They have no business roaming the streets."

"I'm going to kill them all, man."

"Take it easy, pal. Calm down. We need to get the bleeding under control. You're lucky the bullet didn't hit an artery," I said, pushing back the driver's seat and reclining it all the way. "Lie down."

"Yeah, alright," he said, lying down, taking a deep breath.

I was getting out a new piece of gauze when Adriel's text landed on my phone. Rixon was about to drive off from the site.

"Rixon's on the move. I'll have to go get him," I said.

"How'll you do it alone?"

The plan was for Brick to drive the pickup into the middle of the road, forcing Rixon to stop. I would then walk over and grab him.

"I'll just go stand in the middle of the road. It's not as if he'll run me over," I replied.

"Not a great plan."

"It'll have to do. We don't have time."

"I don't want to wimp out now. I'm sure I can manage," he said, trying to get up.

"Forget it. You've been shot. That's not wimping out," I said, restraining him. "I've got enough dead people on my hands, as it is. We don't want you losing more blood and going into shock."

I grabbed fresh pieces of gauze and put them on his shoulder.

"Here, hold this and keep pressing. I'll be back in a few minutes."

"Good luck," he replied.

When I turned the corner and moved towards the road, I could already hear the car coming from the site. I walked into the middle of the road, waving him to stop. Rixon wasn't going too fast. He braked and came to a stop a few feet from me.

"What's going on?" he asked in an irritated tone, sticking his head out the car window.

I walked towards him, drew my gun, and pointed it at his head.

"Turn off the ignition and give me the key."

He complied immediately.

I went over to the passenger side, got in, and handed him the key.

"Drive around to the back of the bar."

"What do you want? I'm not carrying any money."

"Shut up and do what I say," I said, pressing the gun into his ribs.

"Please, what do you want?" he asked, sounding very scared.

I pressed the Glock further into his ribs. That must have hurt.

"Do what I say and you'll come out of this alive. Or I shoot you now. Your choice?"

He shut up and drove around the bar to the back.

"Stop beside the van."

Rixon complied.

"Get out," I ordered.

As soon as Rixon got out, his eyes got fixated on the dead man lying beside the pickup.

"There's another one of your Mexican pals in the van," I told him.

I wanted him to be scared for his life before I began questioning him. His eyes grew wider as he looked at the second body.

"I don't have any Mexican pals..."

"Shut up and move."

I roughly pushed him towards the bar's back entrance.

"Hands against the wall," I ordered, before frisking him. I took out his wallet and cell phone, pushed him inside the corridor, and shoved him into the restroom.

"There's nowhere to escape. So, don't bother. I need information from you and you're going to give it. If that happens quickly, you might stay alive. Think about it until I come back for you," I said, before locking the door and walking out.

I came out and examined Brick. He looked pale and needed to get to a doctor. I couldn't take a shot man to hospital in the pickup with bullet holes in the windscreen. I called Chico.

"Hey, Marshal, I've been meaning to..."

"Chico, listen to me," I cut him before he could begin giving me a status report of how his day had been going. "I need your help."

"You need my help? Really? Bro, I'm flattered. What can I do for you?"

"Meet me behind the bar. The old one, not the new one at the hotel."

"Got it, Marshal. You want me to come packed? I've got a..."

"No. Just get here fast. Brick is injured."

"Oh, right. On my way."

I called Adriel next.

"All going as planned?" he answered with a question.

"Slight complication. We got Rixon. But we bumped into a couple of cartel guys. Brick's been shot."

"Serious?"

"No, he'll be fine. I've called Chico to take him to a doc."

"And the two guys?"

"Dead."

"Hmm... what's the plan?"

"I'll question Rixon. Be with you in under an hour."

"Roger that."

I checked up on Brick. He was lying quietly, eyes closed.

"You need to stay awake, pal. Chico will be here any minute."

"I'll be fine."

I needed to move the body of the second man lying out in the open. I dragged him inside the van and shut the back door. By the time I was done, Chico had arrived.

"Whoa, Marshal, what's going on here? Are those bullet holes in the windscreen?"

"I can't explain now. Just get Brick to a hospital."

"Oh, man, that looks painful," he said as he looked at Brick's shoulder. "What do I tell them if they ask how he got shot."

"I'll call Nash and arrange all that. You don't need to worry about it. When you take him in, just tell them he landed at your diner. You don't know what happened. Brick will say he doesn't remember a thing. They'll think he's in shock. Nash will take care of the rest."

"Alright, boss. You know best," he replied.

We helped Brick get out of the pickup and into Chico's truck. And they were off.

I next called Nash. He wasn't too happy about having to work with minimal information. But he agreed to go to the hospital and sort things out. I promised to fill him in on everything before the night was over.

It was finally time to question Rixon.

CHAPTER 21

I didn't have time to fool around with Rixon. I needed answers. Fast.

I unlocked the restroom. Rixon was standing in the far corner, looking scared. He looked all primed for questioning. I decided to enhance the effect by taking him outside, opening the back door of the van, and showing him the two bodies.

"Take a look at these two. You're ending up with them if I don't get what I want."

His face lost color, and for a moment, I thought he was going to pass out. I nudged him inside the bar and pushed him to a table in the corner. I took a seat opposite him.

"You know who I am?" I asked him.

"No. And I don't want to know. You can see that, right? I don't know your name, where you've come from... I don't care to ever remember your face. I won't ever identify you. Ask me anything you want, I swear I'll tell you. I have some money, I can get it for you. But please don't hurt me."

The man was scared for his life, sure I was going to kill him. I decided to play on his fear. That would be the fastest way to get him talking.

"I'm the one who killed your two pals lying dead outside."

"I don't mean to disrespect you, sir, but I think you have me confused with someone else. I'm a scientist. A chemist. I don't know any gangsters."

"Who said anything about gangsters?"

"Uh, those two, uh, bodies outside..."

"Those two gentlemen in the van? I never said they were gangsters. I have a feeling you know them."

"No."

"So you're a tough cookie? Won't talk easily? Those two outside were the same. Wouldn't listen to reason. I had to finally kill them. But you're different, aren't you? You're a scientist. So, let's play a game. Have you heard of the Five Finger Fillet?"

"No," he said, a feeling of dread in his voice, as if he could guess the game wasn't going to be much fun.

"It's simple. You'll put your hand palm-down on this table, fingers spread. You see this knife?" I showed him the razor-sharp blade of my boot knife. "I'll stab the table between your fingers. The more you lie, the faster my knife will get, the greater the chance I'll miss the table and stab one of your fingers. So, scientist, try and calculate how many fingers you'll have left by the time this interrogation is over."

"Please, no..." he pleaded, dread written large on his face as he bunched both hands into fists and put them between his legs.

"You don't get it. Not playing isn't an option. Playing it safely definitely is one. I'm pretty good at it so long as you don't force me to go fast. I guarantee you won't lose a single finger if you're honest. Here, I'll show you."

I put my hand on the table, spread my fingers, and began stabbing the table between them. This was something I had gotten really good at, at a point in life where proving I was a badass had seemed very important. Young and dumb, as they say. But once you attain that level of motor co-ordination and dexterity, the knife becomes an extension of your hand. But for someone new to it, even watching another person perform it is nerve-wracking.

I spread out my fingers and began the rhythmic stabbing motion. Slow at first, the first stab outside the thumb, the sixth stab outside the little finger, and back, and back again... increasing the speed. Rixon watched in fascinated horror, flinching every now and then.

I suddenly stopped, stabbed the knife hard in the middle of the table, and left it there. I got up, went behind him, grabbed his hand and forced it on the table. He was trying to keep his fingers bunched up in a fist, but a little pressure with my thumb on the back of his wrist forced his fingers to uncurl. I began the dance with him, holding his hand firm on the table, making slow but forceful stabs between each finger.

"Now here's the deal, scientist. I'll ask you some questions. I know the answers to many of them. Every time you lie, the speed of the knife will go up. I've got full control at a slow speed, but if you force me to go too fast, I can't guarantee you'll leave the room with all your fingers. Only the truth will set you free. Is that clear?"

"Yes... yes... of course. I won't lie. Please stop."

"How long have you been a meth cook?"

"What? No, I'm a chemist. You've got me wrong."

I began stabbing faster.

"No, no, please. Sorry. I used to cook for the Dawsons. But now there are others doing it. I swear."

I slowed down a bit.

"For the Dawsons maybe, what about the Mexicans?"

"I don't want to do that, I swear. They're forcing me to go with them. I swear. Please stop. Please," he began sobbing.

I took his hand away in a quick motion and stabbed hard into the table, where his palm had been half a second ago. He looked at the knife in horror as I went to the other side of the table and took a seat facing him.

"Now look at me. This is not over. I'm giving you a breather to tell the truth. Lie once more and it begins again. Got it?"

"Yes."

"What were you doing at the casino today? Think carefully before you answer," I said, placing the tip of my index finger on the heft of the knife standing erect on the table, half an inch of its blade embedded in the wood.

"I was making sure the meth lab is uninstalled properly," he said in a resigned tone.

"Why is it being uninstalled?"

"It's being taken to Arizona. The cartel is going to be taking over production there."

"Las Hermosas?" I asked more to let him know I knew things, than to get his confirmation.

He seemed surprised I knew that. A further slump in his shoulders told me he had given up trying to lie.

"Yes," he replied.

"And they're taking you with them?"

"I don't want to go... but, yes," he replied in a defeated tone.

"But why go to the trouble of uninstalling the lab and taking it all the way. Surely they make enough money from the meth to buy new equipment."

"This is high quality state-of-the-art equipment made for pharma manufacturers. You can't just walk into a store and buy it off the shelf."

"Hmm... How long have you been cooking at the site?"

"I'm not..."

"Yeah, I know, the boys you trained," I said, cutting him off.

"Four... five months. It used to be in a workshop in the old town before that."

"Where's the lab located in the site?"

"There's a main casino hall in the middle of it."

"That entire hall is a cooking lab?"

"You've seen it?" he asked, sounding surprised. "They aren't using the entire hall. The lab was in maybe around half the space."

"How come no one noticed it all these months. There must be weird smells, gases coming out."

"As I said, it's a state-of-the-art lab," he said, with a touch of pride. "Not some small-time rolling kitchen. We had the best equipment, the best air filtration system, it was just odorless air that came out of it. We're pharmaceutical manufacturers, after all."

"Don't kid yourself. You were pharmaceutical manufacturers. Once. Now you're just a bunch of meth cooks and dealers. And with the Mexicans coming into this picture, it's curtains for any pretensions of respectability you had."

"Who are you? Am I allowed to ask that... but, no... sorry... forget I asked. I don't want to know."

"Right. Forget that. Where are the uninstalled lab components? And where's the Dawsons' stock of meth?"

"Baxter will kill me if I tell you."

"You really want to play that game again?" I asked him, looking pointedly at the knife.

"No."

"Come clean and I'll let you go. No one will know we talked. After tonight, it's not going to matter. That whole operation is going to fold up. You won't need to go to Arizona. You want that, don't you?"

"Yes."

"Then, talk. Where are the uninstalled meth lab components? And where's the stock of meth?"

"The lab's lying disassembled and packed in the main hall. As for the meth, there are rooms at the back of the site, next to the butte. They lead to a secure below-ground level, like a bunker. That's where the stock is—all 2,000 pounds of it."

"2,000 pounds? No wonder the site's being guarded like it's Fort Knox."

"In street value, I believe that's around $100 million."

"Jesus! How much were you cooking?"

"Around 700-800 pounds a month."

"And the Mexicans were moving all that?"

"Not all. That's why they're left with that huge stock. The cartel will scale up the operation from Arizona."

"And none of the construction workers noticed it all these months?"

"There wasn't any construction going on these past months. It only began last week. After they decided to transfer all the cooking to the cartel."

"When do they pack all the stuff in the trucks?"

"They just began, after the day shift got over."

"How many men do they have in there?"

"Are you planning to steal all that stuff?" he asked me, his eyes getting a little crafty.

"Maybe. Now you want to know more about me?"

"No, I don't. You won't harm me, will you?"

"I've got no particular love for the Dawsons or the cartel. But I'll let you get out of here once you've told me all I want to know. After that, you're on your own. I won't let anyone know you squealed. That's all I can offer you."

"That's good enough. Thanks. They've got six men at the site right now. But more Mexicans are coming over tonight."

"When?"

"I really don't know that. My guess would be not for another 2-3 hours. They'll escort the trucks out of the state."

"And the van with the bodies, where is it?"

"What van? Bodies? I swear I don't know."

"Where's Charlie?"

Rixon fell silent.

"Didn't you hear my question?"

"I don't know about Charlie," he replied.

"And we're back to playing our game again," I said, reaching for the knife.

"No, no. Please. Listen to me. Charlie has run off somewhere. I don't know where."

"Go on."

"I didn't know what his deal was, until the day he ran off. But he was a good man. I liked him. When he told me there were men looking to kill him and begged me for help, I did. I told him I'd cover for him for a few hours. And he ran. Didn't even want to tell his girlfriend. He was scared she would become a target as well."

"And you? You didn't get in trouble?"

"Jasper called me while we were having the conversation. Told me men would come looking for Charlie and I should point him out to them. I told him I wasn't sure where he was but I'd go look in the factory. Charlie ran off and I pretended to look for him."

"So, he's alive?"

"I think so. But don't know for sure."

"And what about those gangsters? Who were they?"

"A tough looking bunch from up north. Seattle, I think. They made a fuss when I told them I couldn't find Charlie. They checked every inch of the factory, but finally left."

"And Jasper knows that?"

"No. Those guys left town. Jasper assumed they'd taken him with them. There was too much happening. He never asked to confirm."

"What about Lou?"

"I don't know about him. But I'm guessing he was in a similar situation as Charlie. Either took off or some gang took him. Both things happened on the same day, so I guess they're related."

"And Carter?"

"How do you know all these people? Are you a cop?"

"You want me to show you those bodies lying outside again?"

"Right. Dumb question. You can't be a cop."

"Yeah. So, what do you know about Carter?"

"I have no idea. I know this guy was in town. He was making Jasper very nervous. But I don't have any idea. I assumed he'd gone away."

"No. He didn't. Jasper kidnapped him. Could he be at the casino?"

"Hmm... I don't know. I haven't been to those rooms and bunker for a while. They're locked and guarded all the time. They didn't even let me in there today."

"Alright. You're free to leave."

"What? Really? Why, thank you... so much."

"Go on home and lie low. When are you supposed to be in Arizona?"

"I leave tomorrow."

"You won't need to. But don't even think of talking to Jasper or the Mexicans. I've got all this recorded," I said, showing him the phone I had been holding under the table. "I won't tell on you. But if I find you played a double game with me, they'll certainly get to know you squealed. I'm sure you understand you don't have a chance after that."

"Yes, of course. I understand. I won't talk to anyone. I'm just going to go home, get drunk. I swear. I've had enough of all this. You won't tell them, right?"

"You have my word. Now go on home."

"Can I ask who you are?"

"You better not."

He nodded and walked out.

It was time for me to join Adriel at the butte. Our bumping into the Mexicans, Brick getting shot... things weren't going exactly as planned. I could no longer ride around hidden in the backseat of the pickup. I would have to drive myself. And that too in a truck with bullet holes in the windscreen. But there wasn't any other option.

The good thing was it had gotten dark again. I wouldn't be as visible. I got in the driver's seat, put on a baseball cap with the bill pulled low, and headed towards town to take the long-winded detour to the butte.

CHAPTER 22

I arrived at the back of the butte and parked the pickup well away from the road. Finding the location of the climbing rope in the dark didn't prove to be a problem. As soon as I called Adriel, he looked down from the top of the butte and pointed out the exact spot with his flashlight. It took less than ten minutes to join him at the top.

"How's Brick?" asked Adriel.

"He'll live."

"Good. Got what you needed from Rixon?"

"He sang like a canary. But didn't have any idea about Carter. Nor about Lou. The other witness who disappeared, Charlie, is alive. He got wind that his old crew was looking to grab him. Managed to skip town in time without telling anyone, not even his girlfriend. Rixon helped him get away."

"He did? Not as bad as the rest of them?"

"He's no saint, but not an out-and-out criminal. One of those fence-sitters. Made a quick buck by helping the Dawsons set up the cooking operation. But likes to think of himself as a scientist. But I do believe he helped Charlie get away. But nothing on Lou. He's most likely been grabbed by his old crew in Texas. If that's the case, it wouldn't have ended well."

Adriel nodded in a resigned manner.

"Focus on Carter," he said. "I'm sure we'll get a clearer idea about everything soon. So, what's the plan?"

"There's a chance Carter might be down there. I'll have to go down and investigate."

"There's been a lot of activity after Rixon left. The regular construction staff have left the site. Only six guys down there. All of them armed," Adriel said, handing me the binoculars as we lay flat near the edge to watch the site. "Two guys at the main gate. Four of them loading the trucks. Two carrying packs from the rooms at the back, loading them onto one. The other two transferring stuff from the central hall, loading the other truck."

I was interested in the trucks and the rooms at the back, the ones leading to the below-ground level. Rixon had told me the entrance to the rooms was usually locked and guarded. But it was lying wide open. The problem was the men were moving between the rooms and the truck. Accessing the trucks or the rooms would be difficult. I didn't want to alert the Mexicans.

"What's the plan?" Adriel asked me.

"We've got to do a couple of things. Install trackers on both trucks and check out the rooms at the back. You take the trucks and I'll check out the rooms. But zero engagement. We get in and out like ghosts."

"Why the trucks?"

"They're transferring their entire meth stock. 2,000 pounds."

"2,000? No wonder security is tight," Adriel commented.

"I'd ideally have disabled the trucks. But that's complicated. Difficult to do it discreetly. But trackers are easy. Once they're in place, I'll give the coordinates to Flynn. He'll get DEA to make the bust."

"What about the rooms at the back?"

"They lead to a secure below-ground level. Kind of a bunker. They've got their meth stocked there. But there's a possibility they could be holding Carter there. The problem is all these guys moving between the rooms and the trucks."

"They've been at it for an hour. I bet they'll take a break."

"I hope you're right. I want to get this done before reinforcements arrive. Rixon said the cartel is sending more men for escorting the trucks."

"Maybe we don't need to wait for their break. I've been watching their pattern. There are windows of opportunity every now and then, when all four are either at the trucks or at the rooms or central hall. Let's get down, take positions, and dive in and out as soon as we get the chance."

"Let's get going then," I said, taking out the trackers from my pocket. "So, the plan is, we part ways as soon as we touch ground, you take the trucks and I'll head to the bunker. As soon as we are done, we climb back up straightaway. No point hanging around."

"Roger that."

"These are the stick and leave versions," I said, handing Adriel the trackers. "Magnetic as well as adhesive sticking. Plop them into any of the tire wells. They won't come off."

"Sounds simple," he replied, pocketing them.

We set up the rope in the back corner of the site nearer the trucks. That part lay in almost complete darkness. Security was airtight on the front and sides of the site, but they weren't that bothered by the back because of the butte. They didn't think there could be a breach from the back. We parted ways the moment we touched bottom.

Watching the men undetected wasn't really an issue. There were many mounds of loose earth created by the excavators during the day. I watched their movements for around ten minutes before an opportunity arose, when one of the men had just reached a truck and the second one was moving towards it. I would have a couple of minutes to get in and out undetected.

I walked soundlessly towards the rooms. The structure gave the appearance of a long rectangular hall from the outside, with only one entrance and no windows. But when I entered, I saw there were three interconnected rooms laid out in a straight line. And once you entered, there was no other way out.

I didn't have time to linger. The first room was the security center, a large desk facing the entrance, three large monitors with multiple feeds from the security cameras, each monitor displaying feeds from six cameras. The feed on the first two monitors was from 12 security cameras located on the perimeter fence. The third monitor was receiving images from cameras installed inside the site. Three in the central hall, one near the trucks, the other two near the main gates.

The second room was mostly bare, except for a couple of chairs in a corner. The third room looked like a rest area for the guards. There were a couple of makeshift beds, a couch, two chairs and a table. There were narrow ventilator windows near the top of the back wall in each room, not even wide enough for a man to squeeze through. All of them were blacked out and shut tight.

In the far corner of the third room was a heavy metallic door. Wide open. Steps beyond the door led to the below-ground level. Big packs of what I assumed was meth were lying stacked at the bottom of the steps. It would take the men about 6-7 more rounds to finish loading all the remaining packs. About half an hour's work. More if they took a break.

There were stacks of empty shelves at one end of the room. A gun cabinet next to it. I could make out a few shotguns and rifles. The below-ground space was essentially a big, secure room. Not even a ventilator window. Only one entrance or exit— through the metal door. As Rixon had said, it was more of a bunker. But no sign of Carter anywhere.

As I walked through the rooms towards the entrance, I decided to make peepholes in the blacked-out ventilator windows of each room. A few, quick scratches with a knife were enough to scrape some black paint off, creating small openings, enough to get a view of the lighted interiors from the darkness outside. I wasn't sure if I was coming back to the place again that night. But the way things had been changing, I wanted to be prepared for anything.

I moved quickly from the third to the second and finally, the first room, the one with the monitors. I realized I had taken too long to scout the area when I heard steps coming towards the door. I ducked behind the big desk. The two men came in and went straight towards the bunker.

I crawled out from under the desk, slipped out the entrance, and was back in the shadows again.

I waited for the next window of opportunity, when all four men would be away from the trucks.

The chance came ten minutes later, when the men decided to take a break. All four walked inside the rooms. By then, I was already tied into the rope. I didn't waste a second—attached my mechanical ascender and began climbing. When I reached the top, Adriel was already there, waiting for me to show up.

"How did it go?" he asked me.

"Nothing. No sign of Carter. That thing at the end of those rooms is a bunker. All metal and concrete. The remaining stock of meth is in there. But nothing else."

"Now what?"

"I'm getting the feeling the Dawsons might have him locked up in one of their houses. They're heavily guarded. High fences. Guards at the gate. Not what you expect from a home."

"Houses? They don't live together?"

"No. There are three houses in the compound. Almost identical. Baxter in one, Jasper and Grady in the other, Daphne in the third."

"Hmm... and you think Daphne's on the level?"

"I think so... no, actually, I'm almost certain. I initially thought she was playing me. But I think she's genuinely stuck with them."

"So, why don't you straight out ask her?"

"Ask what?"

"If they've got Carter hidden at the houses."

"I did. She says she doesn't know. I know she's scared of them. She might be hiding things. But it didn't feel like she was lying about this... How did it go with the trucks?"

"No problem. Trackers installed on both trucks. One of them is a refrigerated truck. I wonder why?"

"I'm sure it's got the van with the bodies inside it. I'd forgotten about it. The tracker I put on the van shows it's still on the site. Must be inside that truck."

"Van inside the truck?"

"I guess there wasn't a choice. The bodies would have started decomposing. They would have taken care of the bodies last night, but I didn't let them. The Dawsons wouldn't want them dumped in their casino, now that they're trying to go legit. I guess the cartel must be taking them wherever they dump bodies. I'm sure they must have some place."

"You think there are a dozen bodies in there?"

"Yes. We'll nail those bastards. The DEA will clamp down on that truck with the meth. The state troopers will be all over the bodies. End of the road for the Dawsons and the cartel, at least their operation in the States."

"They've sure had it coming. So, what now? Pay the Dawsons a visit?"

"Yes, let's see what they've got hidden in there?"

CHAPTER 23

We rappelled down the rope and touched ground. I checked my phone as we walked towards Adriel's pickup. There were a couple of missed calls. One from Flynn. The other from Mark Murphy—my deputy when I headed the Special Operations Group at the Marshals. A real hothead, but a good man to have by your side. I guessed he must have been holed up with the SOG team at Vegas. He wasn't a man known for his patience.

I called Flynn first.

"Good timing, Blaze, I just got off the phone with Murphy," Flynn said the moment he took the call.

"Mark?"

"Yup. You know how he gets—I'm having a hard time holding him back. He can't get why he and the boys can't just blast their way into Little Butte."

"Oh, boy, I have a missed call from him. I know what that's going to be about. Once he gets something in his head..."

"I know. But first things first, how's it going?"

"I'm close. I'll find Carter."

"That's what I needed to hear. What did you find?"

"I know what happened to him. The Dawsons ordered the kidnapping. The police chief and another cop were involved. I have good reason to believe Carter's alive and being held somewhere. I've been looking all over town. Not too many places left where he could possibly be. I should get to him tonight."

"Excellent. What can I do from my end? I have already moved Murphy's team closer. They're at a motel off the I-93 just north of Alamo. Waiting for your signal. Raring to go. They can be with you within 45 minutes."

"That's good. I'm sending you the coordinates for a couple of trackers I placed on two trucks. It's pure gold, so far as ending the Dawsons is concerned. Not just them, but the cartel as well."

"What's in the trucks?"

"One of them's carrying 2,000 pounds of meth."

"2,000 pounds? Oh boy, DEA are going to go nuts over this."

"Exactly. And wait till you hear about the second truck. It's one of those refrigerated ones. Carrying a dozen bodies. The bikers and sicarios I mentioned last night. I don't know what they plan to do with them, but the Dawsons are trying to make sure the town goes completely legit from tomorrow. The cartel is taking them to wherever they dump bodies of their victims."

"Jesus! Where the hell do they think they are? This is not Juarez!"

"Exactly. I can't believe all this has been going on in this sleepy little place."

"This is big. It'll be one for the FBI and highway troopers. I'll start making the calls, Blaze. What's your plan now?"

"I'll go check the Dawsons' houses. They're located in a secure compound. They've surely got something to hide. I have a feeling Carter might be hidden there."

"Be careful. I'll get on with my calls. Let me know if you need anything."

"Roger that."

I turned to Adriel.

"Flynn's on it. These trucks aren't going anywhere once they move out of here."

"Good," Adriel replied. "And thanks for getting the ventilation sorted. I wasn't getting enough fresh air while driving," he added, looking pointedly at the four bullet holes in his pickup's windscreen.

"Just four small holes, Adriel. You won't even notice them," I said, laughing.

"Must have been a rifle. A handgun bullet would have made wider cracks. We wouldn't have been able to see enough to drive."

"Bang on. It was an AR-15."

We were about to get into the pickup when I got another call. It was Murphy.

"Hey, Cowboy! I'm getting a feeling you're ignoring my calls."

"Murphy, you Irish hothead. I thought you'd have learnt to be patient now that you're a big shot, heading your own unit," I said as I took his call.

"Big shot my ass. Don't you go hogging all the action alone. Stop making us sit on our asses, man."

"Good to see you're still the committed pacifist," I replied, chuckling.

"Yeah, right. And didn't I tell you, Cowboy, you wouldn't be able to stay away from the Marshals."

"Seriously, pal, I had retired. But couldn't stay away when Flynn told me Carter had been kidnapped."

"I know. How's the investigation coming along? I've heard you're setting a new record for body count in a single investigation. Flynn's been shitting bricks."

"I didn't really expect this, Murph. There's weird shit going on here. I didn't expect Mexican cartel presence so far north of the border. Almost feels like we're in El Paso. And they're sending in reinforcements tonight."

"No shit. But no worries, bro, we've got your back. That's why I vetoed Flynn's decision to stay put in Vegas. That was way too far."

"Flynn told me it was his decision to get you closer to Little Butte," I said, chuckling. "I'm surprised he hasn't fired you yet."

"Yeah, right, says the cowboy who could barely toe the line... It was more than two hours away, man. Not good enough when the cartel's involved. Now we're less than 45 minutes from you. Just say the word, bro. We'll come guns blazing."

"Thanks, pal. Good to know you guys are around. There's one more place I need to scope out. They might have hidden Carter there. The moment I get an idea of his location, I'll give you the word. We'll put an end to this cartel shit."

"You got it, Blaze. We'll be waiting for your signal."

"Roger that."

I filled Adriel in on the conversation with Murphy. I had just removed my climbing harness when I received a text from Daphne, asking me to call.

I signaled to Adriel before taking the call. He nodded, got in the pickup, while I remained outside in the cool evening air, and called her.

"Hey Axel, please hold on a second," she said.

I could hear background voices. It sounded like she was moving somewhere quiet to take the call.

"Hi, sorry, I'm in the hospital. There were too many people around," she said as she came back on the call.

"Hospital? What's up, Daphne?"

"There's been an incident. Jasper and Grady have been getting all worked up over some of their boys going missing. You know Hank, the one you knocked out today?"

"Yes, the one going for Clarise?"

"Yes, him. And the second guy who rushed at you—Percy. They've gone missing. Jasper got it into his head that Clarise would know what happened. And that stupid oaf Grady does whatever Jasper tells him to do."

"They went after Clarise?" I asked, struggling to keep calm.

"Yes, I'm so sorry. I intervened as soon as I came to know."

"Not your fault, Daphne. Is she hurt?"

"Yes."

"How bad?"

"She's fine now."

"How bad was it, Daphne?" I tried my best not to sound angry.

"She was knocked out. Concussion. But the doctor has cleared her. Keeping her overnight."

"Grady punched her?"

"Yes," she replied in a guilty voice.

"I'm not blaming you, Daphne. What those two do has nothing to do with you."

"I just can't believe how low they can get."

"Where did this happen?"

"In the hotel bar. They asked Billy to fetch her from the salon. You know Clarise, she doesn't back down. She marched right in. I was in the back room. Billy immediately told me, and I rushed out. But she'd been knocked out by then."

"Where are those two now?" I asked as calmly as I could.

"I don't know. I pulled a gun on them. So they left the hotel. I then brought Clarise to the hospital."

"Good for you. Is there anyone around to keep an eye on her?"

"Well, I'm here. Not leaving her side until I'm sure she'll be safe. Nash is sending over Betsy. Not sure if you know her."

"Kind of. I know she's not dirty like Graves."

"Yeah, right. Betsy will be here all night. Ellie and Mabel are coming over as well."

"Good. She should be fine. Now, Daphne, I need to ask you to do a couple of things."

"Uh, OK, go ahead."

"Jasper, Grady and Baxter are going to go down tonight. Big time. I don't want you to be around when that happens. You need to leave town."

"It's almost funny... a couple of hours ago, I was the one asking you to leave town."

"I know."

"What're you going to do?"

"What I do best, what I'm trained to do—take down the bad guys. But I don't want you to get caught in the crossfire. Even if they manage to stay alive, they are going to prison for a really long time. They won't own a thing in Little Butte before the night is over. It's all going down. You get what I'm saying?"

"Yes. I knew there was no escaping this. I told you."

"I know. But it's not the end of the road for you. This is your chance to get out. Leave this place. Start a new life."

She fell silent.

"Daphne, I need to hear you say yes."

"Let me think about it, Axel. What's the other thing you wanted?"

"I've found out Charlie is alive."

"Really? Clarise will be thrilled. This is what she might need to make a quick recovery."

"I don't know where he is. He skipped town to get away from the gangsters looking for him. Ran away without a trace. But I'll track him down."

"Oh. That's good. I'm sick of all this mayhem. Good to hear something positive for a change. But... he left Clarise? Without any message... any goodbye..."

"For her own safety. He was under witness protection. That's the way these guys are told to operate. Not put anyone else at risk. He did it for her safety."

"Uh-huh."

"Once Clarise is out of sedation, tell Ellie to let her know this. She's been through a lot. She has a right to know."

"I will."

"And Daphne..."

"Yes?"

"Are you done thinking?"

"Yes."

"And?"

"I'll leave as soon as Betsy is here."

"Leave town?"

"Yes."

"For good?"

"Yes."

"Good. Don't go home or to the hotel. Things are going to get crazy soon. Just get in a car and leave. Can you do that?"

"Yes."

"Good."

"Axel."

"Yes?"

"Will I see you again?"

"Remember what I said the last time we talked?"

"Uh, you were talking about buying me a drink?"

"Exactly."

"I have no idea where I'll be."

"You know I used to be a Marshal?"

"Yes?"

"Finding fugitives is what we do best."

Daphne laughed.

"I'll find you."

"I guess you will," she replied.

Time was running out. The moment the call ended, I got into the pickup. Adriel was already in the driver's seat. We headed for the Dawson's houses.

CHAPTER 24

We had barely begun moving when I got another call. It was Dewey. I wasn't really in the mood to talk to the kid. I was guessing he maybe wanted a pat on the back for having completed his "mission".

"Man, I need to turn off the phone now," I muttered to myself.

But I took the call. It was a good thing I did.

"Mr. Blaze, Axel, you need to come here, quick. They're torturing Quint. Oh God, what do I do? I didn't know who to call."

"Calm down, Dewey. Who's torturing Quint?"

"Jasper and Grady. And a bunch of gangsters inside the store."

"Where are you right now?"

"On the roof, looking in through the skylight. When I got back, Jasper's pickup was parked outside the store. It's past closing time but there were lights on inside. I knew something was wrong. I climbed onto the roof and looked in. Quint's in a bad way, Axel. He's badly beaten up. Blood all over his face. I don't know what to do."

"Don't worry. I'm on my way. Be there in ten minutes. How many men are there?"

"I see six, including Jasper and Grady."

"Where's the way to the roof? Back of the store?"

"Yes, there's an iron step ladder."

"OK. Listen to me carefully. Stay where you are. Look out for anyone else in there... the weapons they have. Put your phone on vibrate. Wait for my call. Got it?"

"Yes sir."

I turned to Adriel.

"It's time to take off the gloves. This is going to be no holds barred."

"Got it. Where?"

"Quint's store. Grab the rifle. We'll have to take them all out."

While Adriel was grabbing his rifle, my phone buzzed again. The number was Quint's. I was sure it would be Jasper at the other end, trying to lure me into the store.

"Hello?"

"Mr. Blaze," Quint spoke my name in that formal way, in a weak voice, almost a whisper. The phone was on speaker mode. Others were listening in. He was trying his best to give me a clue.

"Quint? You alright?"

"Yes. Where are you?" he asked, his voice sounding very strained.

"I was about to head into town. Grab a bite," I said, trying to sound very casual.

"Can you come to the store?"

"Sure. Want me to come now?"

"Yes. Mr. Blaze, it's urgent."

"No problem, I'm on the other end of town. It shouldn't take me more than 15 minutes, Mr. Madison."

I was hoping he would get what I was trying to convey—that I understood something was up. He wasn't sounding good. Hope would give him strength.

"Thanks," he replied, gasping, before the phone got disconnected.

I called Dewey.

"Hello, Axel?" he whispered into the phone.

"Dewey, I just got a call from Quint."

"From Quint?"

"Yes, listen to me carefully. I've told him I'm coming over in 15 minutes. Jasper will most probably move the pickup to someplace it won't be visible when I come. Don't assume they're going away. Stay where you are. Don't make a sound. I'll meet you on the roof in ten minutes. Got it?"

"Yes."

I asked Adriel to swap seats with me, jumped into the driver's seat, and drove fast towards the store, avoiding the road leading through town. I knew there would be men looking out for us.

We approached the store from the direction of the highway, driving towards town. I switched off the lights half a mile before where I planned to stop. We passed the three Dawson houses and the pharma factory. The store lay five hundred yards further on. I stopped the pickup a hundred yards before it. Darkness had set in completely.

The area between where I had stopped and the store was largely unbuilt. We left the road and moved carefully in the shadows. There was just one pickup standing in the parking lot. Must have been Quint's. We kept advancing in the shadows. As we neared the store, we began moving along the side wall of the store, taking care not to make a sound.

We reached the edge of the wall and were about to turn into the area at the back of the store when I saw two men standing in the darkness, looking up. They were looking at Dewey, who was coming down the steps, carefully feeling each rung before taking a step down. He was making too much noise for someone moving so carefully.

The two men had guns slung around their bodies but weren't holding them. They didn't really need to, for a slightly-built kid like Dewey. I held out my hand, indicating to Adriel, who was a step behind me. The men were around 20 feet away. Adriel was carrying a rifle. I had my Glock but didn't have a suppressor. Taking a shot was out of the question.

Adriel took out two throwing knives from his boot sheaths and handed me one. These were serious knives he had crafted himself. Made of carbon steel, about 12 inches in length, perfectly balanced and heavy—weighing over a pound each. These were deadly weapons, meant to kill.

Adriel would take out the first guy and move out of the way, leaving the second one for me. Dewey was almost within grasping distance of the two men. Adriel stepped out, threw a knife at the first guy. Twelve inches of razor-sharp carbon steel flew towards the man's neck. As soon as he threw the knife, Adriel cleared the way for me, not waiting to see the result. He didn't need to. When Adriel threw a knife, it landed exactly where it was meant to land. The man's death was a foregone conclusion—the knife went in deep into his neck. He had begun going down when I stepped forward and made an identical throw at the second guy. Both men were down on the ground before Dewey even realized what was up.

I was able to clamp my hand on his mouth before he could open it to make a sound.

"I told you to stay up on the roof," I whispered, taking away the hand.

"Sorry, I was getting scared. I heard some noises below and was afraid someone would come up and grab me."

"And you thought the best idea was to come down?"

"Sorry, I didn't think. I just thought I'd run off to the road and wait for you there."

"Never mind. Get back up. We'll follow you."

Adriel had checked around the corner in the meantime. There was no one else outside. The rest of the men were waiting inside for me to make an appearance.

Adriel retrieved the knives and we began following Dewey up the ladder. We crouched by the skylight to look inside.

My blood boiled when I saw what they had done to Quint. He was sitting hunched, tied to a chair in front of a desk near the reception counter. I couldn't make out if he was conscious. His face was bloody. Even the white hair on the side of the head visible from my angle was streaked with blood. A hammer and a large screwdriver were lying on the desk in front of Quint. I knew they must have been used on him.

The skylight didn't have a view of the complete store. There wasn't a clear line of sight to the store entrance. Five men, including Jasper and Grady, were visible in the area around the reception counter. One of the men was Luca, Hector's bodyguard, who I had almost put down earlier when he tried to grab me. He must surely be looking forward to having me at his mercy.

I knew I would be frisked the moment I entered. The only weapons I could carry undetected were the two boot knives. The sheaths on my boots were adjustable and I moved them to the inside of the boots. Anyone frisking me would feel the edge of the boots, but not the knives.

Adriel and I agreed on a strategy. We couldn't take the chance of Adriel shooting anyone unless he was sure there weren't any other gunmen outside his line of sight.

Our plan was based on all of them wanting to gather in the middle to have a go at me. We decided that the moment I was sure all armed men were within the line of sight of the skylight, I would raise my hand to give him a signal, either a V sign or a raised knife. The second I did that, Adriel would take out any men carrying a gun. I would deal with the rest.

I was ready to go. I nodded to them and made my way down. Walked briskly towards my pickup and got in. Half a minute later, I braked loudly in front of the store entrance. No one inside would be in any doubt that I had arrived.

The main door was shut, although there was light inside, filtering out through the display window on the right side of the entrance. As soon as I knocked, the door opened. I found a rifle barrel pointed straight at my chest. Luca, the bodyguard, was carrying his favorite MP5 submachine gun, which he pointed with satisfaction at my face.

I acted surprised, as if I expected Quint to open the door. I raised my hands and was roughly pulled inside. A third guy frisked me.

There were seven men in all. Two men with AR-15s positioned near the entrance. That's why we couldn't see them from the roof. Problem was, when I was pushed inside the store, they remained standing near the door.

"Oh, lookee here, it's the Marshal man. How was Vegas? Had fun? Thought you could fool us?" Jasper spoke in a mocking voice.

"You shouldn't have gone so far," I replied, looking at Quint. "There's no coming back from this," I added, my voice laced with threat and menace.

"I don't believe this guy," Jasper replied, looking at Luca. "He still thinks he can make threats."

I ignored him and kept looking at Quint. He was barely conscious, tied to the chair, which was what seemed to be preventing him from falling face down onto the desk.

Quint's face was all bloodied from a deep gash above the left eyebrow. The left eye was swollen and closed shut. Two fingers of the left hand looked smashed—someone had used a hammer on them. There was a stab wound on the shoulder, probably with the screwdriver. If I had any doubts about what to do with those men, they disappeared when I saw Quint's condition—none of them was going to get out of that place alive.

"Quint!" I called out to him.

Quint raised his head slightly, tried looking at me, and whispered, "Sorry".

"I'm here. You're going to be fine."

"You really think so?" Jasper asked in a mocking voice.

"Why drag him into this?" I asked Jasper in a calm voice.

Years of practice had taught me not to let my anger take control of me. I had learned to channel it. When the time was right, the men around me would feel its full force.

"No one in town dares go against the Dawsons. He had to be taught a lesson," Jasper replied in a gloating voice.

"And you needed to torture an old man to prove how tough you all are?"

"The old fool wouldn't tell on you. We had to beat it out of him."

"Who did this to him?"

"Grady and Luca," Jasper replied, almost chuckling. "They love beating the shit out of people."

"You shouldn't have done that," I said coldly, looking at the two.

My voice was thick with menace.

"Oh, but we did. And now you're going to experience it first hand," Jasper replied, looking at Luca.

Luca let go of his gun and picked the hammer. Inflicting pain on me would be the highlight of his evening. The gun was still slung around his body, but he barely noticed it. His focus was on me and the hammer in his hand.

The other two Mexicans weren't holding any guns. But they were packing handguns in the backs of their pants. I would need to take those two out before signaling Adriel.

The two men by the door, holding the AR-15s, were also getting interested in what their gang was planning to do with me, and were slowly coming forward to get a view. I needed to increase the entertainment level to get them closer. Three more steps forward, and they would be within Adriel's sights.

"You like seeing people getting beaten up, you little weasel? Too pussy to do it yourself?" I mocked Jasper.

He lost his smile. I turned to Grady.

"And you, big guy, you like hitting women? Makes you feel like a tough guy?" I braced myself for the punch that I knew would follow.

Grady had been bristling to have a go at me all day. He finally got the chance. Pushed Jasper aside and swung a mighty fist at me, directly at my face. I tried to dodge it, but with men crowding me from behind, I couldn't completely avoid being hit. It was a glancing blow, but it jarred my head. I could taste blood in my mouth. The AR-15 guys had moved forward another couple of steps.

"How's that feel? Tough enough for you?" Grady asked in his gruff voice.

I was clearing my head when he attacked me again, driving a solid punch into my stomach. I saw the punch coming, but the guys behind me stopped me from getting away. All I could do was tense up my core. He was a bear of a man. His fist drove into me like a hammer.

"Not so talkative now, are we, Marshal boy?" Jasper chimed in.

Once I was done gasping, I replied in a mocking tone, looking pointedly at his right hand, "How's that finger, tough guy?"

His index and middle fingers were in a splint and bandaged together. "Made you cry, didn't it?"

"Leave him to me, Jasper. I'll make him shut up once and for all," Grady said, looking at Jasper, as he grabbed the hammer from Luca.

Had the hammer landed, it would have been curtains for me. He was looking to kill and could have easily crushed my skull. But he didn't really have much of a chance. The other men moved back when Grady swung back his arm holding the hammer to begin a wide swing. He took too long to take the swing.

Grady's entire front body was open for me to strike. I could take my pick—groin, solar plexus, throat... A kick to the groin would be satisfying. But with four guys around me, chances were someone could decide to swipe my other leg from under me—I could land hard on my ass. I needed to be in control.

I decided to go for the throat. A chisel fist strike. It's not exactly a fist—the knuckle joints remain straight. But the fingers are folded at their middle joint, the proximal interphalangeal joint, transforming the fingers into three sharp poking devices. It's like wearing brass knuckles. Punch the hand straight out into the throat of your opponent, just below the Adam's apple, so the full force of your swing is transferred from your pointed finger joints into the soft part of your adversary's throat, crushing the larynx and the windpipe. Chances are, the man won't get up, ever.

After what Grady had done to Quint, I didn't want him to get up, ever.

I struck at his throat with every ounce of strength I had. Grady didn't make any sound. He stood still for a couple of seconds. His hand holding the hammer opened involuntarily. The hammer clattered loudly as it fell on the floor. It was as if his life was seeping out of him. He couldn't even lift his hand to clutch his throat. Just stood there a few seconds, trying to breathe.

Everyone froze for those five seconds, just watching him, their focus having strayed from me. The two guys with the AR-15s had moved almost to the center of the room. Exactly where I needed them to be.

It was time to signal Adriel. I bent and grabbed my boot knives. They were in my hands before anyone even began to realize what was going on. I raised my right hand with the knife pointing straight up, turned around on my heels and slashed the neck of one of the two men standing behind me, slicing deep through the carotid and jugular. Blood spurted out of the deep gash.

I heard two quick shots from Adriel's rifle just as my knife moved in an arc towards the man's neck. I didn't need to look to make sure that the two men with the AR-15s had been taken out. When Adriel shoots a man, the man dies. Simple as that. Shit like shots missing targets or rifles getting jammed don't happen to people like him.

I stabbed the second man in the solar plexus, just below the center of the ribcage with the knife in my left hand. I heard the third shot as I pushed the knife into him. That must have been Luca going down. I stabbed him in the throat with the other knife to finish him off.

I turned to find Luca on the ground, dead. A neat hole made in his head as the 6.5mm Creedmoor cartridge, travelling at almost thrice the speed of sound, whizzed through his skull, entering his forehead and exiting the bottom of his skull. The two men with the AR-15s were lying a few feet behind him. Both shot clean through the head. Grady was on the ground as well. Dead.

Jasper was the only one left standing.

CHAPTER 25

My face was the face of death. I had worn that mask many times in the past. It struck fear in the hearts of my enemies. Jasper froze in terror as I turned towards him, the bloody knives held firmly in my hands.

I knew Adriel and Dewey would attend to Quint. I deliberately avoided looking towards him, keeping my eyes on Jasper, accentuating the fear in his heart, as I took slow, deliberate steps, the knives pointed towards him. Jasper moved back in mortal fear, matching each step I took towards him. We kept moving along the aisle between the stacks of shelves. Finally, he had his back against the wall.

I came up to him, standing face to face, looking into his eyes as I wiped the bloody knives on his shirt.

"Where's Carter?" I asked him, my voice cold as ice.

"Wh... wh... what? Wh... who..." he stammered. His mind was in turmoil, trying to decide the best way to stay alive—pretending not to know about Carter and hoping I would believe him; or telling me everything about him. I needed to help him arrive at the right choice. Fast. The time for bullshit was over.

I didn't say a word. Sheathed one knife back in the boot. Grabbed his right hand, which was already bandaged, with his index and middle fingers in a splint. I placed his hand on a desk, palm down, and slammed the knife into the bandage between the two fingers. It sliced some skin and flesh off one finger as the knife got embedded in the wood. A tinge of red appeared on the bandage. The injury wasn't serious, but the action of the knife slamming between his fingers, drawing blood, scared the life out of the already terrified man.

I ignored his whimpering, pulled out the knife, placed the knife tip on the back of his palm, pressed on it a bit to break the skin, and looked at him.

"Where's Carter?" I asked again, in the same emotionless voice.

"Wait, wait, I'll tell you. He's at the casino. Don't..." he was staring transfixed at the knife, "please..."

"He's not at the casino. I checked."

I pressed on the knife a little, drawing more blood. He gasped in pain.

"He's there. I swear. Please... wait... listen to me... Hector's men are taking him there right now. I talked to him just before you arrived."

"Where was he before that?"

"In the basement in our house. He's been there all these days."

"Why take him to the casino?"

"You've been making our guys disappear. Hank, Percy, Mexicans... Hector doesn't trust us. He wants everything to be at the casino before his guys come to take it all away."

"They'll take Carter as well?"

"I'm not sure. Probably, yes. Hector's playing all the shots."

"When are his guys coming?"

"I don't know. Sometime tonight."

The look on his face told me he was trying to bluff me. I pressed further on the knife. About a quarter of an inch of the blade sunk between the metacarpal bones on the back of Jasper's palm. He screamed.

"When are Hector's guys arriving at the casino?" I repeated the question.

"In about an hour. Definitely within two hours."

"Where are they coming from?"

"Arizona."

"Las Hermosas?"

"Yes," he replied, looking surprised that I knew.

"Where are they taking the trucks?"

"Back to Arizona."

"Where will they hold Carter at the casino?"

"There's a bunker at the back. That's the only secure place. I'll tell you everything. I swear. Take the knife away, please! It really hurts," he was almost sobbing.

I ignored his pleas.

"When's Hector planning to kill him?"

"He's not going to kill him."

I pressed on the knife.

"Please, I swear. Pops doesn't want him killed. He'll convince Hector to let him go. I'll convince him. Please."

"No need to convince Hector. He'll end up with a bullet in his head before the night is over," I said in a matter-of-fact tone.

Jasper gave me a scared look.

"Why did you guys attack Quint?" I asked Jasper.

"He was helping you."

"How did you know?"

"Those men at the gas station. The ones you messed up today. They were keeping an eye on everything from the gas station."

I wanted to kick myself for putting Quint in danger. But I kept my emotions in check.

"Now listen to me carefully. You're going to call Hector. Tell him I'm dead. Convince him you need to get information from Carter. Convince him not to kill Carter until you've talked to him."

"I can try, but I don't know if he'll listen to me. I really don't have much influence on him."

"Figure out a way if you want to stay alive. If Carter comes out of this alive, you will live. Or else, you've seen what I'm capable of. I will kill you myself. Do you get that?"

"Yes... yes, completely."

I finally moved the knife away. Jasper held his hand tenderly.

"Is Grady dead?" he asked me.

"Yes."

"Oh, man," he replied, his voice breaking.

"Turn around. Hands against the wall."

He immediately complied. I frisked him. He had no weapons on him. He relied on Grady and the cartel for muscle. Now that they were gone, he was out of options. I kept his phone with me.

"Stay here. I'll be back in a few minutes. If I find you've moved even an inch, you don't want to find out what I'll do."

"I'm not going anywhere. I swear."

I walked back to check on Quint. Adriel and Dewey were attending to him. Adriel had cut the rope binding Quint and was holding him steady. Dewey was helping him sip some water. Quint looked at me as I knelt beside him. His one open eye had a bit more life than it had a few minutes ago.

"Have you called 911?" I asked Dewey.

"Yes. Ambulance is on its way."

"I'm feeling better than I look," Quint said, trying to inject some strength in his voice.

"I know you're tough, Quint. But this is my fault."

"Rubbish," he whispered. "You're fighting our fight. Don't even think about it."

"It's all going to be over tonight. You'll wake to a new dawn tomorrow. That's a promise."

"That'll more than make up for all this," he replied, looking at his battered hand.

I gave a slight squeeze to his shoulder, got up, and signaled Dewey to come over near the counter.

"You alright, Dewey?"

"Yes. I was just sitting on the roof. You were the one getting beaten up down here. Are you fine?"

"Just a couple of light knocks. Not a big deal. Can you get me the keys for the garage? I need to get my pickup out of there."

"Sure thing."

He went behind the counter and handed me the keys.

"Thanks. Better get back to Quint now."

"Yes, of course," he said and went back.

I signaled Adriel to join me.

"You alright, kid?" Adriel asked, looking at me searchingly.

"Yes, Adriel. It had to be done."

"I know. So long as you're clear on that... this is war."

"You don't have to worry about that."

"I won't. So, what's the plan now?"

"We've got a location on Carter. They've moved him to the casino."

"Casino?" Adriel sounded surprised.

"They must have taken him there same time we drove to this place. They've been holding him in their basement all this time."

"We would have got to him, either way. Where's he now? The bunker?"

"Most probably, yes. I'm getting Jasper to call Hector. Confirm the location. Tell him I'm dead. Let him relax before we spring a surprise on him."

"You sure he won't warn Hector?"

"He's too scared to try anything. I'll have him on speaker to make sure," I replied.

"So it's back to the butte again? The best bet would be to do a repeat of what we just did an hour ago—up the butte, descend into the site from the back, and get Carter. And then fight our way out," Adriel said.

"There's also the option of entering through the main gate hidden in Jasper's pickup. But once we're in, getting to the bunker won't be easy in a frontal assault. There'll be at least ten armed men there."

"I agree," Adriel replied. "Best to get Carter, then make a stealth attack and fight our way out. Better than fighting our way in," he added.

"I'll get Jasper to make the call now. Quint's got a small office at the back. I'll take Jasper there. Keep an eye out so no one bursts into the room in the middle of the call."

"Sure."

I walked back to Jasper and asked him to follow me to Quint's office. I drew my knife as I closed the door of Quint's office behind us. Jasper's eyes grew wide.

"Thought about what you're going to say to Hector?" I asked him.

"Uh, yes."

"If Hector gets the slightest hint that something's not right, I will plunge this into your throat. There are six bodies lying out there. One more won't make the slightest difference. You get that?"

"Yes. Completely."

"Right. Call Hector. Put the phone on speaker. If Carter comes out of this alive, you stay alive."

He nodded and made the call.

"*Bueno*?" Hector said as he answered the phone.

"Hector, it's Jasper."

"You have good news for me?"

"Yes. It's all done," Jasper replied.

"You have got Blaze?"

"Yes. He's dead."

"Dead? I wanted to watch him die. Where's Luca?"

"Sorry. He's taking care of the bodies."

"*No importa*. So long as he's out of the way. Now we can get down to real business. We will be leaving in an hour. You better come down fast."

"Yes, I'll be there very soon. What about that man Carter? He is still alive, right?"

"That Marshal?"

"Yes."

"He's still breathing. But not for long. He will soon be saying hello to Blaze."

"Don't. Please. I have to get some information from him," Jasper asked him.

"What information?"

"Things he may have told others when he was investigating. It's best to be sure there'll be nothing leading people back here."

"Why do you care? You will have nothing left here to cause you problems once we're gone. And there will be no trace left of him once we put him in a barrel of acid."

"But still, best to be sure," Jasper replied, looking at me with an alarmed look on his face.

"OK. I'll keep him alive until you come. He will be more than ready to talk by the time Carlos is through with him."

My eyes hardened. Jasper became more nervous when he saw my expression.

"Uh, I do need to talk to him. Please tell Carlos to wait."

"We'll see. We have got another one we have to get talking. One biker who escaped from my men last night."

"Biker?"

"Yes, they killed the others but this one wasn't with them. We caught him when he was admitted to hospital with a gunshot wound. Your cop, Birdie, alerted us and we grabbed him. He hasn't told us how he got shot. But no one stays silent when Carlos uses his knife."

"Uh, right."

"You're bringing the body of Blaze with you?"

"Yes. Of course."

"OK," Hector said and disconnected the phone.

Jasper looked at me fearfully. I had no more use for him. I needed to leave for the casino immediately. I didn't want them to have enough time to do serious damage to Carter and Brick.

I asked Adriel to keep an eye on Jasper. Then walked over to where Grady and Luca were lying, almost beside each other. I frisked them for phones and kept them in my pocket. I didn't want Baxter or Hector finding out what had happened at Quint's place. Not until I broke the news to them myself.

Then I walked towards the store entrance to call Flynn and Murphy.

"What's the news?" Flynn asked me as soon as he took the call.

"I've got Carter's location," I said, relief clearly audible in my voice.

"Finally! You have no idea how I've been waiting to hear those words. Good work, Blaze."

"I still need to get him out alive. He's being held by the cartel."

"Oh... so, what's the plan? Time to send in SOG?" Flynn asked me.

"Yes. But I won't wait for them. Cartel reinforcements are coming in within an hour. I don't have time to lose. I'm heading over there now."

"Do that. I'll get on the phone with highway troopers in Nevada. We'll set up roadblocks. I've got the map in front of me. If cartel's coming from Tucson, they'll come through Vegas and take the I-93."

"Yes. Best have a roadblock set up as soon as they get off I-93 towards Little Butte. They'll have heavy artillery."

"I know. We'll be ready. Leave that to me. You best coordinate directly with Murphy."

"Will do."

"I've got everything set up to intercept the trucks. We're tracking them. They haven't moved from the site yet. When they do, we'll be ready."

"Good. I'll call Murphy."

"All the best, Blaze. Go, get Carter."

"Roger that."

I ended the call. Made another one to Murphy.

"Hey, Cowboy, what's up?" Murphy asked as soon as he took the call.

"Ready for some action, Murph?"

"Hell, yeah," he replied. "Boys, time to rock and roll," he called out to the rest of the SOG team. I could hear them whooping in the background.

"Hear that?" Murphy shouted into the phone.

"Sounds like they're ready to party. I'll text you the coordinates after this call. It's a construction site. Secure perimeter with security cameras. The cartel is holding Carter there. I'm heading there now. See you boys when you arrive."

"All the best. Go get him. We'll raise hell as soon as we get there."

"Get moving then. Time to show them what SOG's all about."

"Yeah."

I ended the call and walked back in. Paramedics had arrived and were attending to Quint.

The cops arrived next. I wanted to give Nash a heads up about roadblocks being put up by highway troopers. But I was worried about being seen by Graves and Birdie. Any plan to rescue Carter would only work if I had surprise on my side, so long as Hector believed I was dead. The moment Graves or Birdie got wind of my being in town and alive, they would alert Baxter. Those two needed to be taken out of circulation until I got to Carter. Even if it meant kidnapping them.

I saw Nash walking in with another cop I hadn't seen before. No sign of Birdie or Graves yet. I took Nash aside.

"How's Quint?" he asked me as soon as he saw me.

"He's going to be alright. They worked him over real bad, but he'll be fine."

"Who was it?"

"Jasper, Grady and the Mexicans."

Nash looked inside. He could see the bodies lying there.

"You killed them all?"

"All except Jasper."

"There wasn't any other option?"

"No, there wasn't. They were going to kill Quint and me. Go check out what they did to Quint."

"Hmm... I get that, but every time I see you, there are a few more bodies I have to deal with."

"It's all coming to an end, Nash. I'll take you through everything in detail, but for now, you've got other things to worry about. There are cartel reinforcements on their way to town. They aren't just coming for a routine visit. You need to be prepared."

"How do you know that?"

"I know. Trust me."

"When?"

"Within an hour. Highway troopers are being informed by my office as we speak. They'll be setting up roadblocks out of town, just off the I-93. You need to coordinate with them."

"Alright. I assume you're off on another mission I don't have a clue about."

"The last one, Nash. Then it's over," I said. "Are Graves and Birdie coming here?"

"Graves has gone silent. No idea where he's disappeared. Birdie's on his way. Is that a problem?"

"No, it's fine. They can't do much now. And you'll soon be throwing their asses in prison. I've got enough proof for that," I said.

No matter how understanding Nash was with me, there was no way I could confide in him I was planning to abduct his fellow cop.

"One more thing," I said. "Jasper is tied up back there behind the shelves. Throw him in lockup, will you?"

"Gladly."

"And no calls for him. Baxter thinks I'm dead. He shouldn't know otherwise until I reveal it to him myself."

"Got it."

Nash walked inside the hardware store. I motioned to Adriel. It was time to move.

When we turned to walk towards the entrance, I saw Birdie standing there. He looked surprised when he saw me, then tried to hide it by turning around. He began walking out, fishing in his pocket for his phone. I followed him at a quick pace and called out to him.

"Officer, I need to show you something," I shouted to him as soon as I exited the store.

Birdie turned and looked at me.

"I need to make an urgent call. Police matter. Show me later," he replied.

"There are two bodies by the wall around the corner," I pointed toward the back of the store. "Better secure the area," I persisted.

He still wasn't convinced and looked double-minded. I walked to the corner and pointed towards the darkness.

"This man looks Mexican. Not sure about the other one."

That piqued Birdie's interest. He finally decided to take a look. The moment he rounded the corner, I came up behind him, and wrapped my arm around his neck. Went for a carotid artery choke. A simple hold, pressing on the carotid arteries on both sides of a man's neck, interrupting the blood flow to the brain, making him pass out within seconds.

My right arm went around Birdie's neck, elbow bent in front of his neck, forearm coming around the other side of his neck and locking onto my left bicep, my left hand moving to the back of his neck, pressing his head forward. My right bicep pushed into his right carotid artery, my forearm pressed his left carotid. Birdie went limp within seconds.

Adriel had followed me around the corner by then.

"Change of plan?" he asked.

"Just a little tweak."

"Like kidnapping a cop?"

"Yup. He'll squeal to Baxter if I let him loose."

"Right."

"Can't let Nash or anyone else see me. I'll get my pickup and dump him in the back."

I used Birdie's own cuffs on him, took his gun, phone and radio, threw him in the back, and pulled the tonneau cover over him. Adriel got into the passenger seat and I began driving towards the back of the butte.

It was finally time to get Carter.

CHAPTER 26

Adriel and I would be going up against more than ten armed men. And they would be holding Carter and Brick hostage. Both would be hurt and weak. The element of surprise would be the only thing working in our favor.

We planned as we drove towards the butte. It would be best to split up, with Adriel staying on top in sniper position. That would give us a tactical advantage. There was also a chance of cartel reinforcements arriving before the roadblocks were in place. It wouldn't help if both of us were pinned under heavy fire.

I would descend using the same route I took earlier and make my way to the back of the bunker. We wouldn't engage the enemy until Carter's position was confirmed.

Birdie had woken up by the time we reached the back of the butte. He was starting to make a noise, kicking against the sides and the cover. There wasn't anyone around to hear him, but I didn't have patience for the weasel.

I opened the cover and grabbed him by his collars. He had begun to warn me, saying, "I'm a cop. You're going to be in troub..." He never got a chance to finish the sentence. I slammed his head against the side of the pickup, knocking him out. Then slid back the cover and locked it.

I packed as much firepower as I could carry. Placed the Glock in the holster in the back of my jeans. I put the suppressor, spare magazines, and a couple of two-way radios in a body bag. Slung the bag as well as the suppressed Colt 9mm submachine gun across my back.

Adriel had already slung his rifle across his back. We got into our climbing harnesses. I fixed my mechanical ascender to the rope and began to climb. When I was about a third of the way up, Adriel began following me.

Once I was at the top, I walked over to the other side and examined the construction site. I expected around ten men down there—the six we had seen earlier, loading the trucks and manning the gate; and Baxter, Hector and his bodyguard, Carlos, and maybe one or two more.

All activity around the trucks had stopped. They were packed and ready to go as soon as Hector's men arrived.

There was no sign of Hector or Baxter. I could see four men near the entrance. Two inside the guard's cabin beside the gate. The other two stood outside, smoking. We couldn't see anyone else. They were either in the rooms over the bunker or in the central hall.

There was a cop car parked just inside the gate. Baxter must have placed Graves on escort duty for the trucks. No wonder he had gone silent. He couldn't let Nash or the other cops know where he would be for the next few hours. That worked in my favor. He wouldn't have listened in to any messages from dispatch about the incident at Quint's store. Parked beside the cop car was Hector's Hummer.

Adriel had joined me in the meantime and had begun setting up the long-range rifle. Everything within the site, except the hall's main door as well as a ten-yard area in front of it, was within Adriel's range. I handed him a radio, then secured my mic and earpiece.

The front and side perimeters of the boundary walls were well lighted. The lights were at such an angle that the wall of the butte above the bunker was illuminated. The only way to descend undetected was from the other end, near the trucks. Then make my way across the base of the butte to the other end. I needed to reach the back side of the rooms and get a view inside using the peep holes I had created earlier in the ventilator windows.

I nodded to Adriel and began descending. Touched bottom in a couple of minutes.

I stayed back in the shadows and moved towards the rooms. Once I reached the area behind them, I peeked into the room at the far side, the one with the entrance to the bunker. There wasn't anyone in there. But the door to the bunker was closed. There was no way of knowing if there was anyone locked in there.

The next room was empty as well. The third room had all the monitors receiving the feed from the security cameras. There were two men sitting behind the monitors. One of them was Spencer, Baxter's third bodyguard. The one I had met in the morning in the abandoned gas station. His right arm, the one I had broken, was in a cast.

The only way to confirm the location of Carter was to take the men out, then check the bunker and the camera feeds.

I drew my Glock and screwed the suppressor on. Took a final look around before stepping into the room, gun pointed straight at the second man's head—the one-armed Spencer was much less of a threat.

"Don't make a move," I ordered in a sharp voice. "Hands where I can see them."

The man froze for a second. Then his left hand began coming up. The right arm was still under the table. I let off a shot, the bullet nicking the top of his left ear. I had the suppressor on and was not too concerned about the sound being heard in the central hall.

"I won't ask again."

The man complied immediately. Both arms shot straight up. Spencer was already the picture of obedience—his left arm was all the way up before I shot half the other guy's ear off.

"Get up. Move away from the table," I ordered the second man. Once he was clear of the table, I snapped, "Hands against the wall."

I frisked him. He was carrying a Beretta 9mm.

"Don't move," I ordered him.

I signaled Spencer to join the other man by the wall. While I was frisking Spencer, the second man tried taking a swing at me. Poorly executed move. I clipped him hard on the side of the head with the Glock. He fell unconscious on the floor.

"You planning to take a swing as well?" I asked Spencer.

"No," he replied, vigorously shaking his head.

I went behind the table. There was a shotgun in a narrow shelf below the top. And a bunch of keys.

"Keep your hand against the wall. Don't move until I tell you to."

Spencer nodded and kept standing facing the wall. I looked at the monitor showing the feed from inside the hall. It was a large structure, square in shape, with a high central ceiling. There was a large, empty central area, where the gambling tables would eventually be located. Three sides of the hall were arranged on two floors. Two staircases from either side of the main entrance led to the upper floor. You could go up one staircase, walk around three sides of the upper floor, and come down the other staircase.

Two sides of the hall had rows of rooms facing each other across the empty area in the middle. Eight rooms on each side, four on the ground level and four more on top of them. All sixteen rooms looked identical. Each room had a door at one end, and a rectangular dark-glassed window close to the door.

There were only three cameras installed inside the hall—one above the entrance, a second on the wall opposite, and the third above an enclosed area, the location of which I couldn't figure out.

A man was standing guard just inside the entrance. I couldn't see anyone else. All other men were inside the rooms.

"Come here, take this seat," I ordered Spencer, indicating the seat beside me.

The bully I had encountered in the morning had become an obedient young man. I kept the Glock pointed at his midriff as I interrogated him about the feed.

"I don't want to hurt you more. Get that?"

"Yes," he replied, nodding.

"I've got some questions. Give me straight answers and we need not have any more unpleasantness. OK?"

"Yes."

"How many cameras are there within the hall?"

"Three."

"Where is this third camera located?" I pointed to the feed from the camera installed in an enclosed area.

"It's above the back entrance."

"Is the entrance locked?"

"No, they've been using it to load the trucks."

"How many men are there inside the hall?"

"Seven... maybe eight... I'm not hundred percent sure," he replied.

"Is there a cop in there?"

"Uh, yes... Graves."

"What about the man, Carter? Is he alive?"

"Uh... yes... are you a cop?"

"Maybe."

"Look, Officer, you've got to believe me, I've got nothing to do with what's going on in there. Those guys are psychos. I didn't sign up for all that."

"You're part of them, Spencer. There's nothing like 'those guys'."

"I'm not, Officer. You've got to believe me. I signed up to be Baxter's bodyguard. I play rough at times, knock guys about, but I never killed anyone in my life. I swear, I'm not like them killers," he said, looking at the knocked-out man.

"We'll talk about that later."

"But listen, don't you remember from the morning ... I never tried shooting you or anything ... I didn't even grab the shotgun. I would just have pushed you around a bit... if you hadn't gone all Rambo on me and put my ass on the ground."

"Maybe. I don't care. All I care about is getting Carter out alive, get it?"

"Yes. Are you here for him?"

"Yeah. Now, here's the deal... if Carter comes out of this alive, you live, simple as that. Got it? Don't talk, just nod," I said.

He nodded vigorously.

"None of those guys in there will be alive ten minutes from now. Don't be under the illusion I'll think twice about putting a bullet in you. If you want to live, tell me exactly what's going on in there."

"I'll tell you everything. They've got two guys tied up in that room," he said, pointing to one of the rooms on the ground level. "One's Carter, the other's a biker. Both are in a bad shape. There's this guy—Carlos. He's a full-on psycho."

"Are they all in that room?"

"No, only that nutcase Carlos, Hector, Baxter and two other Mexican guys. They were torturing the biker when he passed out. I couldn't take it and got out. Said I wasn't feeling well. They laughed at me."

"Who else is in the hall?"

"There's this guy by the front entrance. Graves too couldn't deal with what those psychos were doing to the biker and went to another room. He's in that room in the corner, next to the room where they've got Carter," Spencer said, pointing to the screen. "There's a passage beside the room, leading to the back entrance."

"Any other men?"

"No. But a lot of cartel guys are expected soon."

That gave me a bit more confidence he was telling the truth. A plan was beginning to take shape in my mind. A frontal assault would almost certainly mean Carter and Brick getting shot. I would have to draw Hector and his men out of that room. Once I was inside the room, that would be the time to come out with guns blazing.

"What's Hector's phone number?" I asked Spencer.

"I don't know. I swear. You can check my phone."

"Will this guy have it on his phone?"

"I don't know. I doubt it. We both work for Baxter. Nothing to do with Hector."

"What's Baxter's number?"

"That I have. Here," he handed me his phone. Baxter's number was on the screen. I saved it on my phone, but kept Spencer's phone with me.

"What's in the bunker at the back?"

"Nothing. They had all the meth in there. That's all been loaded onto the trucks."

"Open the bunker," I told Spencer, handing him the bunch of keys.

I caught the unconscious man by the foot and dragged him behind me as I followed Spencer.

"Throw him inside," I told Spencer.

He surely didn't have much love for the man. Caught him by the collar with one hand and dragged him inside the bunker.

"I'm going to lock you in."

"I did tell you everything truthfully."

"I'll get to know in the next few minutes. If that's the case, it'll help your case. Stay put here until then," I said as I closed and locked the door.

I talked to Adriel on the radio as I walked out.

"I've found Carter's location. He's being held in the hall."

"Roger that."

"I'm heading in now. Through the back entrance directly below you. You see any movement anywhere else?" I asked Adriel.

"That's a negative. The only men visible are the four at the gate—two inside the cabin and two standing by the gate."

"Good. Wait for my signal. The second I tell you to, take out the two standing by the gate. I'm banking on the sound of the shots to get Hector away from Carter."

"You want all four down?"

"Your call. If the men inside the cabin start posing a threat, take them out. But fire two extra shots, just for effect."

"Roger that.

"I have neutralized two men. Seven more to go inside the hall."

"Good luck."

I walked towards the back of the hall, the side facing the butte, away from the line of sight of the men at the gate.

Spencer had been telling the truth. The back entrance was open. The door led into a passage. At the end of the passage was another door with a small glass window within it. Beyond it lay the empty central area of the hall. According to Spencer, Graves was in the room next to the door. I walked back towards the rear entrance and called Baxter.

"Baxter. Who's this?" he asked in his deep voice.

"They call me Blaze."

Baxter was lost for words. It didn't take a lot of imagination to guess why. He had been expecting his sons to drag my body and throw it in front of him.

"Lost your voice, Baxter?" I asked him.

"Where are Jasper and Grady?"

"Take a guess."

He remained silent.

"I told you I don't make trouble unless someone messes with me. You should have listened," I spoke in a cold voice.

"You think you'll get away in one piece? I'm going to hunt you down."

Anger had begun to replace the disbelief in his voice. I could hear someone in the background asking him who he was talking to.

"Sure, you try hunting me down," I replied. "Now better hand the phone to your boss."

"I have no boss. I own this town," he thundered.

"Yeah, right. Keep pretending you're in charge. Give the phone to Hector. He'll have your hide if he doesn't get to hear what I'm about to tell him."

Baxter handed the phone to Hector. I could hear faint traces of words exchanged between them. Hector knew it was me on the phone when he got on the call.

"So you're still living," Hector said.

"What did you expect? That your man Luca would bring you my body? You need to get smarter, Hector."

"Luca is dead?"

"I told you what I do with rattlers that try to bite me."

"You are very lucky to be alive. Also very foolish. You should have used this chance to disappear. Now the cartel is going to come after you. You will know its power. I will kill you with my hands, slowly and painfully."

"I'll save you the bother, tough guy. I'm coming to you. Actually, I'm about to ram through the gates of the casino. Time to finish this business."

Hector placed his hand on the phone and whispered something to someone. I put the phone on mute and talked to Adriel on the radio.

"Adriel, in ten seconds, shoot the two men."

"Roger that," he replied.

I unmuted the phone at the same moment as Hector said, "You're bluffing."

"You'll find out in a few seconds. I'm coming in. Stop me if you can," I said and disconnected the call.

I walked over to the door to watch their movements in the hall just as the first two shots rang out. Five men rushed out of the room. Hector, Carlos and Baxter moved swiftly towards the main entrance of the hall while the other two men rushed across the hall to a room at the other end to grab weapons. The men were halfway across the hall when two more shots rang out. All of them broke into a run towards the other end.

At the same time, the door to the room next to me opened and Graves walked out, looking confused. I moved behind him and pressed my gun into his gut. He didn't make a sound. I pushed Graves towards the room from which Hector and the others had just rushed out. The door to the room was already open.

Hector and his men were too busy peering out the main entrance towards the gates. Hector shouted out to the man guarding the entrance to go towards the gate and check. I knew the entrance was blocked from Adriel's view. But once the man walked about ten yards towards the gate, he would be within Adriel's cross hairs.

Four seconds after the man stepped out, a bullet took him down. Hector cursed as the men gathered at the entrance, trying to make sense of what was going on outside.

Meanwhile, I pushed Graves into the room, using him as a human shield in case there was another gunman in there.

But there wasn't. There were just two men in the room, tied to chairs. One of them looked unconscious, head slumped forward. It was Brick. The other man was conscious. Bruised and battered, but conscious. I had finally found Carter.

"You took your time, Cowboy," Carter said in a weak voice, bravely trying to smile.

"You're a hard man to find, pal," I said, barely able to contain the relief in my voice.

Two more shots rang out at that moment. I guessed the two men in the cabin must have tried shooting back at Adriel.

"All four down. And a fifth as well," I heard Adriel's confirmation in my earpiece.

"Roger that. Maintain position. I have located Carter," I replied.

I knew the others would rush back in as soon as they realized someone was taking potshots at them from the top of the butte.

I slammed Graves against a wall, cuffed his hands behind him, and pushed him down on the floor. His face had the resigned expression of a man who knew his game was over.

I took out a boot knife and sliced through the ropes binding Carter.

"Get in the corner, Carter. They'll be coming in guns blazing any second now," I said as I cut the ropes binding Brick and dragged his limp form towards the corner.

Spencer had been right. Carlos was a psycho. Brick had multiple shallow stabs on his torso, shallow enough not to kill but cause a lot of pain. His wounded shoulder, where he had been shot earlier, had been opened up with a knife.

I turned to find Carter trying to take a step but falling down. I hadn't realized one of his legs was broken. But I didn't have time to be gentle with him.

"Sorry, pal. Bullets will be whizzing around soon," I said as I grabbed him under the shoulders and almost dumped him beside Brick. Then I turned around, shot out the lights inside the room, and rushed towards the window to watch the men outside.

All five men were back inside the hall. They had figured out there was a shooter on top of the butte but had no clue I was already inside the room. They entered the room next to the main entrance and came out armed with MP5 submachine guns. Five against one. Not great odds, especially with their heavy artillery. But I still had surprise on my side.

Hector, Carlos and a third man took up position near the entrance while Baxter and the fifth man walked towards the room. After blowing out the room lights, I was in comparative darkness. I could see them clearly through the dark glass, but they couldn't see inside.

I took out the Colt 9mm SMG from my body bag, placed the stock firmly in my shoulder, and waited, ready for them. The man accompanying Baxter was the first one to walk in. I waited until he had stepped inside the room and Baxter was in the doorway. Then I shot the first man right between his eyes.

Baxter began turning and stepping back at the same time, trying to get out of my line of fire. While he was turning, he was also lining up the MP5 on me. He was quick for a man his age. But not fast enough. I shot him through his left knee, the bullet ripped through the knee and lodged in the right one. Baxter fell onto his side on the floor, half in and half out of the room. He lost his grip on the MP5, but it was slung across his body and fell next to him.

At that exact moment, Hector, Carlos and the third man finally realized what was going on and let out three simultaneous bursts from their MP5s. I ducked. Bullets shattered the dark glass of the window beside the room's door before thudding into the back wall.

But I hadn't taken my eyes off Baxter. He had begun lining his gun on me as I fell. I fired three quick shots into him. From the low angle on the floor, the bullets entered his body around the abdomen and tore through his heart. Death was instantaneous.

"You don't have a chance, Marshal, my men are going to be here any minute," Hector shouted from the other end of the hall.

"No one's coming to save you. There are roadblocks all across town. It's just the three of you," I shouted back.

"You're bluffing."

"You don't learn, Hector. You said the same thing two minutes ago. Seven of your men have died since then. Give yourself up, if you want to live. Last chance."

"You won't catch me, *cabrón*. No one fucks with the cartel. You and anyone you care for will die. I promise you that."

"Keep dreaming."

My words were met with bursts of gunfire. I pressed myself against the wall and peered out. One of the men had taken advantage of the cover of gunfire to run up the staircase. He had taken up position on the upper floor directly across the room we were in. He began firing and had me pinned against the wall. I couldn't return fire even when I saw Hector and Carlos rushing out the front entrance.

I guessed what they were up to. One of them would divert Adriel's attention while the other made a dash for the trucks. Once one of them got to the trucks, Adriel could do little from his near vertical angle. I needed to take out the third man to go after them.

"Need a hand, Blaze?" Carter asked me.

"Sure," I said, helping him to take position beside the window and handing him a gun. "Fire off a few shots through the window. Divert his attention. I'll be by the door. I'll take him out as soon as he fires at you."

"Sure thing."

"Don't expose yourself, Carter. Just a few quick shots. OK? We don't want you getting killed after all this trouble finding you."

"Don't worry, Cowboy. Just be ready to take him down."

"Right. Now," I yelled.

Carter let off a few quick shots towards the man on the upper floor and dived back down. As soon as the man began firing towards Carter's position, I shot him.

"Bingo. Stay here. I'm going after the others," I shouted to Carter before rushing out.

I checked my impulse to run towards the main entrance. I didn't know Hector and Carlos's position outside the entrance. They could easily be waiting to shoot me down while I was running across the hall.

When I heard the sound of gunfire outside, I ran towards the back entrance. I exited the back and ran towards the front. I found Carlos standing outside the entrance, hidden from Adriel's view. He had chucked an empty magazine and was replacing it with a fresh one. I shot him in the head. Point blank.

"One of them's got to the trucks," Adriel whispered in my earpiece.

"Roger that," I replied.

I heard the sound of a truck starting at the same time. I ran to the other side of the hall and planted myself firmly in the path of the truck. Fifty yards separated me from the truck.

Hector shifted into gear but did not move immediately. He kept revving the engine for a few seconds.

I had the gun pointed straight out, rock steady in my hands, the stock extended and nestled firmly in my shoulder, my right cheek pressed against it, eyes looking through the front sight, waiting for him to make a move. The Colt had been a faithful companion on many operations. I didn't have the slightest doubt about its accuracy. Or my ability to take out a man at fifty yards. I wanted Hector to make the first move. Give him a false sense of security—thinking he could actually get away with the truck.

Hector pressed the accelerator as the truck began moving towards me. He was hunched behind the wheel, only the top part of his head from the eyes up visible, giving me less of a target to shoot at.

I shot him a second after he began to move. The bullet pierced the windscreen and smashed into Hector's forehead. I didn't need to check if he was dead. I took a few steps sideways to get out of the path of the slow-moving truck. It passed me, hit the Hummer, dragged it into the cop car, before finally coming to a stop.

"Time to come down, Adriel. Mission accomplished," I said into the mic.

"Roger that. Well done, kid."

I walked to the truck, pulled Hector's body, and dumped it on the ground. Searched his pockets and got his phone. I used his thumb to unlock the phone and set it to permanent unlock. Then put it in my pocket.

I called Nash. Told him it was all over. Asked him to rush over with an ambulance. Then walked back inside the hall and let the feeling of relief wash all over me.

I had found Carter. Mission accomplished.

EPILOGUE

The large glass doors of the bank shut behind me as I entered the foyer. The sounds of the street in downtown Nashville were replaced by discreetly playing piped music. I took a seat on a set of fixed chairs arranged by the wall.

The counters weren't too busy that time of the morning. Behind the counters was a row of four cabins. All with transparent front walls made of glass. Three of the cabins were occupied. Two of them had a banker seated at one side of a desk, talking with clients seated on the other side.

The main desk was unoccupied in the third one. The banker, a gorgeous woman, sat on a couch placed against one wall, listening intently to her client.

My eyes looked at the sign hanging on top of the cabin. It said Deputy Manager. The name below it sounded half familiar. Daphne Madison. She was finally free to cast away the name imposed upon her—Dawson.

Daphne was every bit as attractive as I remembered her. The tumbling curls of honey blonde hair caressed the flawless skin of her finely chiseled face. I sat there looking at her, feeling satisfied that she was safe, back in a place she was comfortable in, doing something fruitful that she liked doing.

But she couldn't know I had found her. Not yet. Something I found in Hector's phone prevented me from doing that. Hector had texted my name and photo to Raúl Machado—the boss of the SDC cartel, located beyond the reach of the DEA and the Marshals. I knew a storm was coming. I wasn't scared. Facing killers had become a way of life. But I couldn't let someone close to me get caught in the eye of the storm. That had happened once. Never again. I would wait for the storm to come. Pluck its eye out.

A couple of minutes later, I got up and walked out through the glass doors. I would be back. When the time was right.

****

LETHAL FORCE
Axel Blaze Thriller
(Book Two)

When Blaze takes out a Mexican cartel's operations in Nevada, the cartel sends hitmen after him and everyone he cares about. Bad move. What the cartel doesn't realize is, it has messed with a Lethal Force.

HARD TARGET
(Book Three)

At an isolated gas station in Kentucky's Appalachia, Blaze stumbles upon an execution about to go down. Blaze's intervention gets a pack of mercenaries after him. What the hunters don't realize is, when it comes to deadly sport, Blaze is a master of the game.

MEAN STREETS
(Book Four)

Midnight in New York City. A car stops at an intersection. Blaze sees a girl in the back giving him a distress hand signal. The chase that begins in Manhattan takes Blaze on a treacherous journey through the underbelly of the city that never sleeps.

UNCHAINED FURY
(Book Five)

Blaze lands in San Francisco. There is a contract out on him and his team. Floated by the Cady brothers—ruthless arms dealers who will stop at nothing to get revenge. But they made a mistake. When the game becomes no holds barred, when nothing is off limits, there's nothing to hold back Blaze's fury.

NO ESCAPE (Book Six)
(Releasing December 2023)

Chaos erupts in Bison Creek, Wyoming. Two slain officers. Blood-soaked ex-Marine Logan Davis on the scene. There's a sinister link between a cult and Boston-based investors. Powerful forces intent on burying the truth. Davis calls the one man he knows will move heaven and earth to dig it out—Blaze.

Made in the USA
Las Vegas, NV
29 September 2023

78312556R00187